THEY WHO FELL

KEVIN KNEUPPER

Liked the book? Two other novels in the series are in the works, so if
you want to get a heads up as to when they're being released, please
sign up for my mailing list at http://eepurl.com/IrhLP. I don't e-mail
for anything other than new releases, so you won't get any spam.

To the girl with the gum on her butt.

CHAPTER ONE

"DON'T SPEAK. IT'S IMPORTANT NOT to speak." Jana listened attentively to Sam as he rattled off instructions. She tried to project calm and poise—the image in her head of the ideal servant. Her face complied, but her eyes betrayed her. It was the eyes that always screamed fear.

"Unless spoken to," Peter piped in helpfully.

"Unless spoken to," agreed Sam, "and even then, say as little as possible." There wasn't much time, now. Everyone moved with a sense of urgency around the kitchen, knowing they had but minutes to finish the preparations for the next course. Pots clanged, ovens roared with flame, and dishes were loaded with delicacies tailored with care to the whims of the individual diners, insomuch as they could be predicted. The servants rushed about under Sam's watchful eye; one here arranging little globs of meat into careful patterns on the plates, another there holding forks to the air and inspecting for splotches that might have been missed in the wash.

"Less is more," advised Peter. "Definitely more," said

Sam. Platitudes, to be sure, but sometimes they anchor the mind. The novice needs a safe harbor, a place to return to in the event of panic and uncertainty. They all knew this was Jana's first time. No matter how much she'd insisted she was old enough and ready enough, it put them all on edge. They'd have sheltered her longer if they could have. But needs must, and what they needed now was a replacement server.

"Do whatever you're told. You get told to jump, you jump. You get told to dance, you dance." Sam was trying to cover every contingency. Jana had heard this all before, recurring whispers in the dark since as long as she could remember.

"Do it fast," added Peter. Their voices acquired an insistent edge as the seconds inched by, closer and closer to the moment they all knew was coming.

"No delays. You can't delay. And don't react to the conversation. They'll see. They want to pretend like you're not there," Sam said. "Usually," Peter interrupted.

"Usually," Sam continued. "It's better when they pretend. You want to be in the background. A prop." A tall order for Jana.

It wasn't her looks that were the problem. She was pretty, in a girl-next-door kind of way, but not so much so that it would be a distraction. And it certainly wasn't her demeanor. She was quiet, bordering on mousey. Most of the younger ones were, if they'd been brought up after the Fall. No, the problem was that Jana had never served before. She'd be new to the diners, someone they'd never seen and someone whose novelty might attract their interest. In times of order and restraint, unwanted

6

attention is a mere nuisance. But in times of disorder and lawlessness, attention can be a dangerous thing.

"Seen and not heard," said Peter.

"Not even seen. Not even noticed," said Sam.

It was always possible. Sometimes even probable, depending on the mood of the room. But the divide between advice and aspirations was beginning to blur. Whether any of them drew the attention of the diners was a matter of chance. Sometimes they'd be absorbed in conversation or reminiscences, too interested in each other to bother with a servile nothing scurrying about in the background. And sometimes they'd be bored. Anything could happen when they were bored.

"Don't stay longer than you have to. Serve the food. Stay 'til it's done," said Sam.

"But then leave," said Peter. "Leave as soon as it's polite to. Quietly."

Noise was never wise. Plates can clink, forks can clank, and—god help you—glass can break. This seemed the least of the risks, but it had to be said. Jana wasn't likely to stay, and she certainly could be trusted not to speak out of turn. But there's always nerves. Shaky fingers couldn't be controlled, and they'd all had them before. The only thing to do was hope—hope nothing dropped, and pray you didn't falter. Silently, of course. Prayer was the worst thing you could do.

"Quietly. Professionally. No matter what happens," said Sam. Jana had practiced, to be sure. She'd memorized the ritual of serving a course. Which seat to go to, which diner would be where, and what to do in a thousand contingencies. She'd been working at it for months. But there's nothing like the real thing, and the pressure just isn't the same. The sense of unease in the room rose as their time drew nearer. It was down to moments, now, and Sam gave Jana his last bit of advice as the servers exited the kitchen in a solemn, careful procession of foodstuffs and libations: "And whatever you do—whatever you do—don't look them in the eyes."

Jana gave a last, wistful glance into the kitchen as its door swung shut. It was a haven of safety in many ways, if only for the cloak of anonymity it provided. Blame for problems with the food tended to fall on the servers as messengers. There were fewer opportunities for error. And, of course, you weren't being watched. The servers plodded through the halls in silence, focused intently on their tasks. There wasn't much to look at in any event. The interiors were bare and blackened, scorched by flame, and the idea of brightening them with decor for the servants' benefit was considered frivolous. Jana pursed her lips, running the injunctions of the other servers through her head as she walked. It helped distract from thoughts of what could happen, or what had happened to servers during meals past.

A din from the distance grew louder as they approached the entryway to the dining chamber, rising until the doors opened and it became a scattered cacophony of laughter, stories, and chit-chat. To Jana's ears, it was indistinguishable from the familiar sound of the servants supping among themselves—except for the palpable tension she felt, and the periodic fluttering of wings.

CHAPTER TWO

"THERE'S MOVEMENT. I CAN'T TELL how many. At most, three. Still grounded." The voice crackled over the walkie-talkie, breaking a bored silence that had overtaken the room. William Holt hadn't been a hunter before the Fall, otherwise he might have been used to the tedious monotony he felt while awaiting his prey. He might even have enjoyed it. This sport, though, was different. A hunter at least waits in comfort, safe in his blind with only the anticipation of the kill to distract him from his thoughts. But ducks or deer or fish can't strike at their pursuer. Miss your shot and they simply flee, leaving you to your patient vigil. Holt, on the other hand, was hunting a predator. His nerves never quite turned off, no matter how quiet things seemed to be. He always had to be on edge, ready to react at a moment's notice. The periodic messages from Faye, the spotter, made his stomach ball just a bit in anticipation every time something came through.

"Three's too many," Holt radioed back. "Hell, two's too many. If we can't confirm the number, we pass." He'd grown cautious over years of fighting. He wasn't always like that—a tall, brawny, dark-haired former policeman, he'd been a rule-breaker coming out of the academy. Like most of his classmates, he wanted to take on the bad guys. He was good, they were evil, and stodgy older cops who'd given up their ideals to push paper weren't going to stand in his way. It was all a fantasy, but the young can be forgiven for thinking they'll conquer the world. Policing turned out not to bear much resemblance to war, if one could call it that. They did, as a matter of pride. But this was less a war and more a small tit after a long series of tats. He'd ended up having a lot in common with the criminals he'd chased—confronting a vastly more powerful foe, the best he could reasonably hope for was to act, flee, and avoid getting caught.

Next to Holt sat Scott Daxton, better known to the members of their cell as Dax. A pudgy, bespectacled, and out-of-shape geek, Dax was an unlikely choice for what amounted to an assassination. But beggars can't be choosers, and there weren't many people left to fill the role. No one was really sure how many had survived, but the consensus was that it was in the tens of millions at most. And even among those that remained, the fighting spirit was dwindling. Most people had concluded that things were hopeless. The major cities were rubble, and it was too dangerous to congregate in larger groups. The orgy of violence immediately after the Fall had wiped out most anyone who had a desire to resist. And while comparatively few people had actually been killed directly, billions had starved or succumbed to disease once the world's governments imploded. Holt took who he could, and it wasn't that Dax was useless. He knew how to access what was left of the Internet, he was great with technology, and he had connections. In any kind of combat, though, he'd just be a liability.

Dax fidgeted, anxious to end the wait. "We oughta try at some point. It's been days. It'll never be perfect. If it doesn't work, we get underground and we're gone." The subways and sewers were the only truly safe means of movement. This had once been a thriving city, and its residents had once considered themselves the center of the universe—or at least the parts of it they knew of. The few that remained knew better, now. What was left of New York City was mostly a husk. Buildings had collapsed, had been ransacked, or had simply been abandoned. The only permanently inhabited structure for miles around was the Perch.

Its inhabitants didn't call it that, but the nickname had spread quickly, spat from the mouths of those dispossessed of their homes. A dark, towering structure, the Perch loomed over what remained of the city. Black spires jutted upward from its sides, poking at the skies in defiance and giving it the look of a gnarled, metallic cactus. Lights could be seen sporadically at points, but it wasn't clear from the exterior how much was living space and how much was dedicated to some other purpose. Construction had begun shortly after the Fall, once its residents accepted that things were never going back to the way they'd used to be. After a few years the thing was done, blighting the skyline and signaling the end of the city as its people had known it.

The area immediately around the Perch was mostly

debris. Any nearby buildings had been scavenged for useful materials during its construction, and what wasn't needed was simply left in piles on the ground. A few miles or so away, many of the buildings still stood, but they were in questionable condition. Most were too dangerous to live in, but a few people still tried, even then. Holt and his cell encountered them from time to time while they moved through the city's remains. People can be stubborn, and reluctant to accept that their lives have changed for good. Some still dreamed that one day things might return to normal, and that they'd be left to rebuild as they saw fit. Others just couldn't conceive of a life lived someplace else. Their friends, families, and jobs all in the past, they preferred to try to survive in their homes rather than crawling about in a forest someplace and learning an entirely new way of living.

A new voice came across the airwaves—Dustin Thane, the one they'd tapped to deliver the final blow. "We can do two. Knock one down and he's mine. Y'all just have to keep the other one off me long enough for us to kill him and bail."

Thane wanted to fight, always. His hair was bleached blonde, cropped short, and his face was covered in a dark stubble that never seemed to cross the line from scruff to beard. He was an attack dog, spoiling for battle and the rush of adrenaline that came with it, and he'd probably have ended up in prison if it weren't for the Fall. He was the type who had trouble restraining himself, and always chose to escalate a confrontation rather than be the one to back down. Holt had his hands full trying to manage him. Thane had gotten better about things, and the cell hadn't been together for very long, which gave Holt reason to hope. And finding someone willing to fight these days was harder and harder, after all. But this wasn't meant to be a grand, glorious battle. It wasn't even meant to be a fair fight. Valor was a fine enough thing, but it was discretion that got you home safely.

"No. It's one, or it's a no-go," Holt radioed back.

"I don't usually agree with Thane," said Dax, "but we have to try at some point. We lugged these all the way up here. They're heavy. It'd be a huge pain in the ass to carry them back out again." Dax gestured to a thick metal footlocker at the center of the room. Inside were several Stinger missiles, along with their launcher. They were small, shoulder-fired, and designed such that they could be used by a single person. They weren't nearly as heavy as Dax implied, but in the end it's all relative. He'd been covered in sweat carrying the footlocker up here, and he didn't relish thoughts of repeating the task.

"No. It's my call. Thane can only handle one of them. We'd have to ground them both, and even if we did they wouldn't stay down for long. This is all about patience, and only taking the easy shots. We're here to fight dirty. Besides," Holt said with a smirk, "it's not the worst thing in the world if you have to exercise some more."

Dax's face reddened as he turned his focus back to his laptop, and to coded messages from other cells around the world. He knew he wasn't cut out for battle. He didn't have the experience, didn't have the athleticism, and didn't have the talent for it. But inside he still fantasized about being one of them. A reckless warrior like Thane, or a decisive leader like Holt. He looked up to them both, despite the teasing, and did whatever he could to get close to the action. Mostly that meant a supporting role, helping with the planning and watching the Internet for news or for anything that might help them somehow. The enemy was generally oblivious to human technology. It either didn't interest them, or just wasn't one of their natural talents. They'd learned enough to strike at power plants and datacenters, but they were always a few steps behind, and it didn't look like they'd ever shut things down entirely.

Holt waited in silence, staring at the Perch out of the broken windows of the abandoned building they were hiding in. He'd never been close to it. He could have tried, if he'd been inclined to. There were people inside. The Vichies. Sometimes they still let more in. But you had to make a trade that he'd never been interested in making. You could get access to relative comfort and relative safety, and you wouldn't be on your own. But you wouldn't be free, and you'd have to check your dignity at the door.

Almost an hour passed before the next update from Faye. "This might be it, boys. There's one standing at the edges, facing west. Looks like he's all alone."

Holt picked up the walkie-talkie to radio back. "Watch him. If he—"

"He's in the air! He's in the air! Heading straight down the alley!" Faye's voice was flush with excitement. She was alone in a sniper's nest, and had been for days. She was patient enough, but she'd been itching for something to happen to break up the monotony.

"Everyone get ready. If I get a shot, I'm taking it,"

Holt replied. "Faye, watch for where he drops. I want Thane moving in ASAP. Otherwise we're on silent."

Dax scanned the skies with a pair of binoculars, while Holt prepped the launcher. They'd get one shot, with a narrow window. They had to hit him in just the right place, or he'd go to ground too far away for Thane to reach him in time. And while a Stinger could take out an airplane, it wouldn't do more than stun one of them. Someone would have to be up close and personal to deliver the killing blow. Get there too late, and the target would have recovered—and he wouldn't be in the mood for mercy.

"There! There! I can see him!" Dax gestured excitedly, pointing at a small, black dot weaving through the air between them and the Perch. "An angel."

You could call them that, although many called them demons instead. That might be just as apt a description, given how they'd acted since the Fall. To the survivors of the carnage they'd inflicted, the only real difference between angels and demons was where they'd landed when they fell. It certainly looked like an angel. Feathered wings spread wide, it glided towards them, heading towards the street of surviving buildings that Holt had selected as their point of ambush.

"I see him." Holt swung the launcher over his shoulder, steadying it and pointing it outwards through the window. He looked again for the target, caught it with his eyes, and lined up the sight. He waited a few more seconds. Just a little closer, and they had a better chance. He kept the angel in the sight for another moment, listened for the beeping noise that indicated he had a lock, and fired. A small cloud of smoke billowed into the air around them, traces of the trail that spewed from behind the missile as it honed in on the target. Following the heat signature, the missile adjusted, tracking the angel as it flew. The angel bobbed up and down in the air, either hearing the burst of sound from the missile's launch or seeing its smoke as it approached. But it was too late for evasion. The missile hit, and the angel was engulfed in flames as a ball of fire lit up the air in between the row of buildings. The angel fell, again, sending up a plume of asphalt as it crashed into the streets below.

CHAPTER THREE

"**T**HERE WERE FOUR OF US. Held at bay for hours. Bolt after bolt ripped through the air around us. We were outgunned, outnumbered." Uzziel had told this story many times before, but his dinner companions tolerated it without any complaint. Most of their own stories were just as stale, and Uzziel had gotten quite masterful at the telling after years of practice. His audience had all lived for at least a few thousand years, and they were used to repetition. Besides, Uzziel was a warrior, and these were likely to be the last war stories he'd get a chance to tell. The rebellion was over, and the prospect of any future glories now gone. All that was left was to glorify the past.

Uzziel was short and stocky, with mad little eyes that saw menace in everything. He stroked his thick, black beard as he continued to regale the others. "We were damned determined, though. It was at the height of things. And I don't have to tell any of you, but we were in no mood to let the Crystal Towers stand."

"Symbol of oppression," said Rhamiel as he sipped

from his wine. Rhamiel looked substantially younger than Uzziel, although that didn't mean much with their kind. He had an aloof air, born of vanity. Virtually all of the angels had at least dabbled in sin since the Fall, if not plunged into it, and that had been Rhamiel's vice of choice.

"That it was, Rhamiel. We were going to torch those towers, Maker be damned. Sachiel was clipped as we entered. Lost control. He had to glide down, to a hard landing. But we kept going. We fought through a row of constructs. Came to a door, a reinforced door. And we pounded and pounded, and we burst through. And what did we find?"

"The Maker's own son, Uzziel? Returned at last?" Ecanus smirked as he interrupted. Ecanus was slight of frame, and didn't look big enough to be very threatening. But he had a reputation among the servants for unprovoked outbursts, and they all tried to give him a wide berth.

"Better," said Uzziel. "One damned cherub. His fat little fingers clutching the defense controls."

"And you turned the other cheek, of course?" Rhamiel asked, idly swirling his wine around in a golden, jewel-encrusted goblet.

"Ha! No, that we did not. We stuffed him into a barrel of ammunition and lit it on fire. Then we razed the towers, and moved on to the Ethereal Gardens." Uzziel laughed heartily, and turned to demolishing the contents of the plate in front of him.

Behind them, the servants moved in. Their actions were carefully choreographed, almost a dance. *Take the fork, then replace. Remove the plate, bring it to Sam. Get the next course, put it down, then backs to the wall.* Jana ran the list through her head, over and over. Things had to look good. Most of the diners didn't care, but a few were particular. You can't please everyone, but the servers had to try.

Jana glanced up quickly, taking in the room. Around a dozen of them were seated at the long, formal dining table in front of her. Ornate tableware was lined before the diners, ready to receive the intricately prepared delicacies they'd be served. Everything was a mish-mash, a schizophrenic menu guided solely by Sam's guesses as to the diner's preferences for the evening. A roasted hog sat at one end of the table, stuffed with apples and sugars and waiting for Uzziel's attentions. Noodles of various kinds ruled the center of the table, and a vegetable medley of eggplant and zucchini slices finished things off at the other end. Imposing red banners bearing the symbol of some heavenly faction had been hastily hung along the walls, a nod to Uzziel's penchant for war-making.

Sam's admonition against making eye contact was a good one. Seeing an angel would have been unsettling in and of itself. But these angels had fallen, and most of them hadn't made it through quite intact. They all bore scars of some sort. Most had burnt skin, twisted tissues that covered most of their bodies. Their wings ranged in color from a light soot to a charred black. Many had sustained damage to their faces during the Fall, and they could be sensitive about it. Give one of them the wrong sort of look, and they'd give you a scar of your own.

Jana moved behind one of the chairs, standing at

the ready. She'd drawn Nefta, who tended to be one of the more reasonable ones, and had thus been considered a good choice for Jana's maiden service. It was all relative, of course, and any one of them could explode if their mood dictated it. Some of the angels seemed to have descended into full blown psychopathy after the Fall, treating humans as playthings in a sandbox they were frustrated to be confined to. Others could even approach kindness. They'd all spent centuries in service of humanity in one way or another, and old habits die hard. But they still had an air of superiority about them whenever they interacted with their former charges. It could manifest itself as something closer to paternalism or something closer to disgust, but it was always there.

Jana stood, waiting, and looked to Sam. Dressed formally and standing at attention, Sam was a leader and a mentor. What was left of his thinning hair was graying prematurely, a byproduct of the stresses of his duties. The lines on his face were etched into a permanent expression of worry. A little older than the others, and a lot wiser, Sam acted as a conductor of sorts. He stood at the back of the dining room, carefully watching the flow of the conversation for the right time. It wouldn't do to interrupt a story or a joke by collecting the plates too soon. You had to lean over the table to do that, and you had to be seen. Whoever was speaking might take offense; whoever was listening might be distracted. Sam watched, saw the conversation enter a lull, and gave a slight nod to the other servers. It was subtle, and you'd miss it if you weren't watching closely. Fortunately none of them did, and they approached the table in unison.

Jana reached for Nefta's fork, replacing it with a fresh one. She then removed the plate, keeping her eyes locked on a point she'd selected at random on the table in front of her. She couldn't see any movement from the periphery, which was a good sign. Nefta had picked at her food, leaving most of it on the plate—a bad one. Hungry angels could be angry angels. If she disliked the food, she might hold Jana responsible. Or she could simply be brooding, or any of dozens of other explanations that Jana couldn't help but begin running through in her head. She forced herself to stop, to focus on the task at hand.

She walked the plate back to Sam, following a line of other servers. One by one, they approached a stainless steel cart next to him, deposited their plate and its contents as quietly as they could, and resumed their places behind the chair of the diner they were serving for the evening. As Jana approached, Sam eyed Nefta's plate nervously. They exchanged a quick look of worry as she scraped the food into a bin on the cart. There was nothing he could do, but she at least had his sympathies. She carefully stacked the plate, then pivoted, returning to her place to await the arrival of the next course. Sam rolled the cart out of the room, staring downward and trying to look as submissive as possible. The best servers projected a practiced air of obsequiousness, which seemed to draw the least negative attention.

"Ecanus, I hear you had a little foray into the world of man recently," said Rhamiel. "Anything exciting? Or is the Maker's pet creation as dull as it's always been?"

"The only excitement out there is what we make

for ourselves," Ecanus replied. "I went southwest with Tavael, a few days flight. We found some smaller camps, but the fun's gone from those. I came up with something much more entertaining than mindless slaughter. Not to name names, Uzziel."

Uzziel responded with something between a grunt and a growl. His slaughter was anything but mindless. He'd been of high rank in the Heavens, the rough equivalent to a general. He left the tower only for sorties, planned missions with a checklist of goals designed to keep the remains of humanity disorganized and panicked.

"We found a hidden path they were using to travel between encampments. It was buried in a forest, and you almost couldn't see it. But Tavael has good eyes. We landed, picked a place of ambush, and started confronting travelers along the path. We asked them riddles." Ecanus paused, smiling. Jana listened, but dared not look up. It was hard not to flinch if you looked at him directly, and any look could be interpreted as a stare. Ecanus had more scarring than most, and his face had been ruined. Red blotches blurred into pocks and dents, and all that was left of his hair were a few scattered, lonely tufts. His wings were singed a dark black, making him resemble an angry, half-broiled raven that had escaped from some farmer's stew.

"Riddles?" asked Nefta. "You've never been the intellectual sort. Where did you even come up with them?" Ecanus had been strictly a foot soldier before the Fall, with no sign of a bent towards puzzles.

"I'm not. And we simply made them up. What has

three hands, a mouth, and cannot breathe?" He waited patiently as his audience pondered the question.

"Some sort of clock?" guessed Uzziel.

"Perhaps," said Ecanus. "I don't really know. We made up the riddles; we didn't bother to come up with the answers. The results were splendid. We'd surprise someone, pose the riddle, and demand that they answer or die. They'd sputter, think, and then take a guess. We'd confer, and make them wait awhile. They had such hope in their eyes, that we might be considering sparing them. That maybe they'd guessed correctly. Then we'd laugh, and kill them all anyway. It was incredible fun."

He took a drink, surveying the room. None of the servers looked up, although they all knew the story had been told at least partly for their benefit. Ecanus reveled in cruelty, but most of the other angels expected at least some restraint in dealing with their servants. Getting them trained took time, and the supply wasn't unlimited. Psychological torture, though, left no visible scars.

"Cute," Rhamiel said. "I suppose it gives an added bit of artistic touch to the violence. But you really should branch out. The Maker prohibited so much. You ought to at least taste some of the other vices, otherwise you'll never appreciate their virtues."

Jana couldn't help herself. She looked up. Rhamiel's gaze was fixed directly on her as he spoke. There was something in his eyes, and she couldn't tell exactly what. They were a bright, shimmering blue, and they seemed to draw you into them. He had a cold predator's stare, but there was a playful twinkle in them, too. The contrast was unnerving. It didn't help that his vanity was justified. Of all the angels she'd seen, Rhamiel had been least affected by the Fall. His face was flawless, and other than some slight scarring on his hands he was the picture of angelic perfection. He had a taste for the formal, and wore an opulent bronze chest plate that showed off his well-developed physique. His wings were virtually undamaged, flush with feathers that shimmered with a light grey tint. Jana looked down quickly, hoping to dodge his stare. However he might look, they could all be deadly. She knew that with them she had to assume a mask of meekness, no matter what she might be feeling inside.

No one else seemed to notice Jana's faux pas, though Nefta seemed to have noticed Rhamiel's fixation. Jana could see her drumming her fingers against the table and tensing her wings against the back of her chair. She hoped Nefta's irritation wasn't being directed her way, but there was no way to tell from behind. She knew she couldn't look up again, and so she focused on the floor as Ecanus continued on, glaring at Rhamiel and contorting the scar tissue on his face into a burnt, wrinkled scowl. "I didn't rebel just to dirty myself with some glorified chimpanzee. If the Covenant hadn't—"

"Ecanus!" bellowed Uzziel from across the table. The room fell silent.

"Some things aren't discussed in mixed company," said Nefta icily. "I'd expect even the lowest and crudest among us to have more tact than that. It's a wonder you aren't invited to dinner more often." There an awkward pause in the conversation. Ecanus's eyes narrowed to slits, and his face puffed and twitched as he fumed, clanking his utensils loudly and continuing to eat. The other angels focused on their food, pointedly ignoring him.

The silence broke only when Sam returned, pushing a fresh cart containing the next course. The servers looked to him for guidance, terrified. Recognizing the tension, he began service at once. Again Jana lined up, waiting to receive a fresh plate. She hoped it was more to Nefta's liking. She ran things through to herself, one more time. *Just get the plate, turn, and stand behind her in your place. Watch for your cue.* That part went smoothly. She made it safely back and positioned herself behind Nefta. She stood at attention, waiting for everyone else to return. Then Sam nodded, and they all stepped forward as one.

Jana reached in front of Nefta, carefully placing the plate in front of her. She thought she could see Nefta staring at her, but couldn't be sure. She'd learned her lesson, and her eyes kept a laser focus on the plate. As she backed away, she heard it. A clink from across the room.

She backed herself against the wall, where she was supposed to be. So did everyone but Daniel, one of the other servers. A few years older than Jana, he'd helped her practice some, and had been filled with advice on how to avoid an incident. Now he stood chained to the table by Ecanus's grip. He'd had made some error delivering the plate, and had knocked it against the table ever so slightly. The food was intact. Maybe nudged around the plate, but that was enough. Ecanus now held his wrist, forcing his arm against the table.

"Pick a finger," said Ecanus. Daniel remained paralyzed, unable to respond.

"Pick one, or I'll take them all."

Daniel stuck out his pinkie, clutched the rest into a tight fist, and closed his eyes.

"Wise choice," said Ecanus, as he unsheathed a flaming knife from his belt. The knife flickered as he raised it into the air, and sparks flew as he brought it down onto the table.

CHAPTER FOUR

"SIT HIM DOWN. SIT HIM down. Let go, boy. Let me take a look." Sam pushed Daniel into a chair, trying to calm him. Daniel released his injured hand, giving it over to Sam for inspection. Daniel's face still bore a look of complete shock. Far worse things could have happened, but he hadn't been expecting any of them. He'd never caused offense, and had never suffered more than a mild verbal scolding.

"Is he okay?" asked Jana, hovering at the edges of the commotion and trying to get a peek. There wasn't much any of them could do. The wound had instantly cauterized, and in any event no one had been bold enough to ask Ecanus to return the finger. But they cared about him, so they put on a show, and they hoped that it might calm him down. Ecanus could do as he pleased, and there was nothing that could stop him or any of the others from coming down to the servant's quarters to continue the fun if they were so inclined.

"It hurts. It's on fire. How am I going to keep working? I'll drop things," said Daniel. His eyes welled with tears, and he couldn't keep himself from sneaking glimpses at his charred skin. None of the other servers could, either. Something about tragedy draws the eyes, whether it's a need to process the horror or some animal instinct to learn lessons from the missteps of those around us.

"You'll be fine. It wasn't your fault. You were just there," said Jana. She tried to sound soothing, hoping it might calm him down.

"If he'd really been angry with you, he'd have taken the hand," said Sam. Cold comfort, but true. Ecanus wasn't known to forgive a slight.

"Give him space. Give him space. Go clean things up now, and let me tend to him." Sam shooed the crowd of servers out of the room. They'd made their sympathies known, and it was time to get back to work.

Peter led the way back to the kitchen, and Jana followed. Peter was thin, almost to the point of being sickly. Younger than Sam, he had ambitions of climbing the ranks, such as they were. There weren't many rungs on that ladder, and it seemed a little silly to Jana. There were no perks to leadership here, only peril. But he kept at it anyway, directing the others and using any opportunity to take charge. Men find comfort in hierarchies, and things always look more comfortable at the top. He wasn't the kind of man you'd expect to see running things, but he had a tenaciousness to him. He had the temperament of a determined little terrier that won't let go of someone's ankle, convinced its prey will eventually succumb to the nipping no matter their size.

"Let's get started on the dishes," said Peter. "We want them sparkling. There could be an inspection at any moment, and we all know what would happen if we failed." There had never been an inspection, not by the angels. They didn't care for details, and didn't care to sully themselves or their reputations by making a trip to the kitchens for something as inconsequential as dishware. They preferred to manage by watching for errors and punishing them, swiftly and savagely. Sam would scour the dishes to ensure they were clean, and probably several times. But his wrath they could handle.

Jana soaked a stack of plates in a wooden bucket, boiling away the grime. There weren't a lot of amenities there, but they did have fire. Sometimes it was from wood, sometimes from paper, and sometimes from coal, if they were lucky. The angels allowed caravans of necessary supplies into the tower under strict supervision. The humans living there weren't their only servants. Others outside were in their service as well, and did whatever was needed to keep their masters content. It was much more dangerous out there. Angels often couldn't tell humans apart, or affected not to be able to. And many on the outside would relish the chance to settle their quarrels with the angels by having a friendly chat with those who served them.

Jana mixed in some dish soap and began scrubbing. Plenty of goods had survived the Fall, and Sam was diligent about impressing their needs on the scavengers who made the deliveries. If it could arguably contribute to the pleasure of the angels, they were likely to get it. He always had the trump card of threatening to tattle, or simply lying and saying that someone like Ecanus had made a special request. There were limits, though, and the comfort of the servants was a distant priority.

"Someone's taken an interest in you," Peter said to Jana, as a few of the other servers smiled knowingly.

"No one's interested in me," replied Jana. Peter could be insufferably irritating when he wanted to, and she just knew where he was heading.

"Some of us saw," said Peter. "Rhamiel was staring so much, we couldn't help but see."

"I didn't notice," said Jana, trying to get back to her dishes. She'd hoped that Rhamiel's wandering eyes would go unnoticed, but no such luck. Now she'd never live down the teasing, even if she'd survived the meal unscathed. Some of the other girls were already starting to roll their eyes at her and whisper amongst themselves. She'd done nothing to encourage him, but it wouldn't stop them from acting on their envy or trying to knock her down a peg.

"Be careful," said Peter. "You're not the first one he's looked at. I've been doing this a lot longer. You have to watch yourself, or you could end up like poor Daniel. You really want to keep your distance." He loved giving advice, and Jana and the others generally let him. They already knew everything he had to say, but he meant well, and Sam always said that it couldn't hurt to reinforce the basics. The servants' best hope for survival was blind submission, and they did everything they could to ingrain it in themselves as force of habit.

Jana finished her part and dried her hands. "I'll be fine. I was new. It was just a look."

"It's never just a look," said Peter.

She wasn't sure, herself. You could never be too sure, not with them. They hadn't been free for long, and it made them like children in some ways. Many didn't seem to know what to do with themselves. They could be mercurial, flitting from interest to interest, and Peter could be right. Then again, Peter could have interest of his own. It wouldn't be unlike him. He wanted to be more than he was, and a man on the make needs a woman by his side.

The chores done, the servants retired to their quarters. They lived in a spartan common area. Old sleeping bags lined the floors, set off from each other just enough to give a sense of personal space. They each kept a knapsack of personal items or mementos, and there wasn't really room for anything else. It was getting late, and they gathered in the center by a small fire pit. Sam had convinced the servants on the outside to bring in a few wooden logs, and he'd arranged them in a triangle around the fire pit as benches to give them a place to gather and sit together. They didn't get much free time, and didn't have much they could do in it. So they sat together each night, singing songs and telling stories. Mostly they stuck to bland popular favorites from before the Fall. The older servants tended to lead things, working from memory. They were careful—some subjects were taboo, so they had to self-censor. Jana sang along to the songs she knew, but didn't have much of her own to add. She'd been young when the Fall had happened, and her memories from before were fading. They never told stories from after out in the open. Either they wouldn't be interesting or they wouldn't be safe, so the servants opted to just avoid the issue entirely.

As the night went on and the fire dimmed, the crowd around it thinned. One by one, they took to their beds and went to sleep. When it felt late enough, Sam called the night. Jana had waited until the end. She was exhausted, but didn't think she'd be able to sleep. She still felt the nervous energy from earlier in the day, a relic of her adrenaline. It wouldn't always be like this. She just had to adjust. But her first service was a milestone, and though the day hadn't been perfect, she'd heard of worse. She certainly hadn't been the cause of anything, which was about as much as one could hope for. She stood, began the trudge towards her sleeping bag, and went to sleep.

She awoke sometime later, hearing voices. In the shadows of the doorway was a figure, talking to Sam. It didn't have wings, so it couldn't be one of them. It walked closer—a woman. Another servant, from higher up in the tower.

"Jana," the woman said, looking directly at her. "You need to come with me. You're wanted up top."

CHAPTER FIVE

"I GOT HIM. I GOT HIM." Thane's voice came through, and Holt soon saw him from the window, down in the street and sprinting towards the location of the crash. He was carrying a fair amount of gear on his back, but he was making good time. It all came down to a race—Thane's legs against the downed angel's groggy senses.

"I've got eyes on him," radioed Faye. "Definitely a he. And looks like he's completely out. He's still burning, nice and toasty."

"Got it. Keep us posted," replied Holt. He picked up a pair of binoculars, and focused in on the spot that Dax was already excitedly monitoring. It was hazy with smoke, but the outline of the angel was clear. The wings were the giveaway. Sprawling around their bearer, they stretched across the pavement and wobbled from side to side with the wind. Hopefully it was the wind. If the angel was recovering already, then Thane was lost, and it was time to begin a strategic retreat.

Thane ran, breathing heavily and dodging debris and

abandoned cars as he went. He was getting closer, and this was the moment of truth. He could see the body twitching in the distance, just a few dozen yards away. He hesitated, but just for a second. There was never any real doubt about what he would do. He muttered a "fuck it" under his breath and turned his trot into a charge. He closed the distance quickly, ripping off his backpack as he reached the side of his target.

First things first. Thane pulled out a taser, unloading it into the angel's neck. The angel convulsed, his arms jumping, but didn't make any noise. He was still unconscious, and it was hard for Thane to tell the scope of the injuries, if any. The angel wore elaborately decorated ceremonial armor, forged from gold, which the blast had dented in places and melted in others. They'd at least have the satisfaction of ruining him socially, whatever else happened. His neck and face were dotted with burns, but that didn't really mean anything. Odds were those came from the Fall. Thane had seen angels get injured before, and some were weaker than others. It took a lot, and a single missile wasn't likely to do the trick. But they'd planned for that, and the missile was just their opening salvo.

He ripped open his backpack and pulled out the collar. The world's militaries hadn't put up much resistance, other than a few one-sided battles that were mostly for show. But even after the armed forces of every country had been scattered, they kept trying, and someone among their remnants had come up with this. They called it a collar, but it looked more like a heavy neck brace. Around its base was a row of thick, boxy batteries that had been adapted from their original industrial purpose. The interior was lined with a highly conductive metal, circling around the inside to connect with as much skin as possible. Snap it on and deliver the charge, and you could actually kill one of them. It wasn't that you could call angels vulnerable to electricity, exactly. They could endure a lot of it, at levels that would be fatal to any human. It was more that they simply didn't seem to be affected all that much by anything else. Everyone had heard stories about people who claimed to have seen a kill through other means—with grenades, with bombs, and even a tale that was circulating about a man who'd lured one into a bunker filled with dynamite. The stories were secondhand, and probably consisted mostly of exaggeration. But the collar worked, if you could get it on one of them. The stories all agreed on that.

The air whistled nearby, and Thane heard a small thump next to him from the angel. Faye had taken a shot, not that it would help much.

"He moved, Thane. You've got to go faster. I can't keep him down for long." Another whistle, and the angel's head was knocked violently to the side. She could continue pumping bullets into him, but it wouldn't keep him down. Eventually he'd wake, and he'd tear everything in the area apart.

"Hold your fire a sec," radioed Thane. It'd be a shame to get this close just to get killed in the crossfire. He opened the collar, lunging towards the angel and snapping it around his neck. The angel's eyes flashed open. He thrashed about wildly, tossing Thane to the side as he gripped at his own throat. He'd recovered too soon.

The collar was on, but it wasn't active. A second later and the deed would have been done, electricity coursing through the angel's body and sending him to wherever angels went when their lives were finally finished. Thane staggered to his feet, as the angel whipped its wings wildly through the air and tried to remove the thing now fastened around him.

Thane pondered his situation. There weren't any good choices. Run, and he'd be cut down as a coward. Fight, and he'd be cut down as a fool. Then a series of whistles, a series of thumps, and the angel went down again. Faye was firing in quick succession, scoring hit after mostly useless hit. But knocking him down had given Thane the opening. He leapt forward, slamming his hand against a prominent button on the front of the collar. The angel jerked, as Thane pushed himself backward. Contact with the collar was one thing, but once it was running even a brush against the angel's armor was likely to extend the electricity's circuit to Thane himself.

The angel went into a series of spasms, his limbs jerking around uncontrollably. He started making noises, a combination of moans and gurgles. Supposedly they had liked to sing, before they fell. But this was no heavenly choir. Just a low, guttural death rattle, as the collar emptied the current from its batteries directly into the angel's neck. Smoke sizzled from his sides, and after a few more seconds it was all over. Thane had actually done it. The angel was tagged and bagged, and he became one of the few humans since the Fall to do in one of their tormentors.

"It worked," said Holt, watching from above. "Can't believe the damned thing worked."

"People say it's how God fought them," said Dax. "That he was sitting up in the clouds, hurling lightning bolts at them before he cast them down here. It's all silly speculation from old stories, but it inspired people to test it out. Good thing, too, or we'd be defenseless. And I can get more of them. People are selling them online. I've even got the plans, if we could get all the parts." He pulled up a set of schematics on his laptop. It was Greek to Holt, but it looked impressive.

Holt picked up his walkie-talkie, interrupting the whoops and cheers of celebration that had erupted over the airwaves from both Thane and Faye. "Faye. Come on down. Time for us to grab our shit and get moving."

"Okay," said Faye. "It's getting disgusting up here, anyway. Be there in five."

Thane kicked the angel with the toe of his boot, testing him for signs of life. There weren't any, but you couldn't be too careful. He pulled the collar off the body, repacking it. The batteries were done, but they could be recharged, and it wasn't wise to waste things you weren't sure you could replace. He grabbed the angel by the arms and rolled him over, avoiding the heat of the smoldering armor. Bingo. A sword hilt, poking out of a small scabbard on the angel's belt. He tapped the grip a few times with his fingers. It was cool enough, so he grabbed it and pulled.

Fire erupted from the scabbard, and Thane held the sword aloft, marveling at the thing in his hands. The legend was that this was what had been used to bar the gates to the Garden of Eden. Maybe the place did exist, and maybe some lonely angel still stood there in an eternal vigil, not knowing the chaos that had engulfed the world around him. Stranger things had happened. The swords were definitely real, and a familiar instrument of terror. The angels favored them as a weapon, and had cut down countless millions with them. The fire flickered, its tongues reaching out into the air. It was considerably longer than the scabbard, and although it moved, it stayed mostly the same shape.

"Wow. That is one impressive toy." Thane turned at Faye's voice. She looked tired from her time alone in the sniper's nest, running on fumes and excitement. Her long, auburn hair was tucked into a ponytail, and a rifle was strapped to her back. She'd made it down, and was eager to inspect their handiwork.

If you'd met Faye Walker before the Fall, she'd be unrecognizable now. She was an office peon then, pushing papers around a human resources department and giving a large corporation cover against accusations of wrongdoing in their hiring and firing. But she'd spent a few years in the camps afterwards. The camps had been a desperation move, a last-ditch effort of a failing government to put up some kind of resistance. A hastily formed system designed to train ordinary citizens and organize them into militias, the camps had suffered from no shortage of recruits. She'd learned to shoot there, and had developed something of an eagle eye. But groups of people made attractive targets, and they were easily betrayed by anyone looking to join the Vichies on favorable terms. They'd ultimately all been forced to disperse, and she'd operated in a series of smaller cells ever since.

"Like it? I'm gonna slice open another one of 'em with it. Gut him and start mounting heads in a den someplace." Thane practiced a slash through the air, testing it. There was no weight at all, and it felt like he was waving an empty hand.

"Sheath that thing before you lose an arm," said Faye. "You've seen what they can do."

"Fine. Already got my kill for the day, anyway." Bravado aside, Thane was exceedingly careful as he eased the sword back into the scabbard before unbuckling it from the angel's corpse.

"Our kill," said Faye. "You just took care of the reckless part. I'm the one who had to piss in a bottle for two days to make sure you had cover." The role of sniper could be an unpleasant one. The best vantage point might not be the most comfortable one, and you had to be careful how often you moved if you didn't want to get spotted yourself.

Their walkie-talkies screeched in unison with an order from Holt. "Fight over who gets credit later. Get your shit ready and let's get underground."

Faye approached the corpse, giving it a final look. She could still see where there'd been beauty in him, once, but his injuries had mangled him into something else. She'd never seen one up close before. A few times she'd seen them in the distance, soaring above her in the skies. She'd either hid or ran, and hadn't stuck around to see what sort of twisted errands they'd left their nesting place for. She had more courage now than then, but it was still an unsettling sight. She'd grown up before the Fall, raised with stories of angels as loving protectors. The thing before her was a disfigured perversion of her childhood fantasies, turned from guardian into a mad butcher of its own charges.

"Rha-karah," said Faye, almost under her breath.

"You know this guy?" asked Thane.

"Rha-karah shatah-nah," said Faye.

"I never bothered with their names," said Thane. "Don't care what they're called. Don't need to know to kill 'em."

Then Faye just started spewing words. It was as if a dam had broken, and the trickle turned into a flood of incomprehensible verbiage. "Parah nurah shatarah nurah, shata bahka." The words burst out of her uncontrollably and without any breaks. Her face bore a look of complete panic. Her arms hung by her sides limply, as her mouth kept spouting the stream of nonsense. Thane met her eyes, seeing only terror. Then he looked up, and felt it himself.

CHAPTER SIX

"WHAT DO THEY WANT?" ASKED Jana, as she walked alongside the woman. The two continued the upward slog along a central ramp that spiraled around the interior to the upper levels of the tower. The angels rarely used it, preferring to take to the air. But they'd made compromises in designing the place to ensure that one could make their way around on foot as well. They didn't bother to make things easy, and it was a long, circuitous route to the top. Without it, though, the angels would be carrying their own supplies to their own chambers, and they hadn't had much taste for labor since the Fall.

"That's a question for one of them," the woman responded, and continued on in silence. She was middle-aged, with strands of her still-black hair drifting out from underneath the hood of a drab grey cloak. Snippets of purple poked out from underneath at the sleeves and the neck, signals of status that she'd chosen to mask while traveling through the lower levels of the tower.

They were nearing the middle of the structure.

Common areas and common servants were housed near the bottom, to keep the riff raff away from anything or anyone important. A few stories higher up, and you started to see the functional rooms that the angels themselves sometimes had cause to visit—armories, workspaces, and assorted recreational areas. A few of the angels were housed here as well, but only the lowest among them. The angels were all about caste, and arranged themselves according to complicated hierarchies denoting their relative status. Jana had never been able to keep track of it all, and hadn't needed to. Humans were at the bottom, and were expected to show similar deference to every one of them. In the event the angels quarreled amongst themselves, the prudent thing to do was to simply wait quietly and see who won.

"I've never been this high up," said Jana softly, more to herself than anything. The angels had organized their servants according to hierarchies as well. Those outside the tower had the least protection and were considered mercenaries, agents of convenience who were only as valuable as what they could offer. They scavenged for goods the angels might want, bringing them to the tower as tribute in exchange for the promise of immunity from their masters' darker instincts. Mostly they got it, but the angels could be fickle. Those inside the tower were treated as something closer to livestock. They were valuable enough to be preserved, but some were more important than others.

As with the angels, position was everything. Those at the bottom of the tower, such as Jana, were considered useful mostly for scut work. The angels only visited the lower levels to socialize with one another, particularly when their status was unequal. The need for all of them to come down to the servers provided a pretense to avoid bickering over whether any given angel had gained or lost position by ascending or descending to dine. In the middle of the tower was the more skilled labor. Mostly these were craftsmen, along with a few who had talents the angels considered entertaining for one reason or another. At the top lived a smaller group of personal servants, who spent their days tending to an individual angel's every whim. Most of the servants didn't recognize these social distinctions among themselves, as they were all treated equally dismissively. But some of the ones who lived at the top had grown to fancy themselves as superior, mimicking the angels' disdain for those below them.

Another few levels, and they passed a series of gardens. Plants of all sorts were being cultivated, some of which didn't look terrestrial in origin. The angels had fallen along with a random selection of materials and supplies, and perhaps some seeds had been among them. They spoke of it as a kind of memorial to someplace they remembered from home. Sometimes they'd walk through it, pensive and lost within their own heads. Other times it seemed to be used mostly for practical purposes, providing whichever fruits and vegetables happened to be the favorites of the angels living in the tower. Jana looked to the side of the ramp, catching a glimpse of a set of servants pruning flowers to sculpt them into a bizarre design she couldn't recognize.

As they neared the top, the ramp periodically

connected with hallways, lined with living quarters for angels of medium rank. Some of them were just doorways embedded in the outer walls, without any connection to the ramp or to anything else. Likely their occupants valued their privacy, and were happy to make the trade of tending to their own affairs in exchange for keeping their personal spaces totally inaccessible to the help. Jana had heard that there were similar rooms on the outside, which couldn't even be seen unless you were already in the skies.

They walked up the ramp for almost an hour before coming to their destination. The ramp ended at the upper levels, leading into a long, dim corridor lined with imposing wooden doors. As they walked along it, Jana's nerves began to fail. She'd heard stories about some of the things the angels had done, horrible stories. They were always told in a low whisper, and always at night. Each one had the same moral: the only safety lies in absolute deference, no questions asked. It was a peculiar way to be raised, and it had created a peculiar inner turmoil. No matter how much she might chafe at some imperious instruction, something inside her was always screaming to just smile politely and submit.

"They aren't going to hurt me, are they?" said Jana. "Please tell me if they're going to hurt me." She didn't have any options, but a cornered animal will try the inconceivable to escape. Dark thoughts flickered through her head. Maybe she could make it back to the ramp and take a final leap. The woman likely wouldn't be able to stop her, and at least she'd be going out on her own terms. She could deny some angel the glee they'd get from whatever sadistic pleasure they might be up there planning. But then, what happened after? People's conceptions of the afterlife were in flux. Some of the angels had made it a game to drop hints in front of the servants about what things would be like, but they were often contradictory. Sometimes they claimed the gates of heaven had been closed, never again to reopen. Others they promised salvation, but only for their most effective servants. Ecanus had once spun an elaborate tale involving gods from half a dozen unrelated religions and a giant turtle. Sam suspected this was merely their way of passing the time, and often cautioned the servants against believing too much of what they were told.

"I don't know what they're going to do," said the woman. "I do know they'll hurt you if you don't go. So stop being a baby, grow up, and do the things you have to do."

Jana frowned, forgetting her panic. She was hardly a baby. Her fears were real, and more than justified. She kept walking, and spent a few minutes thinking of all of the things she'd say to the woman if only she could. It was all hypothetical. Any chance of a real outburst had been drummed out of her long ago, the product of a lifetime of constant reminders that any careless remark could undo her. Before she'd settled on the most biting potential response in her fantasies, they'd arrived. They stood in front of an imposing, heavy pair of wooden double doors. Their golden handles were fancy metalwork that curled into the shape of some fantastical creature, all teeth and horns and angry eyes. The woman pulled them open and ushered Jana inside.

They entered a large, open lounge. A number of other hallways led off into other places, but this looked like the hub of their social activities. Several angels lazed around on soft velvet couches surrounded by pillows, being waited on by well-dressed attendants as they chatted with each other, drank, or simply stared off into space. Crystal chandeliers hung from the ceilings, sculpted from precious stones that had been hauled to the tower and worked to the angels' specifications by the craftsmen below. The angels were partial to them, as diamond had been a favorite construction material where they came from. Brightly colored paper lanterns were spread around the room, on tables and on walls, and sections of the room glowed blue or green or red from the candles inside. Their colors and symbols belonged to various angelic factions, which had only multiplied since the Fall. Clubs have always been formed mostly for the aura of exclusivity they bestow on their members, and there was nothing the angels loved better than to organize themselves in ways that created envy among outsiders.

The woman led Jana forward, quietly, steering her towards one of the hallways. They were interrupted by a voice as they passed.

"Girl."

Jana froze, paralyzed with indecision. She looked to the woman for guidance, but found none. The woman had stopped, too, but was just standing there passively. Probably she was hoping the same thing as Jana: that she wasn't the one being called to.

"Girl. I remember you. But I didn't catch your name."

There wasn't much to do now but to try to respond

somehow. Jana turned to the voice—it was Rhamiel, relaxing with a friend at a nearby table. They were cordoned off from the others in one of the more exclusive areas, enjoying luxuries that befitted their place at the top of the pecking order. He was staring at her again with those eyes, and it still made Jana uncomfortable. She looked down at the floor. Peter could have been right. Maybe Rhamiel was interested. Some of them seemed as asexual as in the old legends from before the Fall, but others clearly had appetites. Rhamiel's intentions could be anything, and Jana wasn't sure she could fend him off even if she wanted to. And she wasn't entirely sure if she did. There were worse ones who could have taken a liking to her. Certainly worse looking ones.

"I'm Jana," she said, still keeping her eyes locked on the ground in front of her.

"Jana," said Rhamiel. "It's a passable name. Inoffensive, and won't get you killed at least. I couldn't count the number of 'Michaels' who've been put down thanks to their uncreative parents."

Jana stood silently, trying to think through her choices. The conversation didn't call for a response, explicitly, but he could be expecting one. Silence was safest.

"Welcome to high society, Jana," Rhamiel continued. "You don't look like you belong down there, anyhow. Wallowing around in the muck, cleaning grime from plates and rooting around in the leftovers for missing fingers. Come. Sit with us. We'll show you the ropes, and you can entertain us in return. It's tedious up here at times. Someone new would liven up the place." He was smiling now, welcoming, and looked almost friendly.

Jana turned to the woman again, trying to make eye contact and to get some hint as to what to do. But she was studiously ignoring the entire conversation. For a few moments, Jana couldn't decide. Part of her was fascinated, and even wanted to join them. The angels could all be dangerous, but Rhamiel oozed confidence and charm. She'd often wondered what their lives were like up here, and what it would be like to be one of them. She'd never had so much as a kiss, and now here was one of the tower's most well-known residents talking to her. Maybe even flirting with her, if she was reading things right. It was flattering, even if Jana herself found it all somewhat inexplicable.

In the end, she decided to sit. There really wasn't any other choice.

"You've got a little rebellion in you. We like that," said Rhamiel, smirking at the woman who had escorted her up. "Have you met Zuphias? He used to run around inducing miracles before things became unpleasant. I can't tell you how many pieces of toast bore the image of the Maker's son because of him."

Jana believed him, but just for a second. Zuphias must have seen it in her face, because he jumped in quickly. Rhamiel may just have been teasing her, but Zuphias didn't look like he wanted this particular rumor spreading about.

"Nothing as banal as all that," said Zuphias. "Bleeding statues, mostly. A few cases of stigmata. I could show you that one, if you like." He was well-dressed in a scarlet robe that had been precisely tailored to his figure, and he carried himself with an aristocratic bearing. He looked older, his hair graying and fading into a widow's peak. While his face wasn't as clean as Rhamiel's, he had minimal scarring compared to most of the others, with just a few burns running along his jawline.

"No, thank you," said Jana politely. He could have been joking, too, but it was best to assume it was a serious offer.

"Care for something to drink?" said Rhamiel. "I know they don't let you have anything but swill down there. If you're to be joining us, you'll have to upgrade your tastes. It doesn't do to have someone so lovely consigned to our basements." He motioned for one of the other, higher-class servants to approach the table. "Bring us a bottle of wine, from Zuphias's stock. Something nice, to toast to new friends."

The servant darted away to retrieve the wine, as Jana marveled. *She* was being served. By someone who by all rights should be able to order her around, and who otherwise would have considered it beneath him to even speak to her without using an intermediary. She didn't know how to feel about that. Part of her was delighted. She'd been young when she was brought to the tower, and barely remembered her parents. Virtually her entire life had been spent in serfdom. No one had ever fetched things for her or cared about her comfort. On the other hand, she knew full well what it was like to be on the receiving end of those orders.

"Now, girl," said Rhamiel. "What brings you up among us? What troubles are you here to drink away?"

Jana sputtered, nervously trying to start a sentence. She wasn't sure where to begin, or where to go. In the end, she didn't have much of an idea herself, and so not much came out. "I don't know," she said.

"She doesn't know," said Rhamiel, leaning in closer. He flexed his wings, and brushed the tip against her arm as he made himself more comfortable. It sent a chill down her spine. She'd never touched one of them before, and she'd heard stories of all manner of horrible things that could happen if you did it without their permission. She instinctively clasped her arm with her other hand, waiting for whatever the terrible consequence would be. But her skin didn't melt, and demons didn't appear, and she faced nothing more frightening than a brash angel who seemed insistent on toying with her.

"You must know something of what you're doing, else why would you do it?" said Rhamiel.

"Because I have to," said Jana. She couldn't think of any other response, and it was true.

He smiled, and patted her on the shoulder in mock empathy. She flinched, as he'd known she would, and he relished in it as she overcompensated, trying to compose herself by putting on an exaggerated show of nonchalance. He knew he was making her nervous, and he meant to take full advantage of it.

"One never has to do anything," said Rhamiel. "We merely tell ourselves that we do. You might surprise yourself, if you release yourself from the shackles you've imposed." Easy to say, for one in his position. He had all the power, and all the prestige. What he wanted, he got.

She survived at the pleasure of her masters, and got only what she was permitted to have.

She looked up to see her escort, now shooting her a glare. *Now you tell me*, thought Jana. She was hardly an expert on angelic protocol. If the woman hadn't wanted her to sit, she should have let her know beforehand. What was she to do? If she wasn't brave enough to deny Rhamiel herself, how could Jana be expected to? Then she saw someone striding up to them, probably the source of the woman's newfound confidence. She recognized her from below—Nefta. She didn't look pleased. Half her face was broiled from the Fall, the other half was that of a striking blonde beauty, and both sides were set in a scowl. Jana could tell she'd been one of the perfect ones before she'd fallen. Her wings moved, agitated—a disturbing sight. They'd been particularly damaged, and were left looking something like those of a bat, with scattered feathers still clinging to the leathery flaps that remained.

"Rhamiel," said Nefta. "I don't interfere in your affairs, and I expect you not to interfere in mine."

"We're entertaining, not interfering," said Rhamiel, grinning impishly. "You can't ask us not to be good hosts."

"You know what you're doing," said Nefta. "I sent for her, and I don't like being delayed. Girl, come with us."

Jana froze, looking back and forth between the two. Going with Nefta might offend Rhamiel, or even Zuphias. Ignoring her could be fatal. She'd been given a direct order. Rhamiel looked Jana over in silence for a few terrifying seconds, taking a little selfish pleasure in her indecision, and then he did her a kindness.

"Go. We'll share our bottle later, once you're free

from Nefta's clutches. The two of us had plans of our own, in any event. We're to go out into the world, and see what mischief we can stir up." He looked amused, and didn't seem to have taken any offense. Rhamiel stood, and towered over Jana. She'd only seen him seated, but now he was tall, imposing, and moved with a confident strut. He and Zuphias walked away, down one of the corridors and off to one of the many platforms that dotted the exterior.

The woman grabbed Jana's arm roughly, and the two fell in line behind Nefta. Jana could feel the eyes of the room upon her. That kind of attention wouldn't end well, if Sam was to be believed. She'd seen a number of people disappear over the years herself. But then again, maybe some of them were still kicking around in the upper levels. The people here had to come from somewhere. She had a more immediate concern, though: Nefta. Neither she nor her escort seemed happy, and that couldn't be a good thing.

Nefta veered off into a narrow corridor, which wound upward to an isolated chamber. She stood in front of it, waiting impatiently as the woman opened the door for her. Jana followed them inside. They appeared to be in some kind of foyer. The walls were lined with hand-carved wooden masks, depicting a series of faces in intricate and lifelike detail. Jana had only just begun to admire them when she felt something collide with her head, and fell to the floor in a daze.

CHAPTER SEVEN

"THIS ISLAND, HERE," SAID UZZIEL. "A nest of vipers. There's at least two encampments down there in some of the parklands. And there could be hundreds of them scuttling around in the structures nearby."

He'd intercepted Rhamiel and Zuphias on one of the balconies, and was holding a map and gesturing at it excitedly. It was covered in scribblings and notes from either Uzziel or one of his lieutenants—battle plans, perhaps, or just intelligence about the general area. The balcony was small, but it had a perfect view of their surroundings. It had no railings or other protections; just a bare platform, extending outward into space. There were a number of them around the tower, and the angels came to them to think, or brood, or simply to stare out at the skies.

"We'd love to spend the day debating military strategy, Uzziel, we really would," said Rhamiel, brushing away the map. "But this trip is purely for pleasure. An aimless jaunt into the countryside to admire the scenery."

"And I'd promised myself I'd stay out of martial affairs," added Zuphias. "I'm not particularly happy with the results of my last foray into that field."

Uzziel glowered at them both, and thrust his finger at the area of the map that was most heavily scrawled upon. "These are threats. Every one of them a threat. It's vigilance that protects a garrison. I'd conscript the lot of you, if I could muster the support. Instead you dedicate all your lives to loafing."

"Uzziel, look around you," said Rhamiel. "This is hardly some defenseless camp. We're in the skies, far from danger. And a little loafing would more become you. You've too much energy. Why, sloth is one of the sins with the most to commend it. You've done nothing since we arrived but relive old battles and gin up excuses to drill for new ones."

"We'd certainly help you if it became necessary," said Zuphias. "But it's all so dull. I've had more than enough lifetimes of service, myself. You can put aside these labors now. Do something of your own choosing."

"This is labor for ourselves, not for others," said Uzziel. "How do any of you feel safe with enemies around us? We must at least be prepared. That's all I ask. Just do some basic scouting. Just fly past, get me my intelligence, and then idle away as many of your days as you please."

Rhamiel smiled, looking amused. "Perhaps, Uzziel. Perhaps. We've no particular plans, and can make no particular promises. But if we're in the area, and feel so inclined, we'll wander about and report to you immediately if the armies of men are massing around us.

Some armada has doubtless been cleverly disguised down there for the last decade, awaiting the perfect moment to strike."

Uzziel scowled and huffed off. He was used to ruling through authority before the Fall, and hadn't taken well to the need to use persuasion to achieve his ends. Orders were simpler, and they didn't require any thought to the inclinations of their recipients. Now he was a general without an army. The heavenly host was shattered, and the most disciplined of its former soldiers had become the wildest when they suddenly found themselves without their old restraints. Uzziel had been reduced to hectoring anyone with the patience to listen. The angels had been left to their own devices for long enough that convincing them to act in concert was akin to herding cats.

"A final drink, and then let's be off," said Rhamiel, as he motioned to a waiting attendant. Rhamiel and Zuphias both preferred wine. It didn't get them drunk; the angelic constitution was too strong for that. But there was something biblical about it, and they both enjoyed the old classics.

"Perhaps we should perform Uzziel's spywork," said Zuphias. "I won't say the feeling of flight isn't a joy on its own. But it's nice to have plans."

"Plans get rid of all the fun," said Rhamiel. "We'll improvise. You should talk to Ecanus. He's not exactly of our stature, but I've never met someone so creative about his cruelty. He simply follows his own fancies wherever they lead him. He's a tad dark, but there's something to learn from that. We could topple a building, or you could perform some of those miracles you're always going on about." He downed his drink, and approached the edge of the balcony.

They had a perfect view of the ruined city. The skyline was nothing but jagged rows of dilapidated buildings in various states of decline. Rhamiel stood at the brink, facing outward, and lifted his wings. Then he held out his arms and dropped. His wings caught the air, and he began to glide. Zuphias followed shortly, and soon they flew side by side, aimlessly circling the tower.

"Let's follow the wind, and see where it takes us," Rhamiel shouted. They rode a current of air, hardly needing to flap, and drifted lazily over the city. Nothing much happened for a time. The buildings were empty, and the streets were quiet. Rhamiel and Zuphias flew in silence, looking on the crumbling works of man below them. The current was unstable, and veered from street to street. Both were soon lost in flight and in their own thoughts. It was a form of meditation for them—calming, and a welcome break from the politics that often engulfed their home. Neither was much for all that, but many of their comrades felt compelled to busy themselves with petty bickering.

Then Rhamiel spotted it. Something moving on the ground. Just a speck in the distance, but it intrigued him. He motioned to Zuphias, and they flew lower. Closer, now, and the scene became clear. They could see two people, moving. And next to them a body.

"That looks like Abraxos, doesn't it?" asked Rhamiel. Quiet and something of a loner, Abraxos was prone to solitary flights. He'd been the equivalent of a heavenly security guard before the Fall, patrolling its vast boundaries without ever engaging in formal warfare like Uzziel. He was mostly a non-entity to them, but this was too interesting to resist. They moved in, flying lower, and drew their swords.

CHAPTER EIGHT

T HANE COULD SEE THEM IN the distance, up in the skies. Two dots, rapidly approaching, with fire waving from their sides.

"Tongues! She's talkin' tongues!" he shouted into the radio, and lifted Faye over his shoulder.

Holt knew instantly that things had gone bad. Glossolalia was a sure sign you were being targeted from above. Some said it was the true angelic language, but if so, they'd never been heard to speak it. Others thought that it was a trick of the mind—that it was the angels worming their way into the brain somehow, scrambling the synapses temporarily to render their prey vulnerable. What *was* known was that speaking in tongues meant that they were around, and that they had targeted you.

Holt raised a hand to preemptively silence Dax. He was prone to chatter, and this wasn't the time. Then he leaned to the edge of the window, trying to get a good view without giving himself away. He could see Thane entering a nearby building, carrying Faye and hoping to find cover. It wasn't likely to work. The angels knew they were there, and they'd tear the place apart to find them. The angels came into view, drifting in the air over the body. Two of them. They were having some discussion or another between themselves, and leisurely began inspecting the carcass.

"Holt!" Thane's voice came through the radio's static. "Faye's back, but she's not lookin' so hot. Too woozy to fight." Whatever mental connection there was must have broken, either from the distance or from the angel otherwise losing sight of her. But he'd been in her head, and that could be a nerve-racking experience. She'd be shaky and confused, and would need some time to recover.

"Found a closet to hide her in," said Thane. "I'm doubling back. I'll distract them; you get out of here."

Holt barked his response. "Don't be an idiot. They're not even following you yet. Get some distance and we might all get out of here before they get their act together." But Thane was Thane. He'd lost a lot of loved ones, like most. For many people, this sparked a survival instinct, making them increasingly cautious as the years went by and friend after friend joined the dead. The Vichies took this attitude to extremes, willing to lick boots and dutifully act as toadies if it meant even a few more moments were added to their own lives. In Thane, the loss just turned to anger. He actively stoked it. His wounds were emotional, but he was constantly poking at them, nursing his grudges and refusing to allow time to gradually erode the misery of his memories. Holt doubted that Thane would ever let them go. It made him a more dangerous soldier, but also a more reckless one.

Holt could see him now, coming back out of the building through a gash in its side near a collapsed wall. This wasn't about distraction. Thane had the taste of blood in his mouth, and you couldn't just slip the bit back in and expect obedience. He drew the flaming sword he'd retrieved, called out to the two angels, and adopted a fighter's stance.

They looked at him, scoffing, and not entirely sure if what they were seeing was serious. "Poor Abraxos," said the younger looking one. "Driven down into the muck by the Maker, only to die in perhaps the most humiliating way possible. Slain by this little yelping thing with its foul temper. But at least in dying, he set us onto a diversion from the day's dreariness. There's something to be said for that."

Thane's war face was on, and he didn't flinch. "I killed him. Now I'm gonna kill you. Then I'm gonna kill every one of your friends, one by one." He moved towards them, but his steps were more cautious than his words. The angels waved their swords as he approached, teasing him. In all likelihood, either could have finished him off in a few seconds. But they prolonged their play, standing by the body and waiting for him to make the first move. He stopped a few meters away, eyeing them and hoping that the standoff was giving the others enough time to flee. Boundless confidence and blind rage had gotten him this far, but he wasn't a fool. This wasn't a winning fight, but you had to at least throw a punch.

"Thane. Duck." It took a moment for the command from the radio to register and for his thoughts to click.

Thane looked up, locking his eyes on a familiar window in one of the buildings above. Then he turned, and ran.

"What a curious creature. All claws and snarls one moment, and panicked hysteria the next." The older-looking angel watched Thane rushing away, bemused at his sudden loss of confidence. Then a thump and a crackle came from above them. They had just enough time to turn to see something roaring towards them, and then it was inferno all around. They were blown outward, the younger one into a pile of debris and the older one through the windshield of one of the city's many abandoned vehicles.

Holt put down the missile launcher and picked up his walkie-talkie. "They're stunned, but they won't be that way for long. Get Faye and get your ass into a sewer before they're up. Risk her again to play games and I'll kill you myself." The gloves were off, and it was iron underneath. He turned to Dax, who flinched and dropped his eyes. Dax was smart enough to know when it was time to do as he was told. "Get what we need, what we can't live without. Then let's go. Now."

Dax scrambled around, grabbing his laptop and various other assorted sundries and shoving them into a backpack. The room was a mess. It'd been that way when they arrived, but camping out there for this long had left it covered in trash, the old layered beneath the new. Broken glass and soggy old books were mixed with crumbs from their food and balled up dirty clothes. Holt snapped the footlocker shut, kicking it under a table. They'd come back for the launcher if they could, but it was too much to carry on the run. He took another careful peek outside the window. Thane was gone, and presumably had gone back to following orders now that they suited what he wanted to do anyway. The angels were still down, and neither one was moving yet. That gave them at least a few minutes.

"Holt. This is Faye. I'm fine. Thane and I got out and onto another street. There's a subway station up ahead, and if we get stuck we'll hole up there until dark." The city's underground networks were a mess. Many of the old passageways were blocked or had been destroyed. But some paths were still passable, and could be used to travel to the city's edges. From there, you could generally move freely once night had fallen. The angels couldn't see you from above, then, and while some of the Vichies could be a threat, if confronted they often would revert to the same meekness they showed their masters. With many of them, the urge to roll over and expose their bellies when threatened by anyone or anything had become their second nature.

"Thank God," said Dax. He pulled his backpack over his shoulders and looked to Holt for guidance on what to do next.

"We're going downstairs," said Holt. "Stick to the interior of the building until we get to the ground floor. I saw a hole going into the next building in one of the walls. We go through, hide, and wait this thing out until sundown." Dax's eyes bulged to the edges of their sockets, and he started to stammer. Holt heard the flapping, and turned.

The younger angel had recovered. He was outside the window, sword drawn and hovering as he held himself aloft at eye level with Holt. He was handsome—strikingly so, almost perfect except for a trickle of blood flowing across his face from a gash on his forehead. Holt's missile had done something, at least, but that wasn't much comfort to him now.

The angel touched his wound gingerly, withdrawing his hand. He eyed the blood on his fingertips, and then glared at Holt in fury.

"You did this. This face survived the Fall unscathed, and now you've marred it. You've earned an agonizing death for that. Ungrateful little wretch. You can't fathom how long I slaved away for your kind. I saved the ones the Maker thought deserved to be saved, and I killed the ones he thought had to be killed to keep the rest of you safe. All those centuries, all those people, and I've never, *ever*, seen one of you foolish enough to strike me."

"First time for everything," said Holt. "And now there's a second." He pulled a taser from a holster on his belt, aimed directly at the angel's treasured visage, and fired. Wires burst forward, clamping onto the skin of his face and buzzing loudly with energy. The angel dropped his sword and grasped at his head, tumbling downward and jerking the taser out of Holt's hand as he spiraled out of control and into the ground below.

"Move!" Holt yelled, directing Dax down a staircase with an urgent wave of his hand. Dax ran, as quickly as could be expected from him, with Holt close behind. Sometimes the leader must follow, when danger's in the rear, and Holt had always felt an obligation to shoulder the bulk of any risks to his subordinates himself. They raced down the stairs, floor after floor, and finally heard a crashing from above. The angel must have recovered, and was certainly in an awful mood. They could hear him tearing apart the floors above, as they ran to Holt's escape route and crawled through a breach in the brick walls separating their building from the next. Holt led the way—he made it a habit to scout around before selecting a base of operations, and he always had a few contingency plans up his sleeve. They descended into a basement, wound their way through a maze of dusty boxes held in storage for the building's previous residents, and huddled down among them as they listened to the clamor of destruction from above.

CHAPTER NINE

T FELT LIKE THE SOUND had been turned off. Jana's head was spinning, with little blotches of color marring her field of vision, floating into view only to disappear as quickly as they'd come. A muffled voice broke through the barrier in her ears, as the world gradually stabilized. Words began to poke through the fog. It was Nefta, and she was in ill humor. She was raging, going on about Rhamiel and Zuphias and the indignity of seeing a mere servant cuddling close to them like a common harlot. "We'd have turned you to salt in the old days," Jana heard, before Nefta stormed off into her private chambers.

"You're okay. A bit stupid, but you're okay. Just sit still. You'll be fine in just a minute," said the woman who'd brought her into all these troubles.

Jana stuttered, mumbling noises and sounds until a word finally came out. "Why?"

"There's no end to answers to that question," the women said. "Depends what you mean by it. Why'd she hit you? Because you cost her face, probably. You can't get in the middle of their battles. She asked you up here, and you dawdled. You went and talked to one of the others instead. Rhamiel was a particularly bad choice for that, if you didn't want to offend Nefta. You have to know who's who and what's what if you expect to stay up here."

"Stay?" asked Jana, feeling at a swollen welt on her temple as she gradually regained her senses.

"Stay," said the woman, helping Jana to her feet. "You're not going back. Nefta wants you here. With her. She saw something in you, or liked the way you looked, or was just bored. Who knows. But you're a handmaiden, now. And you don't really have much choice in the matter." Most of the angels took personal servants under their wings, training them in their tastes and guaranteeing some consistency in how they were served. It was a comparatively good gig, if you were lucky with respect to whose chambers you ended up in. You were usually off limits to the passing savageries of all of the other angels, who preferred not to openly war with their housemates. And you commanded a certain level of respect from most of the other servants. If the wrong angel chose you, on the other hand, things could get very grim. Whatever neurosis drove them would become your own, defining your every moment as you pandered to their whims and hoped for the best.

"Who are you?" asked Jana, wiping a rivulet of blood from the side of her mouth.

"Now you're suddenly curious?" asked the woman. "You walk for hours without a peep, get where you're going, and then you start wondering how you got there?"

"I didn't know if it was safe to ask," said Jana quietly.

The woman's countenance softened, and she licked her finger to clean a smudge of blood from Jana's cheek. "My name is Cassie," she said. "I've been in Nefta's service for almost a year. I was outside before that."

"I used to be outside, when I was very young," said Jana. "Sam says it's awful now. That no matter how bad things get in here, you don't ever want to be out there."

"That may be," said Cassie. "That may be. Some people aren't cut out for it. I don't know that I was. I came to the gates, they let me in, and Nefta chose me. So here we both are."

Jana looked around, taking in the room. There were a few scattered pieces of furniture, but they were simple and practical. There were chairs to sit at, tables to put things on, and lamps to light the way. Otherwise, the only decoration was the masks. There were rows and rows of them—hundreds, lining every open space on the walls. Each was a face, carved with a variety of expressions that seemed to cover every possible emotional state. They all could have been people, but she supposed it was just as likely that they were angels. They didn't have the scars for it, but then, the angels hadn't always had them either.

"She made them all," said Cassie as Jana stared. "It's kind of her hobby. Don't disturb her when she's doing it. If she wants you then, she'll let you know. She's really not as bad as you're probably thinking. You just have to know the rules. She wants things a certain way, and if you make sure she gets what she wants then we'll all be happy."

"Who are they?" asked Jana, reaching forward to touch one of the masks before thinking better of it.

"I couldn't tell you. And I wouldn't ask. It's fine to talk openly with me. But you have to be cautious when you're talking to any of them, even her. If they want to keep something inside, you have to let them. If they want you to know something, they'll make sure you know. Nefta can be... harsh. She doesn't have the mean streak that some of them do. But she expects obedience, and she'll punish you if she thinks you're out of line." Cassie put her arm around Jana's side, gently guiding her away from the wall and leading her on a tour of Nefta's suite.

"This room is for the cleaning," said Cassie. Various garments were bundled in baskets around the room, and well-polished pieces of armor were strapped to a few wooden mannequins. The brushes, buckets, and washboards stored there wouldn't have looked out of place a century earlier. The tower didn't have much in the way of modern appliances. The angels couldn't be bothered with human gadgets, and a few millennia of habits would set anyone in their ways. They didn't particularly care about saving the labor of others, either, and were perfectly content to allow their servants to build character by scrubbing away at stains by hand.

Cassie led Jana to another chamber—a large supply closet, filled to the brim with a variety of different cleaning supplies and other materials. Some were manufactured before the Fall, still in their original brightly colored packaging. Others looked homemade. There were stacks of candles and soaps whose irregular shapes and bland colors marked them as having been created after society's collapse. The angels employed a variety of craftsmen to make whatever they could, and their servants on the outside gathered the rest.

"Everything you could need to do your job is in here," said Cassie. "Brooms, mops, soaps, rags. We store it all here, out of the way. You cleaned down there, didn't you? Your quarters were a bit of a mess."

Jana blushed. She felt ashamed and out of place, like she'd climbed too fast and wasn't prepared to actually cling to these dizzying heights. People were dirty, when huddled together, and they didn't have anything like this range of supplies down below. Even if they'd had, there just wasn't time in the busy days to do more than make yourself presentable for the limited occasions when you'd be seen by one of the angels. The rest didn't really matter. The angels didn't care how the other half lived. But Jana was living with one, now, and everyone and everything up here was spick and span.

"We did dishes," said Jana. "Making the food took most of our time."

"That's okay," said Cassie. "You'll learn. Just make sure you let me double-check everything. You'll make mistakes, but I'll fix them."

They walked through a small, unobtrusive door in one of the hallways. It was out of the way, and not likely to attract the attention of guests. Inside was a cramped space with a bunk bed and a couple of storage cabinets. The bottom bunk was clearly Cassie's. A few photos of family or friends had been stuck along the wall next to it, and there was a half-used candle and a few matches on the nearest cabinet. There were even some books, usually considered a frivolity.

"This is our room," said Cassie. "I'm a light sleeper, so you'll have to be quiet if you like to stay up. But I don't expect I'll have problems with that, will I?"

"No, ma'am," said Jana, looking over the space. It wasn't the homey, family-style atmosphere she was used to. She wondered if Cassie was one for stories or singing, but on reflection, suspected that she wasn't.

"What do I tell the others? About what I'm doing?" asked Jana.

"You don't tell them anything, unless you find someone going down there," said Cassie. "And you probably won't. Not for a while, I'm afraid. Once you're up here, they tend to keep you up here. Things are a bit more intimate. The angels aren't as guarded in their own homes. And once you know a few of their confidences, they don't want them spreading beyond to the others. If they trust you enough, and they need something done, you might find an excuse to go down to the lower levels. But it's not a regular thing."

"They're going to worry," said Jana. "They'll want to know I'm okay." For all her friends knew, she could have been sent off to be punished for some perceived slight at the meal. They had little else to talk about, and they were probably coming up with some fantastical explanation even then.

"I let your boss know you were coming up," said Cassie. "And that's all any of them need to know."

Jana frowned for a moment, and then by well-honed instinct her face turned impassive, masking her pain. She sobbed inside, knowing she'd probably never speak to any of them again. Even Sam ordinarily communicated with the upper levels via a series of messengers. He would talk to someone a few stories up, and they'd push things higher and higher. The angels didn't like servants wandering around the tower, and could be testy and confrontational if they saw someone unfamiliar and unescorted. It offended their most treasured sensibility: that there was a place for everyone, and everyone in their place. She started to have a few desperate fantasies. Maybe she'd go down there again someday, like Cassie had. Maybe she'd find some chore that required her to visit from time to time. Maybe in a few years of service, she'd win Nefta's trust and favor and be allowed to do as she pleased, within reason.

She was jarred back to reality by Cassie. "No more time to dawdle. We've got work to do." They scrubbed and cleaned, then. There was no dust, but Jana dusted. The floors were pristine, but Jana mopped them, and then re-mopped them as Cassie found fault after fault. She polished doorknobs, and then was scolded afterwards for leaving her fingerprints on them. She poked the ceilings for cobwebs with brooms, organized foods in the pantry, and cleaned the undersides of furniture on the off-chance that someone might notice. It was an exhausting day.

Cassie turned out not to care much for stories or singing at all. They both went straight to bed, but Jana couldn't shut things off. The day had simply been too much to process. She imagined her friends, and then flinched away from the images, trying to distract herself. Her thoughts were drawn back to Rhamiel, and why he had singled her out. He must have been interested, at least somewhat, or he wouldn't have called her over. He wouldn't have been staring at her. But there was interest in games, and there was real interest, and a vast gulf between the two. Still, someone like that offered real protection. Nefta could say what she would, but she'd never value Jana as anything more than a servant. Rhamiel was strong, and seemed to have the respect of most of the others. If he was interested, he wouldn't let an Ecanus torture her. He wouldn't let Nefta keep her as a slave. She ran things over and over in her head, until exhaustion took over and she slipped into slumber.

She woke from a shove. "Get up," said Cassie. "And get dressed. Not in your rags; in this." Cassie opened a drawer in one of the cabinets, pulling out a fashionable robe favored by many of the upper caste servants. It wasn't flashy enough to upstage the angels, but it was elegant enough that they wouldn't be embarrassed, either. It was more fancy than anything Jana had ever worn. A soft red silk that called to mind a kimono, its hand-sewn needlepoint depicted angels in various scenes of glory.

"Nefta wants us to go with her," said Cassie. "To the Conclave."

CHAPTER TEN

"YOU BASTARDS GET IN, AND you do it quiet," said the ferryman. Holt nodded, and the others boarded his boat. Dax stumbled on the way in, shaking the boat from side to side as he lost his balance. But Thane grabbed hold and steadied him, saving him from more than a few dirty looks from the ferryman. Dax sat down sheepishly, started to blame his lack of coordination on the darkness, and then thought better of it. They were on the shore, just south of the old city. Without all the lights, it was surprising how black things could be. The buildings were just grey silhouettes against the night sky, noticeable mostly by the way they blocked the view of the stars. They were invisible before, but now the sky was lit with constellations that no longer had to compete with the constant glow of urban life.

"Pay me," said the ferryman. "I don't risk my ass for free." He'd worked with Holt for months, but didn't trust him or anyone else. He was an old drunk, when he could be, but booze was in limited supply. He had a thick grey beard, an ideal mask to obscure the perpetual ruddiness of his cheeks. He was crotchety and disagreeable, but he hated the angels, and he knew how to row. He wasn't willing to risk his own skin in combat, but he'd tolerate the comparatively smaller risk of silently moving people and cargo in and out of the city at night. Holt liked him despite his orneriness; the elderly learn to own their faults, which makes them easier for others to bear.

Holt handed him a small bundle—a collection of dried meats and a few pieces of fresh fruit. It'd keep the man going for at least a few days. Food was the only currency anyone much cared about these days, and it was the perishable things that had value. Most ordinary goods were functionally worthless, valued only as much as the labor needed to get them to you. The death toll had far outstripped the physical destruction, and it was the urban areas that had presented the most tempting targets. But once you got out into the suburbs, enough warehouses, stores, and private residences had survived that there were generally more things around than people to use them.

There had been looting, of course. But there's only so much you can carry, and only so much you need for yourself. They were still coming across hoards that people had stashed away in their now-abandoned homes— piles of shoes, once trendy clothes, or useless boxes of electronics. Those things could last for decades. But when the food and medicine had run out, all the stolen televisions in the world didn't do their new owners much good. Industry and transportation had broken down, and without a way to replenish things, people were left to feud and fight until their time simply ran out. The survivors had mainly been those who'd managed to make their way to rural areas. They could grow food there, and had more of it than they needed. Only trickles flowed outward to places like this, far away from any fields of grain.

Holt thought it was all funny, in a sick kind of way. Before the Fall, everyone had envisioned the apocalypse in whatever form it came as a brutal wasteland and a constant battleground between the survivors. It had been that way in some places, but only for a time. If the world resembled anything now, it was less of a battle and more of a frontier. It wasn't that there weren't dangers, because there were many. The angels still roved around inflicting depravities, but mostly at random. The Vichies could well attack you, especially if they found themselves at a clear numerical advantage. But people still interacted and still dealt with each other, even if it was with more suspicion and less trust than before. They tended to live apart, tried to keep their distance from large groups, and weren't exactly trusting of strangers. It was still a risky life, and a shorter one than people were accustomed to, but not much more so on a daily basis than it had been for isolated settlers in centuries past.

The ferryman rifled through his bundle, sniffing at the fruits and taking a few exploratory bites. He muttered to himself, grousing about the lack of proper provisioning these days, but he ultimately was satisfied enough to take up his oars and push away from the shore. Thane helped row with a second set, and they slowly moved away from the edges of the city and out onto the open water.

It'd been hard going to get there. The angels they'd
·ght had been in a fury, wrecking as much as they
·uld before eventually tiring. Holt had still insisted
·at they wait until well after dark before making a run
·r another building. They'd moved from block to block,
·eeping their progress slow to ensure their safety, until
·ventually he and Dax had been able to reunite with
Thane and Faye. Then it was a long, hard trudge to the
outskirts to meet the ferryman.

They kept things silent the entire way. They'd have
been hard to see, just a fleck in the vast waters. But the
angels made people paranoid. Maybe one flying by could
hear them—who was to know? They could do strange
things, sometimes, and had been divine instruments for
so long that it was unclear to mere mortals where their
power ended and God's began. If they could get into
your head, then perhaps they had other ways of finding
you from a distance, too. None of them were sure, so
they just passed the time quietly as best they could. Holt
and Faye scanned the night skies for signs of movement,
while Dax was lost in himself. Thane just rowed.

After a time they arrived, approaching another shore
and then running aground. Staten Island. It was far
enough away from the Perch that there weren't constant
overflights. More importantly, it had forests. In the cities,
there was nothing overhead to block their view, and
movement stood out. But animals still roamed around
the island, and they acted as a sort of chaff, preventing
the angels from simply assuming from a distance that
they'd found someone to harry. Most people had still
moved on to greener pastures, having little reason to

even take the risk. But there were small encampments here and there, and for men like Holt it was a godsend. Without this line of supply, he'd never be able to operate inside the city proper.

"Get off my damned boat, and next time bring me some hooch," said the ferryman as they exited.

"I will, if I can find some," said Holt. "Stay safe. We've been tossing rocks right at the hornet's nest, and they're going to be buzzing around here soon."

"Fuck 'em," said the ferryman, cackling and pushing off in his boat. "Don't have any place else to be, don't really care if they come. Just let me spit in their eyes before I go." He rowed off into the darkness, leaving them there alone on the shore.

They hiked inland, sticking to the sides of buildings when they could. From time to time they had to cross open roads, which was fraught with danger. They went on detour after detour, looking for places that were packed with abandoned cars, and then crawling among them for cover until they were safely to the other side. After a while, it was into the forests and into relative safety. The greenery had run wild since the Fall, extending outward as far as the remaining structures of man would allow. Holt led them with a compass through the woods. There weren't paths, exactly. There were barely enough people here to make them, and only fools would walk along an obviously well-worn passage anyway. But there were marks. Little notches carved into the trees, or rocks that looked out of place. Hobos had used these same kinds of signals decades before: symbols that were unintelligible to the uninitiated, but meant something to Holt. They directed them onward and inward, until they finally arrived at Marv's Colony.

Marv was an eccentric—a rough, tough New Yorker who'd been too old and too fat to join the feeble efforts at a resistance after the Fall. He was slimmer these days by necessity, but maintained the healthy gut that men his age just couldn't seem to get rid of. He was balding on top, with hair running wild at the back to compensate. He'd worked blue collar jobs in the city for years, but when the angels came he fled to the island. Unlike a lot of others, he stayed, retreating with his family to a relatively isolated area of wilderness that had once been a communal farm of some sort. Now it was just buildings and trees, including a sanitarium that had been out of use since long before the Fall. Rumors were that the place was the scene of various brutal murders and child abductions, though no one had ever offered precise details. Those seemed like heinous atrocities then, keeping anyone but the indigent far away. Now such stories would be routine, more to be expected than to be horrified by. Marv wasn't afraid, and he was the one who had discovered the basements, a series of rooms and tunnels under the old sanitarium that served as the home to a half dozen families who survived by setting up a way station for humans passing through the area. You had to be in the know to find it, but Holt was certainly that.

Holt approached the sanitarium slowly, leaving the others some ways behind. Marv could be jumpy around people he didn't know, and while Holt had been there a number of times, the rest of the cell was less familiar. They'd stopped here on the way in, but who knew whether Marv would remember them? Even if he did, it was normally the older children who were stationed somewhere in the upper levels to watch the approaches. A larger group might give them cause to shoot first and tell their parents later.

Walking towards the entrance, Holt stopped near a pile of rusted gurneys and other assorted medical artifacts from another age. Regular guests knew that it was both polite and prudent to await an invitation inside, and this was the appointed place. It wasn't long before he saw a figure in the darkened doorway at the side of the building—Marv, beckoning for him to come forward. Holt gave a signal behind him, and the others slowly approached as well. They walked together to the door, then jogged the last bit as Marv became visibly agitated at the amount of time they were spending out in the open. Manners were nice, but New Yorkers were never much for those anyway, and once their peaceful intent had been signaled it made little sense to tarry where anyone flying overhead could easily spot them.

"You survived!" Marv said with a laugh. "Didn't think I'd be seeing you bastards again. Not tubby for sure." Dax squirmed, but said nothing. He was used to insults, but they paralyzed him with indecision. He'd fume inside, and spend a few hours boiling and plotting revenge. But he never quite had the stomach to fight back in the moment, and thus was ever a promising target.

"We almost didn't," said Holt. "But it was worth it. We bagged one."

"No shit," said Marv, his voice a mixture of awe and skepticism.

"No shit," said Thane, holding up the scabbard of the sword he'd retrieved.

"Well, fuck me," said Marv, eyes widening. "Can't believe you idiots actually got one. Can't believe. Me, I swore you'd be dead. You know, you wanna sell that thing, I can find you a buyer. Lotta people would pay a lot to get one a those."

"Not for sale," said Holt. "We just need a night's room and board. Then we're heading inland for supplies, and for some business I've got to conduct. We're not stopping with just one of them."

"Every one of 'em is gonna be dead," said Thane. "Every goddamned one."

"Okay, killer, you get on that," scoffed Marv. It wasn't that he disagreed with the sentiment. Far from it; Marv was one of the biggest partisans around for the cause of exterminating angels. But he'd seen a lot of would-be guerilla fighters come and go. A scalp was nice, but it was just a start. There were hundreds of angels in the Perch, and it was just one of a dozen such towers scattered around the world. Still others of their kind preferred solitude, and were living on their own in whatever isolated location they fancied. The task was a near impossible one, and while Marv supported it where he could, he wasn't quite as enamored with the idea of the kamikaze approach.

"In the meantime you get in here. The girls have a soup goin'. Squirrel and potato, I think," said Marv. The families there caught what they could, and grew what they could without tipping off anyone who happened to wander by to their presence. Mushrooms were a core staple, as they could be cultivated indoors. For the rest, they simply scattered things around the greenbelt, hiding them in patches of other plants to avoid detection. There were plenty of animals wandering around, but Marv had a strict rule against hunting them. Too conspicuous, he said, and so their meat came mostly from trapping. They stuck to smaller animals, using snares that could be easily disguised and making sure to place them far from the Colony. Marv had come up with a number of clever contrivances to make things easier on the families there. He was always going on about a plan to breed guinea pigs, and pestering Holt to bring him some if he could find them. Holt didn't think it was likely that many had survived, as they weren't the type of creature you'd expect to flourish if left to their own devices. But he always promised anyway, and it seemed to make Marv happy just to make the plans even if they'd probably never come to fruition.

Marv led them into the basements. It was dark through the first part of the tunnels, until they came to a makeshift door made from corrugated metal. He'd pulled it off the side of a shed somewhere, and used it to mask any light from the exterior. He unlatched a wire clasp and pulled it outward just far enough for them to squeeze inside. Past the door was a homey living area for the guests, furnished with mismatched items that had been hauled in from the closest houses, miles away. It was surprisingly well-lit. Marv had installed a generator, and made sure that the place had almost every modern amenity. There wasn't much more hardship than you'd have found at a luxury campsite a few decades before.

He'd even managed to cobble together a hot shower in the corner from spare pipes and an old water heater.

They sat together on a cluster of couches and recliners that Marv had pulled together in the center of the room for entertaining the people that passed through. The other families crowded around to hear the story of the angel's death, and of their narrow escape from his vindictive comrades. Holt even let Thane pull the sword out, which awed children and adults alike. They'd never seen one up close, and most who did never survived. Marv and Holt talked shop for a while, sharing news and gossip. There were other cells, and some had even passed through the Colony recently, but they tried not to talk directly. The theory was that if they didn't know each other, they couldn't betray each other. It worked on that front, but it also prevented coordination and limited the size and scope of their operations.

The night wound down, and eventually everyone wandered off to bed. Marv lent them some sleeping bags and pillows, and they started to settle down for the night.

"Faye, you okay? You've been quiet," said Holt.

"I'm fine," said Faye. "It just felt so strange, the total lack of control. You can't move, you hear the stuff coming out of you, and you can't do anything to stop it. You wonder whether we can really beat them. There's so many. And they can do too much."

"Well, maybe we can't," said Holt. "But there isn't really anything else to do, is there? We could bow to them, but I don't have that in me."

"We've lost it all, though," said Faye. "You know I was engaged? I was supposed to be wiping baby shit and changing diapers right about now. You probably can't even see it in me anymore. I don't even know if he made it, or where he is if he did. There was this perfect little life out there for me, picket fences and everything. And they stole it." She paused, pushing the emotion down into herself so the others wouldn't see. "I don't have anything left but the fight. I know we won't win. But I just don't have anything else left."

They sat quietly with their thoughts, and after a while they all drifted into sleep as the hours passed.

Sometime in the night, Holt awoke to a scratching sound against the metal door. He tapped at Thane, waking him, and both went on alert. Then the sound of voices, a crunching noise, and the door fell backwards into the dark.

CHAPTER ELEVEN

"**A** MENACE! PERILS FROM EVERY SIDE, our own people being slaughtered at our doorstep, and here we sit doing nothing!" thundered Uzziel. He waved his arms about, agitated. Uzziel could speak for hours on the subject of military preparations once he got going, and it had been a common form of entertainment in recent years to prod him into a frenzy and snicker at the results. The mood was more somber, now, and he was milking every moment.

"They were common murderers, Uzziel. Nothing more," said Zuphias, sitting in the first few rows of the audience. He'd recovered, but looked unenthusiastic about the prospects of further fighting.

"Nonsense!" shouted Uzziel, before barreling into a lengthy monologue about the immeasurable benefits of regular drilling and marching.

Jana listened patiently to his bombast for as long as she could before her mind finally began to wander. They were in a large amphitheater, with rows of benches looking down on the rostrum from which Uzziel was currently denouncing the corrupting influence on the Seraphim of the idleness and perfidy of other breeds of angels. Most of the angels in attendance looked bored, and while Jana was no expert on angelic politics, she gathered from the speech that none of the ones Uzziel was complaining of had been permitted to reside in the tower. The angels were clustered in groups, keeping a measurable distance between themselves. Some of the larger ones had their own standard bearers, with massive, colorful banners announcing their affiliations to the others. They knew, already, but for the groups with higher status it didn't do to let the others forget about it.

Cassie and Jana sat behind Nefta, as was protocol. Cassie had said that an unusually large number of angels would be attending the Conclave, and the room certainly seemed to be full. All of them were dressed in their finest, a mish-mash of intricately decorated robes and imposing looking armors. This meeting was seen as an homage to Abraxos by some, and none of them wanted to hear about an important social event secondhand. The others might gossip about whether their absence was intended as some sort of slight, or someone like Uzziel might propose something ludicrous that could be agreed to in an emotional atmosphere if no one were there to oppose it. And besides, it was see and be seen, and everyone wanted to be seen.

Uzziel's speech finally ended with an exhortation to begin building a complicated system of trenches and fortifications around the tower, and a reminder that this was a task too important to be left to house-servants, who might already be plotting all sorts of perfidies of their own. After scattered polite applause, another speaker rose and began monotonously reading from a prepared text about the visual blight caused by irregularly sized doorways in the angels' quarters, and the need to establish a committee to resolve the problem. Perhaps even a subcommittee, should matters not improve expeditiously.

Jana had been warned by Cassie that this could be an intensely boring affair. The Conclave had been formed in a flurry of activity after the tower's founding, and it had been thought that it would serve as a grand political body and act as a bulwark against any interference from Heaven. As the years passed, the angels discovered that they had no appetite for either ruling or being ruled, and that Heaven appeared to have little interest in their activities. Except for a few stalwarts like Uzziel, its regular attendees focused mostly on mundane matters and the resolution of any personal disputes that couldn't be worked out otherwise without escalation to violence. Most had deemed the Conclave to be a farce, and had stopped coming in order to focus on whatever private pursuits they were currently absorbed by. On occasion, though, some matter of import caught the attention of the tower, and the regular meetings allowed them an avenue to air issues among any who were interested.

"I think it is time," said one of the older looking angels, "to get to the matter of honoring Abraxos." Murmurs of assent sprang from around the chamber, a sign that most in the audience found the routine affairs to be just as tiresome as Jana did. Another angel rose, gave a short eulogy, and opened the floor to speakers.

"I should like to speak," rang a voice from behind Jana. She turned her head to see Rhamiel, rising from his seat and approaching the podium. He tilted his head as he walked down the steps to the center of the room, and she could swear he was looking in her direction. Nefta herself seemed to confirm it. While Jana couldn't see her face, her wings visibly tightened and then thrust upward in a quick, angry flap.

"Eulogies are an art filled with the stuff of fantasy. But The Maker warned us against dishonesty, so I shall of course stick to the truth." Rhamiel paused and greeted the audience's laughter with a smile. None of them were prone to honesty unless it suited them, and none could resist a shot against their former master.

"Abraxos was not a dear friend, not to any of us. I do not fault him for it. It was simply his nature. In heaven he wandered around the borderlands on his own, performing services he chose not to discuss. He rebelled for his own reasons, which none of us were privy to. And he spent his days here in solitude, living among us but not of us," continued Rhamiel.

"Many here tire of warfare. A sentiment I understand. But someone has struck at us. A man I have seen, brazen enough to kill one of us and injure two others," said Rhamiel, gathering energy as he spoke.

A voice interrupted, calling out from among the crowd. "Poor Rhamiel! Heaven's ugly duckling, his face now scarred like the rest of us!" Jana saw no scars, and saw no ugliness. He looked as perfect as ever, and any sculptor would have been proud to call him their work. His hands had mild burns, but they only seemed to add character, and weren't all that noticeable anyway. Titters among the audience, however, told Jana that she was missing something. Rhamiel frowned, brushing his forehead with his hand involuntarily. But it was just a moment, and then he was back to dominating the room.

"I'm still the fairest of them all, Orifiel," said Rhamiel, smiling confidently. "My injuries from this scuffle with man are but mild, and whatever I was in Heaven, you'd all trade anything to have had the foresight to protect your own faces. Certainly your swollen, melted nose is nothing to envy." He beamed, and heard no further jests. Jana still didn't see any injuries, but then, she didn't have the angels' standards of beauty.

The sentiments of the room seemed to flip to Rhamiel's side, as members of the crowd jeered at the heckler. Rhamiel reveled in it, railing against the criminals who'd dared attack him and rousing the audience. In the middle of it all, Nefta turned and spoke a word to Cassie.

"Get up, and bring Nefta some water," whispered Cassie. Jana frowned, her face turning to a sulk. The speech was the first interesting thing that had happened in hours, and she wanted to see how it ended. But orders were orders, and Nefta was liable to inflict some punishment on her in front of everyone if she hesitated. She would die from embarrassment, even if nothing else. She got up, and quietly made her way to the back of the assembly, taking care not to obstruct the view of anyone in the audience.

Outside the chamber, she rushed straight to a small station in a nearby room that was manned by some of the mid-level servants. They weren't bound to the service of any particular angel, and so were excluded from the Conclave. Anything needed to fulfill the most common requests was kept here, so as to avoid needless delay. Jana asked for water, and was handed a small leather canteen. She turned, hoping she could make it back in time before the dull droning resumed. Then she saw him.

"Peter!" said Jana, shocked. She was delighted—she'd thought she might never speak to any of her old friends again, and now she had a chance to get word to them that she was safe and well.

"I can't believe you're here!" said Jana. "I only have a minute, but you have to tell everyone. You'll never guess who I'm working for."

"Nefta," said Peter. She stopped, stunned.

"You know I always had a crush on you?" asked Peter. "I should have done something. I was working my way up to it. Getting the confidence. Then you just disappeared. I can work for any of them without a hint of fear, but the idea of making a move on you turned my legs to jelly."

Jana wasn't sure how to take this. She'd never really thought of him that way, and hadn't seen this coming. She'd known, of course, deep down inside. But it was easier to deny it to herself, to pretend that nothing was there. You could never be sure, and there had been no need to broach the issue when it would surely just hurt his feelings. Silent pining harmed no one, but things were out in the open now. She stammered something out, stalling with words to give herself time to collect her thoughts. "Peter, I'm... I'm up here. You're down there. I just don't...."

"You don't understand," said Peter. "I heard. We all heard. The woman. She talked to Sam. She told him she was taking you up. I didn't know exactly where, but I had to try to follow. I should have done it a long time ago, anyway. I'm not meant to be down in the dirt. I'm better than that. We're both better than that. We made it. I'm not at the highest level. But it's just a few floors down from you. Close enough we can visit."

Jana didn't know what to say. She couldn't even understand this. It just wasn't done. Servants at the bottom didn't simply rise in rank by snapping their fingers. "How?" she stuttered.

"I talked to one of them. I pledged fealty," said Peter. "To Ecanus."

CHAPTER TWELVE

BLACK SHAPES MOVED FORWARD, ADVANCING in the darkness. It looked like three, although Holt couldn't be exactly sure. Little light found its way down here from the outside, and at night it was nearly pitch black. He drew his pistol from his belt, groping as he moved, and hoped Thane was seeking cover as well. Marv could be brilliant, in a deviously calculating way. He'd made sure to locate the guest rooms at the outskirts of the basement, between the families' quarters and the exterior. His philosophy was that the welcome visitors should be the first to greet any unwelcome ones. If anyone else found their way inside, Marv himself would get plenty of warning.

Voices whispered to each other, and then a flashlight flicked on and off. They were definitely people. The angels didn't like cramped spaces where they couldn't stretch their wings, and Holt had never heard of any of them carrying flashlights. Another flicker, and he got a clearer look. They were Vichies, slowly creeping their way inside and trying to avoid being detected.

They were easy to identify by their clothing—all white, all the time. Probably it had been originally chosen for its symbolism, as the color most associated with angels in the common lore from before the Fall. It had the added benefit of being conspicuous from above, particularly when everyone in a group was wearing it. It would have been a rarely used color scheme even before the Fall, but now virtually no one else would wear so much as a white undershirt. The Vichies lived in packs and sought safety in numbers. Too many people wanted their heads, and it wasn't uncommon to see a Vichy corpse strung up along the road as a warning to the others about the price of treason.

Holt felt his way behind a sofa—adequate cover, under the circumstances. He leveled his pistol to about where they seemed to be. It was now or never. They'd be approaching where he'd been sleeping, and Faye was probably still deep in her slumber. Dax certainly was. If he'd noticed by now, he wouldn't have been quiet about it. Holt aimed, and waited for the next flash of light to guide his gun.

Then a blinding glare lit up the room, as a streak of fire scythed through the air. Thane had gotten in close without the Vichies noticing. Behind them, even, and he'd swung the angel's sword in an arc that cleanly lopped off one of their heads. As it rolled to the floor, the room was illuminated by the blaze and filled with panic. Holt paused for just a moment, impressed. Then it was back to business, and time to take advantage of the pandemonium. There were two of the Vichies left alive, both armed with assault rifles, but they were in shock at what had just happened. They stared at what was left of their companion, paralyzed and unable to process what was going on. He didn't give them the time to do it. He let loose a burst from his sidearm, downing one of the others.

As the second one fell, the third succumbed to terror. He dropped his gun, collapsing to his knees in submission and placing his hands onto his head. Thane looked like he was about to kill him anyway, but Holt motioned for him to stop. Now the room was filled with whimpers and crying, as the Vichy released a torrent of pleas to spare his life. Faye had woken up and scrambled towards him, kicking away the assault rifles on the floor in case he somehow rediscovered his courage. Dax was still frantically groping around for his glasses. He'd left them somewhere nearby before he'd gone to bed, but for the life of him he couldn't seem to figure out where. His confusion was entirely a product of the sudden commotion, but by the time he'd finally gotten them on it was all over. Part of him felt like he'd missed his chance to play hero, while the rest of him just felt relief that he hadn't been slaughtered in his sleep.

A door behind them creaked open slightly, and Marv poked his head through.

"We've got it under control," said Holt, motioning for him to come forward. Marv entered, leading with the barrel of a military-style shotgun he was frequently bragging about. Soft voices followed into the room from behind him. The families were clearly up and about, but Marv wouldn't let any of them leave their shelter until he was sure things were safe.

"Damn. Boy, you like 'em crispy," said Marv, nodding to Thane. He was still holding the sword, standing over the body of the one he'd dispatched. The corpse's neck was singed to a pitch black, and its head had rolled over towards the surviving Vichy. No one felt like moving it away, and the nervous peeks the Vichy kept taking at it suggested he had no further interest in any kind of conflict.

"I want this one fried, too," said Thane. He waved the sword to point it at the survivor, causing the Vichy to flinch away from the flame in fear. "You and your asshole friends come in here and think you're gonna kill us? Sneakin' around in the dark like a buncha pussies. You're too afraid to fight like men."

It was true, but then, these weren't men. With the room well-lit, they could all see that. They were just boys—still teenagers, scrawny little things who never would have chanced something with someone like Holt or Thane by the light of day. The surviving Vichy's face was sprinkled with uneven patches of stubble, the first sproutings of a nascent manhood he now had questionable odds of ever seeing.

True to his form, the Vichy started begging the second the fire came near him. "It wasn't me! They made me come! We were just looking for some food! We didn't even know you were here! Please!" Sobs replaced pleading, though Thane clearly thought it was all just for show.

"If you're wearin' the white, why do you need food?" said Thane, sneering. "I thought they gave you everything you ever wanted up at the Perch. You need those guns to find food? Guess y'all were just huntin' something down here. Holt, let's just kill this piece of shit and get on with things."

"Let's talk, Marv," said Holt. "Your house, your rules. But this is just some kid. Faye, keep him down and we'll go figure out what we're going to do."

"He's a fuckin' traitor!" shouted Thane. "You know who you work for, you little shit? Who you're helpin'?"

"Thane," said Faye, trying to calm him down.

"No, bullshit! He's one of us and he's helpin' them! I lost so much shit 'cause of people like you. I hadda life, a good life. I was workin' oil patches, I made good money. I had friends, I had a bar I liked to drink at. All that shit's gone. All those guys are dead. Wasn't even the angels that did it. It was you fuckers. You come on through, kill anybody who doesn't give you their stuff, burn anything you don't want. Just so you can bow to those assholes? It's treason. There's only one thing to do with traitors." Thane's eyes flashed, and so did the sword.

"Thane!" Holt shouted, trying to regain control of the situation. It worked. Something in Thane snapped back into focus, and he turned away from the Vichy. He holstered the sword and then stormed out of the room, slamming his fist into the concrete wall and leaving a few smudged, bloody knuckle marks in his wake.

It must have hurt, but keeping things inside would have hurt more. Boys are trained from a young age to suppress their emotions. Something shifts, and one day their childish cries are met not with sympathy or caring but with insults, coldness, and looks of disgust. It's not a pleasant process, but you can't forge a man any other way. Thane was no exception. He'd learned through the years to keep everything within him. He hadn't cried since he was grown, not even as his losses mounted after the Fall. He never talked about what he felt, and an outsider might not think there was anything there to discuss, anyway. But burying things doesn't make them go away. They've got to be let out, and bursts of fury against the occasional object were a fine form of release. Directing his rage at the deserving would have been even better, but Thane didn't always get what he wanted.

Marv gestured to Holt to follow him, and they withdrew to the family quarters, leaving Faye to keep the Vichy from making further trouble. He lay on the ground, tears streaming from his eyes, a boy who had tried to be older than he was. Maybe his friends really had made him do it, as flimsy as his story about searching for food sounded. Maybe they'd just dared him. At his age, that's often enough. Whatever his real motivations, and whatever his intentions had been, he'd made a poor choice in targets and his fate was out of his hands.

Inside, the families were huddled near the door. A few of the men stood guarding the entrance, along with several of the older boys. They had their war faces on, but a serious fighter like Holt could see right through it. Only Marv had the steel for this sort of thing, which was why he was the one holding the Colony together.

"We gotta kill him," said Marv, once he'd gotten Holt aside. "I know you don't like it, but it's what has to be. We gotta just go out there, put a gun to his head, and keep this place safe."

Holt started to speak, but Marv didn't even let him begin. He pulled a pistol from his waistband, offering it to Holt. "Either you do it, or I will."

CHAPTER THIRTEEN

"**P**ETER, YOU FOOL!" SHOUTED JANA, before lowering her voice to a whisper after a few of the other servants turned to stare. "How could you do something like this to yourself? You know what he's like. He'll kill you!"

"It's not like that," said Peter. He leaned in, trying to soothe Jana and keep the others from hearing. "I worked something out. We've got a deal, a good deal. He knows he's hard to work for. But I offered him something he can't get from anyone else: loyalty. His other servants dragged their feet and shirked their duties. He needs someone who can do their job and do it well, without him having to resort to fear or threats. And in exchange he's going to let me live up here. We'll be near each other. You'll still have a friend, and maybe we can be something more in time."

Jana's heart sank. Peter was talking madness, and had let himself be drawn into a warped delusion. She didn't think there was any reason to trust Ecanus, let alone to rashly pledge to him just to climb a few stories higher. The angels took these things very seriously. It was one thing to serve one of them. Any of them could demand that a servant work for them, as Nefta had Jana. But a pledge was something different. It bound the servant, totally and completely, and it was permanent. Jana could still escape, if Nefta let her. But Peter was behaving like a puppy—blinded by unrequited love or ambition, and groping around for anything he thought might satisfy them.

"You didn't even talk to me, Peter," said Jana. "I don't feel that way for you. I don't think I ever would. We grew up together. You're like a brother. We're friends, we really are, but that's it." His face sank, and he looked like he'd been struck. She felt a pang of guilt for hurting him. He could be a bit much, but he meant well. Still, the heart feels what it feels, and Jana just didn't feel it.

"I'm really sorry. You just can't force something like that," said Jana. "You have to find a way to get free. Maybe he'll let you go. You haven't been there for long. Or maybe I could talk to the woman I'm working for. She's close to Nefta. They might be able to do something." She wasn't sure how plausible that was, but Cassie seemed to be protective of her, and she had to try something. She hadn't asked Peter to do this, and never would have let him if she'd known. But that didn't stop her from feeling for his plight, or from wanting to do a little protecting of her own if she could.

Peter shook his head, still looking like he'd been staggered from the blow. "Jana, it's a pledge. He'll expect me to honor it. And I wasn't just doing this for you. I need this. I need to be up here. You know what it's like at the bottom. Things'll be better this way. I know this is a shock. I don't want to rush you. But maybe—"

"Peter," Jana said, stopping him. He was hurt, and clinging to his dream. They're hard to let go of sometimes, and he must have been imagining his world as he thought it could be for a long time. The servants tended to do that. Jana herself had dozens of favored fantasies, and she'd grown up learning to sink into them in her head while her body kept on with the drudgery. Sometimes she was married, raising a throng of rowdy children in a tiny cabin at the base of a range of mountains. Others, she was queen of the tower and adored by all her subjects, human and angel alike. She knew how hard it could be to get suddenly jarred back to reality. Peter had been wounded, and the last thing she wanted to do was twist the knife. She tried to think, to come up with the easiest way to let him down, before a voice from behind her interrupted.

"Chit-chat wasn't part of your instructions. Am I to fetch my own refreshments, leaving the proceedings whenever my thirst is stirred? How does that look to the others?"

Jana turned, and then quickly lowered her head. It was Ecanus, glowering and angry. He looked her up and down suspiciously, and then moved on to Peter.

"Is a romantic rendezvous more important than your obligations?" said Ecanus. "You'd have me sit there, parched, while you tend to your own affairs instead of mine?" He spoke of anger, but his face beamed with a perverse joy. He was thriving on Peter's nervousness, lapping up every bit of it. His wings stretched, imposing and dark. He was small, but he seemed to expand along with them, a bigger and meaner thing than before.

Peter looked as if he was trying to wedge himself backwards into the wall, hunching his shoulders and projecting a defeated air. He stuttered a "no, sir," and then mumbled something unintelligible but deferential sounding. It seemed to satisfy Ecanus, but only for a moment.

"If your needs are more important than mine, I certainly understand. I'm nothing if not forgiving; the Maker taught me that. I'll even show you a compassion. I believe in teaching by example. You think your desires take priority? Well, then today *I'll* be the one to serve *you*," said Ecanus, patting Peter on the shoulder. His smile was warm, and his tone and mannerisms were friendly, but there was a foul glee underneath it all. Peter didn't seem to catch it. He looked uncertain, then relieved, sending a smile over to Jana intended to reassure her that all was well. She didn't buy it for a second, and was a bit baffled that he could. But when someone's found something they'd like to believe in, they'll shut out all the things they'd rather not.

"Water! Bring the poor boy some water! Slake his thirst before you turn to mine!" called Ecanus, snapping at one of the servants manning the refreshment station. They were all huddled together behind a table, nerves on edge. A small, brown-haired boy broke from the group and ran to Ecanus with a canteen, almost tripping over himself before finding his feet in the nick of time. The boy handed it to Ecanus, who unscrewed the top and extended it to Peter.

"Have a drink, then," said Ecanus. "Don't be shy. You're the master today. Your attendant beseeches you, satisfy yourself. Learn what it is to have your needs met by another." He waited, his face all smiles and his eyes all daggers. Peter thanked him, took a sip, and then screwed the top back on. Peter's nervousness was leaving him, and he held out the canteen to the boy.

"You must still be thirsty, child," said Ecanus. "Have some more. It's for your health. Go on." His smile grew a little bigger, and his eyes grew a little nastier. Peter wasn't thirsty, but he supposed it couldn't hurt. He unscrewed the cap of the canteen. Again he took a sip, and again he held it out to the boy.

"Thank you very much, sir," said Peter. "It's very refreshing, and I'm ready to resume my duties."

"More," said Ecanus.

"I'm fine, but I appreciate the kindness," said Peter. "I never even hoped I'd have a master who would put me before himself."

"More," said Ecanus firmly.

Peter stood alone, holding the canteen and giving Jana a pleading, confused look. But she couldn't help him, and couldn't think of anything to do. She wasn't sure how far Nefta's protection extended, or how much it could be relied upon. Even if Ecanus didn't discipline her directly, he might demand that Nefta do it. Or he might simply do as he pleased without care for the consequences. There was no one to stop him here, and no one to turn to. He could kill them and deal with the political aftermath later if he was so inclined, and sanctions from Nefta wouldn't do Jana any good if they were posthumously administered.

There was nothing else for Peter to do but drink. He put the canteen to his lips and began to chug, pausing to wipe his lips and steel himself for the rest. He finished it to the last drop, and then handed it off to the little boy. He looked relieved. His stomach was full, and he was ready to be a servant again.

"Thank you, sir," said Peter. "I'm sure I won't be thirsty for a while."

"Boy," said Ecanus, calling to the child as he was rushing back to the refreshment station. "Bring him another. He looks positively parched."

Now Peter began to turn pale, as it all sank in. The little boy dutifully ran back, holding up a fresh canteen to Peter and then quickly retreating to a safe distance. He held up the canteen and took a few tentative sips, probing to see if Ecanus would tire of the game and let him stop.

"Go on," said Ecanus. "Finish it." His eyes darted back and forth between Peter and Jana, imbibing their fear and their pain.

In the end, all Peter could think of was to try to please him as best he could. He drank frantically, enthusiastically, trying to prove his fealty to Ecanus by following his instructions with fervor. He drank every drop, and then bowed his head and tried his best to seem remorseful for his prior insubordination.

"Thank you, sir," said Peter.

"More," said Ecanus, snapping at the little boy again. "Bring us a jug this time." Again the boy rushed to the refreshments station, and he returned holding a large jug, meant for serving a group. Peter's eyes popped. He was full, and was starting to feel sick. He wasn't sure whether he could finish another. The canteens had been filled to the brim, and there were many, many more were these had come from. But he had to try. He opened the jug, and began to drink. Midway through, he was losing his momentum. He paused, his stomach bulging. He bent over to rest, took a few more sips, and then took another break.

"Keep going," said Ecanus, and so Peter did. He finished the jug, and looked again to Ecanus in defeat.

"More," said Ecanus.

"Please," said Peter. "I'm so, so sorry for my behavior. Please. I was a fool. I'll never do it again. Please."

"You'll drink another, or I'll turn my attentions to her," said Ecanus. Jana shuddered. She'd done nothing to draw his wrath, but that hardly mattered. Ecanus knew weakness when he saw it, and he'd latched upon Peter's weakness for her. Ecanus moved closer to her, flicking his wings about and brushing his blackened feathers against her face. She jumped back; she couldn't help it. The sight of him made her skin crawl. He licked his chapped lips, running the tip of his tongue across them, and grabbed Jana by the nape of her neck. Then he turned to Peter, smiling, and waited.

This time, Peter motioned for the boy himself. He was brought another jug, and he drank. His belly was distended, and Jana could see the bloating underneath his clothes. Water was running down his cheeks, but he kept going. Ecanus cackled, holding Jana's head firmly and aiming it at Peter so that she had no choice but to watch. His breath wafted over her, a putrid smell that made her wrinkle her nose in disgust. She watched helplessly as Peter collapsed to the floor and started choking on the water, his gag reflex kicking in. Ecanus just laughed, finally releasing her only to begin clapping with glee at his hateful handiwork.

CHAPTER FOURTEEN

HOLT HESITATED. HE WAS A lawman at heart, and his instincts were still to follow the law. None of it existed anymore, but that wasn't the point. The law had been a fiction, a set of rules that held sway only because everyone generally agreed which ones had to be followed, which ones could be bent, and which ones could be broken. But people's ideas about those rules were in a state of flux. The more sociopathic elements of humanity simply did as they pleased, but then, they always had. For the rest, times had changed, and some things that would have been unconscionable before were tolerated now. There had always been disputes at the margins about what was and wasn't acceptable conduct, but now there was no arbiter to turn to for a resolution. There were no prisons and no fines, which left only one real form of punishment available to those who felt they'd been wronged.

"He's a kid, Marv," said Holt. He had a touch of compassion in him, even if he had to be careful about showing it nowadays. He'd originally become a cop because he'd wanted to help people. It hadn't always worked out that way, and certainly didn't anymore. People resent discipline, even if it's in their best interests. Sometimes he'd been forced to battle with the ones he was trying to protect. Years of doing it had given him sympathy for the broken ones, trapped inside their pathologies and their self-destruction. The boy had done something very, very wrong, but that didn't mean he couldn't be redeemed. Holt knew from bitter experience that most people never changed. But sometimes they did, especially the young, and there was always hope. He'd seen plenty of it over the years: drunks who went cold turkey, thieves who found religion, and women who finally escaped from relationships that had been vortexes of abuse and pain. He'd had to pull more than one child out of dirty, chaotic places that could barely be called homes. People said it was worth it if you could save just one person, and he tended to think they were right. Marv, on the other hand, adhered to a different school of thought.

"He's a threat is what he is," said Marv. "You wanna just let people break in here? He coulda killed you. Coulda killed me. And he's workin' for them. You let him go, he's comin' back with more, and they might have wings."

"Maybe," said Holt. "They might be coming here anyway. You can't stay. You've all got to go somewhere else for a while. Killing this kid won't change that, and you know it. If he's here, then others are, too."

Marv paused, thinking quietly to himself. He was a paranoiac at heart, and thoughts of threats from above were all-consuming these days. But there were threats down below, too, and he just didn't see a compelling reason for mercy. "I say kill him," said Marv. "You gotta better plan, you do it. Go figure this crap out. I'm getting our shit together, and we're outta here tomorrow. Don't come back if I'm not here. The whole place is gettin' booby trapped, and we're not gonna be back here until the heat is off."

Holt walked back through the family quarters, heading towards the guest rooms. Little children in pajamas with mussed hair poked their heads out from behind half-shut doors, warily watching him and fighting their curious urges. They wanted to see what was going on, but they knew Marv would have their behinds if they tried, so a glimpse of Holt would have to do. The quarters could have been mistaken for any well-decorated suburban living room. Marv had appropriated the furnishings from some of the wealthier areas that were within a day's hike, and must have let the women make most of the decisions. It certainly looked more tasteful than anything he could be expected to come up with on his own, and the decorative candles and abundance of functionless pillows on the furniture were a dead giveaway that he wasn't wholly in charge of this part of the Colony. They'd even installed a homey fireplace, although Marv had never allowed anyone to use it. The fear of being given away by smoke took precedence over attempts to recover a semblance of normalcy. Holt suspected that the families wouldn't be happy about leaving the nest they'd created, but they'd made bigger sacrifices before.

The door swung open to the guest quarters, and the Vichy was still on the floor, tears drying. The collar of his rumpled white shirt was stained with drops of blood, and the rest was muddied with dirt from the ground. It was ill-fitting on his teenage body, anyway; he'd probably salvaged it from some businessman's closet. His pants were much the same, well-worn sweats with their string pulled tight around his waist. But something white was something white, and he had to show his allegiance if he wanted to be one of them. Faye stood over him, calmly watching and pointing one of the Vichies' own assault rifles at his head.

"What's the word?" asked Faye, keeping her eyes on the Vichy as she spoke.

"Don't know yet," said Holt. "Marv wants you dead, kid. You're in his house. You come into a man's house without permission these days, you can't expect him to let you come out of it alive."

The Vichy looked up at him, his face sinking into anguish. He probed for some sign of his fate, but couldn't find any. Holt had been a pretty good amateur poker player before the Fall, and had generally cleaned up when it was just the boys playing for beer money. Holt had no intention of killing him, but the Vichy didn't need to know that. He'd participated in a few "scared straight" programs in his day, and knew that a taste of life's consequences was often just the thing to convince a boy to assume the responsibilities of a man. They always started out playing tough, trying to beat their chest the loudest and prove they were somebody. They never understood the subtleties of manhood. Holt had the icy confidence that came from years of challenges, knowing from experience that the more a man blustered, the shakier his position was. Acts of bravado were a feint, a search for weakness that was abandoned the instant it ran into strength. The boy was well past that stage after his run-in with them. He was broken down, and it was time to rebuild him.

"Get up, kid," said Holt. "We're going outside."

The caterwauling started up again at once. The Vichy bawled about his family, his good intentions, and how he'd never be seen again in these parts if only he were set free. Holt just grabbed his arm, pulling him up and pushing him forward. Faye followed them from behind, gun at the ready. They passed through the darkened passages and out towards the moonlight, the Vichy begging the entire way.

"Hold up," said Holt. "Shoot him if he makes any noise." He shoved the Vichy against a wall just inside, and motioned to Faye to play guard. The Vichy began softly whimpering, but she seemed to tacitly understand that it didn't count. Holt walked to a nearby window, let his eyes adjust, and then scanned the surroundings for a few minutes. Nothing was moving and nothing seemed to be out of place. He couldn't be certain what was out in the forest, but the tree line was some distance away, and anyone in it would have to be a pretty good shot to pose a threat in the dark. A rusted tractor from the Colony's farming days that had been scuttled in the middle of some nearby brush was the most obvious hiding place, but Holt knew it was infested with wasps, and no one would be hiding there for long. He was fairly sure that the Vichies had been alone; their fumbling home invasion didn't suggest much planning. But it was safest to be prepared, and his years since the Fall had made him all about precautions. When he was satisfied that there wasn't some hidden sentry, he dragged the Vichy outside and kept him moving, pistol at his back.

Holt walked him towards some open grass, away from the Colony and well away from the forest's border. The last thing he needed was a chase through the woods before they'd gotten things squared, and it was too dark outside for them to be easily visible from up in the skies. The Vichy kept silent this time, cowed by the earlier warning. Their feet disappeared into the brush, and when they were far enough away Holt roughly shoved him to the ground. The Vichy was all terror, shivering in fright. He looked around for some kind of escape, but found none—only grass, his captors, and an orchestra of crickets.

"Faye here thinks you're a traitor," said Holt. "Isn't that right, Faye?"

"I'm not. I swear I'm not," said the boy.

"You're a Vichy, aren't you? You're sure dressed like one," said Faye. She was barking at him, milking the role. If Holt wanted to be the good cop, she had no problem being the bad one.

"We're servants. We're just servants," said the boy nervously. The Vichies shied away from the name themselves. It tarred them with treasons past from before the Fall, and they preferred to think of themselves as pragmatic survivors just doing what had to be done.

"Servants don't carry guns," said Holt. "Soldiers carry guns. What were you doing poking around after your fellow humans?"

"You're fighting for the other side," said Faye. "That's what a traitor does, isn't it? Takes up arms against his people? And for what? So you can be somebody's pet?"

"No, no, no. No. It's scary out here," said the boy. "It's just scary. I didn't want them to kill me. They said they wouldn't kill us, none of 'em. You can't fight 'em, they're too strong. If you do what they say you don't have to hide." His nervous eyes flitted from Faye to Holt, and back again, looking for some sign of their intentions.

"You don't have to hide," said Holt. "Someone else does."

"If you don't fight them, who will?" said Faye. "If you help them, we have to fight you, too. Ever think about that?"

"We're not helping them," said the boy. "We weren't, we weren't. We just wanted food." He was getting edgy, digging into the ground with his hands and trembling all over. He looked over his shoulder a few times, probably thinking about making a break for it. But there was nowhere to run to. Holt had positioned him well, and it was just low grass all around with at least a mile to any trees.

"That's not what Marv thinks," said Holt. "Marv wants me to kill you. Marv thinks if I let you go, you'll just go back to the Perch. He thinks you'll bring—"

The boy panicked. He charged at Faye, a wild dash from the ground that closed the distance in an instant. Then he was flailing, punching at her and grappling with her for the assault rifle. Holt aimed, but he didn't have a shot. There'd be too great a risk of hitting Faye, especially in the dark. The Vichy had her in close, tossing her to the ground and standing over her. They were both desperately pulling at the gun, a single mass of shadows and jabs locked together in struggle. Holt rushed over, grabbing at the nearest white he could see to pull the boy off. Then it came. The loud crack of the rifle, and the warm spray of blood across his face.

CHAPTER FIFTEEN

VOMIT COVERED THE GROUND. PETER had ejected the entire contents of his stomach, and pools of dirty water were spreading everywhere. He pushed himself to his feet and stood unsteadily, facing the floor. Any notion that he was something other than a slave was gone. He waited in silence, hoping he could maintain his balance and hoping it was all done. Fortunately, Ecanus seemed to have been satisfied with his fun, and released Jana to turn his attentions back to him.

"Let's go, boy," said Ecanus. "We mustn't dally. There's work to do in my quarters, and it seems the yoke still doesn't fit quite right. No matter. We'll teach you who's master yet, you wait and see." He walked away, with Peter following as quickly as he could. The servants at the refreshment station rushed about to get towels and began wiping away the vomit, trying to eliminate any sign of it before another angel passed by. If anyone thought they'd been remiss in keeping the place clean it'd be their hides, and Ecanus's display had given them a surge in motivation.

Jana was still in shock. This was the single most foolish thing she'd ever seen one of the servants do. She racked her brain, trying to think of something she could do to help, before she remembered—Nefta. She was still waiting back at the Conclave, thirsty, and Jana had been here for far longer than was likely to be tolerable. She grabbed her canteen and ran, praying she could rush back and slip inside before things became too suspicious. But it was too late.

As Jana rounded the corner to the entryway to the Conclave, she saw angels milling around in groups outside. The speeches were done, and the gossip and critiquing was just beginning. It was far more fun to talk about the proceedings than to listen to them, and the angels were busy chattering away. Jana could see Uzziel, surrounded by a half-dozen well-wishers who shared his desire to recreate an earthly version of the heavenly host to fend off the enemies they saw all around them. Flecks of spittle covered his beard as he continued on enthusiastically, rehashing his earlier speech and drawing imaginary plans for barricades in the air with his fingers.

A number of smaller pockets of angels who she didn't recognize stood around in twos and threes, glad-handing and politicking. Some of them didn't get out much, spending most of their time isolated in their quarters, and treated the Conclave as an opportunity to renew their social ties. Others just wanted to grandstand, and she could hear boasts about various interesting distractions they'd come up with to fritter away their ample free time. She weaved through the crowd, dodging wings and gesticulating arms as she tried to find Nefta.

She made her way to the entrance, to a vantage point where she could see her former seat. Nothing. Most of the benches were empty, with just a few dozen of the angels remaining inside the amphitheater, congregating around the rostrum.

She turned to leave, and was interrupted by a call from the very center of the group. "Girl!"

It was Rhamiel, beaming. Apparently his speech had ended well, as he stood among a cluster of angels slapping him on the back in congratulations and leaning forward to offer him suggestions or support. With Rhamiel's cry, all their eyes turned towards the entrance and fixated on her.

"Sneaking out in the middle of the entertainment is bad form, girl. Has Nefta taught you no manners?" said Rhamiel, a little tease in his tone. The angels around him laughed, and fortunately seemed to be in good humor. They were Rhamiel's partisans in whatever political drama the angels were enacting, and didn't seem to be in the mood for cruelties towards the servants just yet.

"Come here! Don't be shy! You're the picture of human beauty, and I've spent the last half an hour educating my detractors on the angelic one," said Rhamiel. Jana's stomach sank. She couldn't leave, and had no idea where Nefta and Cassie had gone to. She wasn't even sure she could find her way back to the chambers. She hadn't paid much attention on the way here, and they'd changed floors once—or was it twice? The hallways and ramps in the tower zigzagged and spiraled into each other according to an architectural aesthetic that didn't make much intuitive sense to humans. While it lent a strange beauty to the place in its own way, it played tricks on her sense of direction, and it wouldn't do to wander around unsupervised.

She walked down the steps to the speaker's platform, the entire crowd watching her the entire way. She felt a mix of shame and fear. She didn't think she was that beautiful, and was worried that his comment might be a prelude to one of their cruel jokes. From time to time, Sam had smuggled in frivolous magazines from before the Fall, and she looked nothing like the women in them. They'd had make-up for their face and tonics for their hair, while the servants in the tower made do with soap and water. Sam always called her a natural beauty, but a compliment from a friend is never truly trusted. She brushed at her hair involuntarily, moving a few wisps to the side that had fallen out of place.

As she approached the group, the other angels seemed to leer at her. She couldn't tell for sure. They were strange creatures, and hard to read sometimes. They seemed to be appraising her, evaluating her as you might a prized farm animal. Rhamiel was the only one who didn't, but his face was inscrutable. It all made her nerves fray. The encounter with Ecanus had deeply disturbed her. She knew how they could be, but back in the kitchens you'd normally only hear about it secondhand. You didn't actually have to see them in action, just the awful aftermath. It was all starting to wear on her. In the games they played, the servants were ever the losers, and she worried about where Rhamiel's toying might lead.

"You seem so withdrawn, girl," said Rhamiel. "There's no need for all that. We've just won a grand victory.

I've convinced the Conclave to organize a raid. Not the wearisome sort of thing that Uzziel keeps demanding, but a real adventure. A reprisal for the scoundrel who did this to my face." He pointed at his forehead to identify the alleged injury. Even up close, she couldn't see anything. She thought for a second that maybe there was a little spot, or a freckle, but then couldn't tell if she was just imagining it.

"It'll be like the old times, before the Maker's son came along," said one of the angels. "He used to have a firmer hand. When someone got up to something, we'd rain down fire or flood the place and drown them like rats. But the boy's been up there for nigh on two millennia, prattling on endlessly about mercy, mercy, mercy. It's what addled the old man's brain, I think."

"Why the sulk on your face?" asked another, sneering at Jana. "You've got the attention of the one who's the talk of the tower. I'd think a girl in your position would be fawning over him, or doing a little curtsy."

"I'm sorry, sir," said Jana, and clumsily attempted one. She couldn't think of what else to do. Sam had always taught her not to deny them anything, and to keep her responses to the bare minimum. They'd tell you if they were expecting more, and if you said too much—well, you'd end up like Peter had.

"That was very cute, girl," said Rhamiel. "A fine attempt. We should have you practice. We're always looking for new entertainments, and I think you've got something about you. A womanly wile I'd love to see more of."

He was grinning, but something was welling up

inside of her. A panic, overtaking her and hammering away from the inside at her self-control. She could feel her breathing quickening, and her heartbeat thudding faster and faster. All she could think about whenever they were talking was Ecanus, gripping her and forcing her to watch his ghoulish show. The curtsy had been too much. It was a performance of its own, and who knew where it would lead? Peter's plight had started off with a sip of water, and Daniel's with a clink of a plate. They would make her dance, and dance, and maybe they wouldn't ever let her stop.

She looked from face to face, and her terror must have showed. The others just laughed louder, but Rhamiel's expression turned from playful to a glint of compassion. He looked hurt at her reaction, like he hadn't expected it, didn't know what was wrong, and didn't know exactly what to do about it.

"This is all new to us, Jana," said Rhamiel. "We haven't been down here long. We're still learning to be ourselves. We were in service for so long. It was all rules, orders, and missions, and we never talked much to your kind. We just did as we were told, and now there's no one who can tell us anything. Why don't you go find Nefta? You shouldn't be running about without her, anyhow."

"Yes, sir," said Jana, scurrying away up the steps as quickly as she could. She thought she'd never really understand what was going on inside them. Rhamiel was a mystery to her, one moment acting as if he wanted to be her master and the next acting as if he wanted to be her friend. She thought maybe he was attracted to her, but she didn't know how she felt about that. He was handsome to be sure, but he was one of them, and it was frightening to know that in the end he could simply do whatever he wanted. And this was all new to her. She hadn't ever had any kind of romantic interests before outside of the fantasies she enacted in her head. She hadn't really had any options. There were a few other men her age in the kitchens, but they were so—*cringing*. They'd been trained all their lives to be submissive, meekly obeying every order they received. So had Jana, and it was probably unfair of her to fault them for it. They wouldn't have survived if they'd been any other way. But yin seeks out yang, and the feminine can't be blamed if it's drawn to the masculine. Rhamiel wasn't the type to crawl on his belly. He wouldn't have rebelled if he was. He and the other angels would have chosen to die before cowering to another, and all their cruelty aside, there was something alluring about that. But there was also danger. She knew she was a moth, but she couldn't tell whether she was being drawn towards a beautiful light or a deadly flame.

She exited the Conclave and went back into the flock outside, jostled around by angels pushing past her who didn't seem to care about whether she was bumped over. Most were taller than her, and she couldn't see over their heads to get a good look at whether Cassie or Nefta had stayed. She couldn't ask one of the angels, but there were a few servants on the sidelines waiting for their masters to finish with their business here. One of them might know, or might be able to direct her back to the chambers. Then from behind, her hair was yanked and her head slammed backward. She wriggled to get free out of instinct, and then went limp as soon as she saw who it was. Nefta, looking furious, with Cassie attending her.

"I saw you with him," said Nefta. "I should think you'd know better by now. You and I are going to have a long, unpleasant talk."

CHAPTER SIXTEEN

HOLT PULLED THE VICHY OFF, slamming him to the ground. But it was too late. The white of his shirt was now splattered with dark splotches, and a growing circle pooled on his chest where the bullet had torn through him. He started hacking, blood foaming from out of his mouth as his arms clutched at the wound. He made sounds, dreadful sounds, things that were a mixture of half-formed words and pleas for help. He wouldn't find any. There were no doctors out here. Holt had some basic emergency medical training from the force, and Marv had a small library of texts he thought useful that included some medical encyclopedias. But this was too serious a wound for them to even attempt to treat.

"Are you okay?" asked Holt, reaching down to Faye to pull her up. She was shaken, but he couldn't see any obvious injuries; the moonlight wasn't bright enough to let him be totally sure.

"I'm fine," said Faye. "I'll be fine. God damn it. Why did he do that?"

Maybe they'd pushed him too far. Holt felt twinges of guilt. He was just a boy, after all. They'd only meant to frighten him. If he'd just waited a little longer, they'd probably have been able to set him free. All he'd have had to do was to understand why this had all been so wrong, and to give them a little intelligence on what the Vichies were up to in the area. But he couldn't or wouldn't wait, or was too scared to. Holt was kicking himself inside. It never got easier, trying to help people out of their own foolishness. He'd thought he could save him, and maybe he could have. Maybe if he'd backed off and played the role a little nicer, the boy wouldn't have been so desperate. Maybe if they'd stood a little further away, he wouldn't have thought his mad attack on Faye would have had any chance of success.

He used to think he'd eventually get numbed to this kind of after the fact questioning and doubt. He knew it didn't really make sense. The boy had made his own decisions, and he was the one who had put them all here. Holt had tried the best thing he knew to get everyone out of that quandary with their lives intact. And nine times out of ten, you couldn't save someone who had committed themselves to treading a darker path. You couldn't just tell them the awful places it led to; they had to find that out for themselves. But he'd still be thinking of what-if's for months, and maybe years. He couldn't help it, and he wasn't sure he wanted to be the kind of person who could.

The noises slowed, then stopped, and the Vichy's eyes went empty. The ground around him was wet with blood, and his expression was locked forever in fear and confusion. Holt started to lead Faye away from the grisly scene, back to the Colony. But on the way her knees gave out. She swayed, dizzy, and collapsed to the ground. She gagged and retched, then dry heaved a few times onto the grass.

"Hey," said Holt, lifting her up. "Hey! You're okay. You're fine. Hold on to me."

"I feel like shit," said Faye. "I think he hit my head."

He thought it must have all been too much. She could have a concussion, and he'd need to check her for that inside. Or it could be a mild form of shock. Sometimes people just couldn't take being that close to another person's death. Faye had assumed the role of sniper in the cell, shooting at her targets from a distance. She said it was because she didn't trust herself in close combat. She wasn't athletic in any way before the Fall, and freely admitted that the average man could overpower her in a fight. She'd killed a Vichy before, though, and didn't seem to have been troubled by it. But he'd been an adult, and the deed had been done from far away as he was threatening another. Holt knew they'd help her through this one. This type of tragedy couldn't be avoided these days, and you had to stick together to cope as best you could.

He led her back to the Colony, and they went inside. Marv ran her through a checklist of symptoms from one of his books, playing at doctor and doing what he could. She seemed to be fine, if still a little shaken, but the signs of a concussion were pretty clearly there. There wasn't much they could do, but Marv dredged up some Tylenol, and Dax volunteered to stay beside her as she slept to keep watch. The rest of them sat up talking and speculating about what the Vichies had been doing there, and the older boys from the families enthusiastically took up guard duties at various windows in the upper levels of the sanitarium. Nothing much happened, and there ended up not being a need for any of it, but Marv was of the opinion that a little more vigilance might have avoided the situation in the first place. Nobody but Faye got much sleep; their adrenaline was still flowing and they couldn't quit thinking about all the excitement.

In the morning, the cell took their leave. Faye was up and feeling better, and their belongings were already packed. They gathered their things together, as Marv directed a flurry of preparations for his own exit. Children ran around searching for their favorite toys, the women fretted about how much of their clothing they'd be able to carry, and the older boys had a grand time installing dangerous traps around the premises to greet anyone who stopped by while they were gone.

"We've got to get on the road," said Holt. "We've got a package to pick up, but then we're going to be heading back to the City to keep up the good fight. We'll check in on the place. If you're not here, we'll leave a note at the trees out by the old bathtubs." Some scavenger had created a pile of them before Marv had ever gotten there, dragged out from the Colony's various buildings, but whoever it was had ended up just leaving them there in a heap of cracked porcelain. Now they were a convenient landmark, located near a copse of trees that Marv used as canvases for the carving of coded messages. If you were just passing through, you could leave him a message there and know that he'd find it.

"Go on, now, and good luck," said Marv. "We'll be gone for at least a few weeks. We've gotta few other spots. They ain't as safe, but I'm staying away and scoutin' the island until I know what's what."

They all said their goodbyes, and Holt led his team onward and outward. They hiked back out into the forest, making their way as far south as they could without leaving its protections. The greenbelts would end, and they'd have to switch to the roads at some point if they wanted to make any time. It wasn't the safest way to travel, but it was still the fastest. And the further they got away from the Perch, the lower the risk. Outside of its immediate vicinity, you might see a solitary angel flying overhead from time to time, but it was nothing like how it could get in the City. There were other dangers, but Holt had a plan for that, too: speed.

When they came to the edges of the forest, they reached a small, hidden tarp just inside that was covered in brush. They'd left it there on the way up, camouflaging their preferred mode of transportation: three motocross bikes, and a four-wheel all-terrain vehicle for Dax. The bikes were faster, but he didn't have the coordination to use them at top speed, and they'd needed something to haul the Stingers with anyway. All of them could go off-road, and Holt had made them all practice various group evasive maneuvers beforehand in case there was an emergency. The roads were clogged with cars, rusting away after having been abandoned in the decade or so that had passed since the angels fell. People had tried to escape all of the cities, all at once, and when a car or two ran out of gas everything behind them had ground to a halt. Even the shoulders were often covered with cars that had tried to go around the traffic snarl, only to create yet another one. But you could usually squeeze through on a small bike, and all of the bridges on the island were still standing and offered the quickest way back to the mainland. They were going to have to be out in the open anyway, and Holt thought that this far south of the Perch it was best to just make a dash for it.

As they pulled out the bikes, Dax insisted on doing a check of each of their engines. He wanted to tinker with them, and to make sure that everything was okay before they started a long distance journey. A mechanical problem out on the road could be a disaster, particularly as one was most likely to happen if they pressed the vehicles' limits during an emergency. He had a little tool kit in a trailer that he'd hitched to the ATV, and he pulled it out and got to work with his inspections while the others milled around.

"You ain't exactly the mechanic type," said Thane. "You work on cars or somethin' before the Fall?"

"Nope," said Dax. "Learned it all from my Dad. He was a blue collar guy, big into cars."

"That apple didn't land too close to that tree, did it?" said Thane.

"He was an asshole and a drunk. But I wanted to be just like him," said Dax. "I thought I'd impress him if I learned how to help him out in the garage. But he and his friends just flicked bottle-caps at my head. I gave it up and spent a bunch of time alone in my room on my computer." There was a tension in his voice. Dax had been nothing like most of his family. They'd considered him an odd duck, poking at motherboards with a soldering iron when he could have been watching a perfectly good football game. Dissimilarity can create distance, and he'd never really connected with any of them. He'd spent most of his boyhood trying to be something he wasn't, something they all seemed to think was better than what came naturally for him. Bookishness got you dirty looks, while athleticism got you pats on the back and proud smiles. The drive to be someone else had never really left him, and it was in large part what had drawn him here, to the cell and their quixotic battles.

"I ended up as a software application developer out in San Francisco," said Dax. "We were working on an app that would automatically like all of your friend's social statuses, so that you could pretend you were paying attention to them without actually having to."

"I'd have used it," said Faye.

"I thought I was going to be a millionaire," said Dax. "But that was before everything all went to shit."

The Fall had come out of nowhere, for the residents of Earth. There'd been no warnings and no time to prepare. One evening streaks of fire started appearing in the skies, all around the globe. The newsrooms initially reported it as a meteor shower, a sudden and freak celestial display. But meteors didn't just appear out of thin air. These objects seemed to materialize from nothing, appearing everywhere at once and with no discernible pattern. As they fell to the ground, darker reports began to trickle in. Videos began circulating of winged beings, screaming in anguish from their burns and creating havoc and destruction wherever they'd landed. At first, things seemed to be contained. Most of them had landed in the vast oceans rather than on land, by simple laws of probability. A few Indian cities were claiming massive casualties, both from violent rampages by a few of the creatures and from the mass hysteria that had resulted among millions of people living together in confined spaces. For the rest of the globe, things seemed to calm down for a day or two as the angels recovered and disappeared into the skies.

No one was sure what had happened, but speculation was rampant. Millions found religion and gathered to worship, while newscasts filled the ticking hours with guesses and commentaries. Governments didn't do much of anything. They seemed paralyzed with indecision, facing something they'd never planned for and didn't have the slightest clue what to do about. They talked in circles about who had the proper authority to respond and how. In the end, it wouldn't have mattered. The angels had fallen, remnants of a heavenly army, and they started doing what armies in disarray tend to do. They regrouped.

Anarchy took hold soon after. The angels began a series of calculated attacks, destroying anything of strategic importance and slaughtering anyone who resisted. It quickly became every man for himself, and most people soon stopped fighting and started focusing on hiding or escaping. The actual warfare didn't last long. The angels began squabbling among themselves immediately after it was clear that their victory was a foregone conclusion, breaking into factions and even attacking each other. That just made things even worse. Rogue angels flew around doing as they pleased, killing people and panicking entire populations. They finally tired of it, settling down in permanent locations like the Perch. They were military-minded enough or bored enough to continue striking at any human military targets, keeping them forever off balance and preventing any kind of organized response to the chaos. Probably the death toll could have been minimized with some basic humanitarian relief, and most people thought it would be as the angels withdrew into themselves and finally left humanity alone.

But that was before the Vichies sold the rest of them out.

CHAPTER SEVENTEEN

"HE'LL HURT YOU," SAID NEFTA. "He can't help it. It's his nature. He'd love you, too, and he'd mean it. But he'd still hurt you in the end, and more than you could bear."

She'd cooled down a little, but she'd been in a fury when she found Jana. After dragging her back to her chambers, Nefta had yelled for what seemed like an eternity before nearly slapping her again. She'd managed to stop herself, and then just brooded in silence for a full quarter of an hour. Jana had been on pins and needles the entire time, worrying about all the terrible punishments she might soon suffer. But now Nefta's voice showed only sadness and concern.

"I know how these things go," said Nefta. "You're following him around like a little girl. You're smitten with him. You've no reason not to be. He's everything you could want on the outside. But the inside is a good deal more complicated."

Jana didn't exactly consider herself smitten. She hadn't been following Rhamiel at all—if anything, he was the one pursuing her. It wasn't that he was uninteresting: he had a strange allure to him, and on paper he was everything she could ever want. She thought he had a kindness to him underneath the outer shell, but the angels could be unfathomable. They did things for reasons she couldn't understand, and more than anything she was worried about the dangers of giving in to his pursuit. Ecanus was an angel, too, and what if Rhamiel had some of that in him? Even Nefta oscillated between anger and kindness, and didn't seem to be able to control herself in the way a normal human adult could. Jana started to tell Nefta that she'd misjudged the situation, but prudence got the better of her. Sometimes it's better to be repentant even if you're in the right.

Nefta slowly paced around the room, running her fingers across a few of the masks on the walls as she went. She stopped at one—a woman, the mask contorted into an expression of despair. She lifted it, stared at it for a bit, and then hung it back in its place along the wall.

"Sit, girl," said Nefta, motioning towards a wooden bench. Jana obliged, and Nefta sat down next to her. It made her uncomfortable. Nefta was close, just like Ecanus had been, and the experience was still giving her jitters. Nefta spoke looking forward, keeping the unscarred side of her face towards Jana. She almost looked normal from this angle, with a few raised bumps from the opposite side of her face the only visible sign of her deformity.

"We weren't always this way, you know," said Nefta. "We were something better, once. You may not believe it, and perhaps I wouldn't in your position. You've only ever known us as we are."

"Do you know what a guardian angel is?" asked Nefta. Jana had heard of them, but only in whispered stories. She knew the angels had all had their duties before the Fall, and Sam had told her that they used to watch people as they slept. What had once been a comforting fable was now a horror story the older servants used to frighten the children. They said the angels used to stand over you while you were in your bed, invisible, and if you weren't careful they still might. You had to mind your words, always, because you never knew when one of them could appear from nowhere with a sword of fire. No one had ever actually seen it happen, but it taught the younger ones a valuable survival skill: how to hold their tongues.

"Yes, ma'am," said Jana. "They see you when you're sleeping, and they know whether you've been naughty or nice. And you mustn't cross them, or they'll pluck out your eyes and replace them with burning lumps of coal." Good stories don't ever die, exactly, but they change as the years go by, and they teach the lessons of the time they're in.

Nefta wrinkled her brow in confusion. "No, dear, that's not quite right. We all had our tasks, assigned by the Maker. He expected us to perform them diligently, something I should hope you'll learn a little about. I was a guardian angel. We watched over people. Not to hurt them, or whatever nonsense they've been filling your ears with down there. We were protectors. Not heaven's most glorious duty, but I thought it the noblest one. Do you see these masks?"

Jana did. There were so many, and Nefta must have spent untold hours carving them. The attention she'd paid to them was striking. Any one of them could have passed for an actual person, if they hadn't been made of wood. They bore the lines of worry, sadness, laughter, or joy that life engraves on all of us, and something of the soul was displayed in the emotions carved into each of them.

"Yes, ma'am. What are they?" said Jana. Then she flinched. Cassie had been very clear that she wasn't to inquire about this particular subject. It was Nefta's business, not hers. But Nefta didn't rage, or raise her fists. She'd gotten command of herself, and seemed to be in the mood to talk.

"They're people," said Nefta. "I watched over every one of them. Century after century, helping them with their struggles with little nudges, protecting them from their follies where I could. It isn't an easy job, mind you. You've a tendency to do as you please regardless of the consequences, your kind. You're certainly no exception."

"I don't mean to be any trouble," said Jana. "My friend...."

"Rhamiel isn't your friend," said Nefta. "I won't make him out to be some kind of monster, because he isn't. Some of the others have become them, but that's simply the way of things. I wonder sometimes if the Maker was in the right in all of this. He wouldn't give us what we wanted, but perhaps we needed something else. Rhamiel may be what you want, but he isn't what you need. He was a guardian angel, too. Did he tell you that?"

"No, ma'am," said Jana. "We really didn't...."

"What you did and didn't do is of no import," said Nefta. "It's what you do now that matters. What you must understand about Rhamiel is that he wasn't always the person you see today. In Heaven he was different. The confidence, the charm, the followers—he had none of that up there. He was actually considered rather plain."

Jana was taken aback. She couldn't even begin to fathom it. Rhamiel was by far the best looking among them, and she'd never seen a human man who could even come close. He looked like someone from one of the magazines she'd seen, walking perfection with no need for calculated photographic angles or tricks of lighting. Nefta must have noticed her reaction, or read something in her body language. She smiled and chuckled to herself.

"You don't believe me? We have different standards of beauty, you and I," said Nefta. "We see beauty in you, sometimes when you can't. We see tiny imperfections in our own faces, ones you'd never notice." Jana wondered how Rhamiel saw her, and whether she'd even recognize herself through his eyes. And if they obsessed over the smallest blemish, how must they feel about their disfigurements?

"The Maker did a little carving himself when he made us," said Nefta. "Our faces were all about symmetries, perfect expressions of who we were inside and who he intended us to be. And look at all of us now." She seemed on the verge of tears. Jana hadn't ever really thought about what this had done to them. The Fall had taken its toll, and the scars weren't just on the outside.

"He was braver than any of us," said Nefta, after a pause to compose herself. "The rest of us fell. Rhamiel was the only one who leapt."

"Leapt?" asked Jana. Nefta had spent a great deal of

time studying human emotion, but she still had much to learn. Her warnings had made Jana genuinely curious, wondering what was in the depths beneath the person Rhamiel had become after the Fall.

"It was during Maion's Stand, the last battle of our rebellion," said Nefta. "The Maker's armies were just mopping things up by then. Everything was in disarray, and we were all demoralized. We'd thought we were on the verge of victory just a few days before. Heaven was on fire, the Celestial City had been razed, and there was even talk of seizing the throne itself. Then the tides turned. Loyalists began to arrive, responding to summons from their duties in distant places. The Maker's forces swelled, and we were beaten back to the outskirts. We all knew things were hopeless. We began to turn on each other, and they exploited it. Everyone could see what they intended. They meant to toss us down, just as they had Lucifer's army before us. Some led a final charge, simply for the glory of it. Others sat and sulked, or tried to flee. We all knew what was coming, and we were all afraid. Everyone except Rhamiel."

"He saw the others being surrounded and thrown into the ether, one by one," said Nefta. "He knew we were all going to burn, and he knew there was no way out. So he grabbed one of the shields we'd pillaged from the armory. It was forged in hellfire, meant for combat inside Lucifer's Pit. He put it in front of him, he went to the edge, and then he jumped. This side of my face, this blotching. Look, girl."

Jana forced herself to. Nefta pointed to her bad side, patched with spots of red and brown. The leathery skin had been loosened and distorted, and parts of it bumped up, forming a permanent swelling. She clearly was sensitive about it, but she had a point to make.

"When they threw me down, I lost control," said Nefta. "I spiraled, my wings useless as I fell faster and faster and burned hotter and hotter. We're strong, very strong, but such heat. It can't be endured for long. I tucked the other side to my shoulder and spared it, but most of me was ruined. Rhamiel was the smart one. The shield bore the brunt of things. His bravery let him be the master of his fall, and he was able to glide and slow his descent. Still hot, but nothing like what the rest of us were subjected to. His wings were singed a bit, and his hands scarred from where he held the edges of the shield. But otherwise he made it through intact."

"And now he's the most beautiful among us. Much of our status derived from it up there, and it's no different down here. Only he's gone from the lower ranks to the top, by his own ingenuity. That's what you must understand, girl. We are all experimenting in sin, and Rhamiel is vain. He cannot help but enjoy his new position. If you chase him, he'll let you catch him. He will love you, and he will care for you, as that is what a guardian angel does. You may think you can tame him, and you can, for a time. But his vanity won't let him sit still. Eventually he'll move on to another, to prove to himself that he can. And then you'll be hurt, and you'll have scars of your own, just like me."

Nefta stood quickly, and her eyes teared up before she pivoted away. She started to head towards her private quarters and then stopped in her tracks.

"You know, I took you up here for a reason," said Nefta. "To protect you. I can see what's to come, even if no one else can. You're in my charge now, and I forbid you to speak to him. Understand me? You will ignore him if you see him. You will not respond to him if he speaks to you. You will stay away. It's what's best for you. The next time you disobey me, the consequences will be severe, and they will be for your own good."

Then she left, muttering to herself as she walked down the hallway: "All this torture and hurt. None of this would have happened if the Maker had just kept his word."

CHAPTER EIGHTEEN

"GIVE HIM A LITTLE LONGER. He's a good guy, but he's not exactly punctual," said Dax.

They were waiting for the Cook, in a used car lot outside of a little town on the outskirts of Trenton. Dax knew him, although mostly from chatting on underground resistance forums on the Internet. They'd worked together briefly, supporting a larger group that had tried a full scale assault on three angels who'd turned downtown Philadelphia into their own private playground. Things hadn't gone well. They'd been particularly nasty ones, warriors with a penchant for kidnapping humans and forcing them into gladiator-style duels for their own entertainment. An actual battle was a dream come true for them, and they'd feigned defeat, baiting the fighters into an attack just to toy with them for hours. Dax had escaped along with most of the support staff, who'd been ordered to stay behind to care for any casualties.

The Cook was an amateur chemist, and had used handbooks he'd downloaded online to teach himself to manufacture a variety of necessities that were no longer being mass produced. One of them was gasoline. People had been able to scavenge it from cars or fuel tanks for a year or two after the angels fell, but it degraded as time went on. It was all gone by now, and if you wanted any, you had to find someone who could make it themselves. The quality was low, it was more ethanol than anything, and it was hell on an engine. In the end, though, none of that really mattered. There were plenty of vehicles, many of which had been left inside garages and were still in pristine condition. But if you wanted to make a long distance trip, you had to find places to refuel along the way. The Cook was friendly, and more importantly, he was free. Most people had given up on resisting, and wouldn't waste valuable resources supporting those who wanted to tilt at windmills. But the Cook was an idealist. You might have to endure a few lectures about his anarchist philosophies, but if you were fighting the angels he'd give you what he could on principle.

"I want to know where this guy is," said Holt.

"I wanna know where we're goin'," said Thane.

Holt had refused to tell them, and Thane had been pestering him about it the entire trip. All he would say is that they needed to conduct some business, they needed to pick something up, and then they were going back to the City. He liked to protect his sources, and many of them wouldn't be happy about dealing with anyone else. He'd been fighting for nearly eight years, and had been a member of groups ranging from large militias to small cells like the one he currently operated in. The same pattern kept repeating itself: they'd lose some people, splinter apart, and then reorganize into smaller and smaller groups. Nothing any of them had tried had been particularly effective, but the one upside was that he'd acquired a wide array of professional contacts over the years. Combined with Dax's virtual friends, they were able to get pretty much anything they needed.

"He said to meet here," said Dax. "I sent him a couple of messages. He's probably on his way, and we'll miss him if we leave." They'd holed up in the sales offices, just inside the windows where the light could still get in. Rows of cars filled the lot, although they'd been heavily weathered and the interiors were covered in broken glass. Inside, the place was a mess. Yellowed papers and old sales brochures were scattered around the ground in between a few of the floor models, still shiny as ever.

They sat there for another hour, playing cards and passing the time. It could be surprisingly boring, now that modern entertainments and distractions had faded away. They'd all grown up absorbed by them, filling every second of their spare time with television, social networking, and games. You could still get some of that, but not on the road, where what limited batteries you had couldn't be wasted on frivolities. One of the hardest things about the Fall was adjusting themselves to find satisfaction without the constant stimulations they were used to. Everyone had their own way of coping. Some people couldn't take it, and had maddened or become unstable as their unoccupied minds went round and round in circles. Others poured themselves into work, even when they didn't really need to. The cell didn't have it quite as bad. Dax always tried to carry a few books, but after a reading or two he tended to lose interest. Holt kept them busy when he could, ordering them to practice or drill during any significant downtime. Thane had never been much for anything but television, anyway, and Faye was sociable enough that she could entertain herself by chatting with the rest of them when she wasn't busy. It still grated, though, and none of them were happy when they had to sit still.

"We're not waiting forever," said Holt. "Daylight's burning and we need to get some gas. I don't want to end up spending the next few weeks hiking. Where's this guy live at?"

"I'm not really supposed to know," said Dax.

"But you do," said Holt.

Dax fidgeted with his hands, pausing and trying to buy time to figure out what to say. After a few seconds, he knew the jig was up. "He'd get really mad," said Dax. "Really, really mad. I was just curious, you know. He was so secretive about it. I wanted to see if I could find out. Like a little game."

"Just tell me where he is," said Holt.

"He's in a trailer park a few miles away. I traced the connection," said Dax. "It wasn't exact, but it got me in the area, and I used some satellite images to pin things down." New satellites weren't being launched, but many of them were still up there, looping around the globe as their orbits gradually decayed. The angels hadn't bothered any of them. They could fly, but as far as anyone could tell they never went beyond the atmosphere. People had speculated, wondering whether there was some barrier they couldn't cross or whether they were even capable of going that far up. A few had proposed fanciful schemes of rebuilding society in orbit, beyond the angels' reach. It was a stretch to begin with, but by the time it was seriously considered the industries necessary for the plan had been decimated. The orbiting remains of various corporate or government space efforts had been commandeered by hackers, used to gather intelligence for resistance or just for personal gain. Dax had been working with some of his connections on an early warning system, hoping to combine satellite imagery with anecdotal reports to get a coherent picture of the angels' activities, but so far there weren't enough people still online to make it very useful.

"Tell your guy we're coming," said Holt.

"He'll completely flip out," said Dax. "He'll—"

"Tell him," said Holt.

Dax sent the message, and then they were off. They drove along the highway until Dax directed them to take an exit to nothing, one of those off-ramps placed every few miles just for a place to turn around. They passed a dingy motel, the sign collapsing and the roof rotting in on itself. A barricade of cars had been positioned in a circle surrounding the doors to a few of the rooms, and they could see movement inside through the windows. Someone had thought it a defensible position, and meant to protect it. Being close to the roads brought danger, but also opportunities. Scavenging was easier, as well as trade. But then, so was brigandry, and there were enough bandits along the interstates that one had to be cautious. Holt signaled to keep going, and they sped away along a dirt road that wound beyond the suburbs and into a set of pastures. They saw it on the side, coming up in the distance: row upon row of trailers, dropped into a field that was now grown wild with grass.

Most of the homes were in poor condition. Time hadn't been kind to them, and they hadn't really been built to last, anyway. Smashed windows showed signs of looting, and a few of the smaller trailers had been overturned. Trash and cheap furniture were strewn all around the main road to the complex, and they had to dodge it all as they drove inside. Even in the best of times the residents of this sort of place had a reputation for unruliness, and those who'd stayed here during the exodus had obviously enjoyed the benefits of lawlessness, at least for a time. A few of the lots were empty, from residents trying to take advantage of their mobility to bring their homes with them. The rest were mostly destroyed; some rusted from the weather, some dented in on themselves, and some gutted by fire.

"He's towards the end," said Dax. "I'll give you one guess as to which one it is."

They didn't need to guess. An army of garden gnomes stood watch outside one of the trailers in the distance, arranged in a phalanx protecting its entrance. An oversized satellite dish took up the rest of the lawn, pointed upward and chattering at the skies. A few pinball machines were overturned on one side of the trailer, their undersides opened to scavenge for parts. Across the street, all that remained of the neighbors' homes were burnt metal shells, with jugs of unidentifiable chemicals scattered around black patches that dotted the grass.

The door to the Cook's trailer was wide open, clanging against the side as it swung with the wind.

"Guess we don't need to knock," said Holt. He dismounted his bike, standing at the edge of the street and watching. Fools rush in, and sometimes angels did, too. But the latter were more durable, and Holt thought the Cook was as unstable as his chemicals. As always, his instinct for caution and deliberation prevailed.

"Hello?" shouted Holt, hand on his gun. He waited a few seconds, but the only response was silence.

"I know he's your boy, but we need gas," said Thane, walking towards the entrance. He had no concern for caution, and his own affinities ran towards instability.

"Maybe we can wait here," said Dax, calling after him. "We probably crossed paths. I bet he's back at the car lot. You can't just go into his house. He gets really worked up about—"

But it was too late. Thane was already inside, poking around in the dark.

"Get in here!" yelled Thane, and interest overpowered the others. They went in, too, to see Thane standing in front of the bathroom door, lit by the glow of a half-dozen computer monitors from the bedroom behind him.

"Take a look," said Thane. They did. It was the Cook, a skinny little man seated on the toilet in an undershirt and his boxers. Splattered blood painted the walls of the bathroom, and his body was covered with wounds. It looked like he'd been gnawed on, with chunks missing everywhere. His eyes were glassy and lifeless, his tongue swollen and sticking out of his mouth.

Holt winced, and Dax rushed outside to escape the scene. Thane poked at one of the wounds, inspecting it.

"Coyotes," he said. "Gotta be coyotes."

"A pack of them, inside a trailer?" said Holt.

"Dogs, then," said Thane. "They go wild and go after anybody." It was true, to a degree. Packs of them skulked around every city, gone feral after they'd been left to fend for themselves. But they weren't exactly brave, and they weren't known to attack a grown man. They certainly wouldn't have left that much of a kill if they'd gotten hungry enough to make it.

"We're gone," said Holt. "Get on the bikes and we'll stop past Trenton and fill up. We'll find something to trade on the way."

"I spy." The voice came from outside, piercing through the walls of the trailer. It didn't sound quite right. It was more hummed than spoken, the words blending together as if from a chorus speaking in unison. Holt drew his pistol, and listened.

"I spy, with my little eyes." The voice came again, and Holt went outside to meet it.

It hovered over Dax, whatever the thing was. Holt had never seen the likes of it—nothing with so many eyes, nothing with so many wings, and nothing with so many teeth.

CHAPTER NINETEEN

JANA WAS EXCITED, SKIPPING AROUND the kitchen as she mopped. The last few weeks had been sheer drudgery, and she was about to get a break.

All she'd done the entire time had been to clean, clean, clean. Cassie kept pointing out faults, or creating chores from nothing, but she just couldn't keep her thoughts on the tasks at hand. It didn't help that Rhamiel was starting to creep into her fantasies. She kept finding him there when she retreated to the cozy cabin in her head with her giggling brood of children. He'd pop through the door and then the children would be his, flapping around her picket fences with tiny wings and sticking their tongues out at her in defiance. She'd switch to her benevolent reign over the tower, and after a bit he'd just follow, barging into her court and announcing himself as its new king. It was frustrating to be unable to control even her own daydreams, but she couldn't help herself.

Towards the end, she'd started thinking about Peter instead, as a distraction from the distractions. She'd tried to raise her concerns about him to Cassie, but was just brushed aside. Cassie said there was nothing they could do, and that the foolhardy had to fend for themselves these days. That didn't stop Jana from plotting elaborate escapes, or dreaming up deals she could make to release Peter from his chains. But then Rhamiel just intruded there, too, taking command in the middle and freeing Peter himself. She kept coming back to Nefta's warnings, but they weren't exactly helping. They'd only made him more fascinating. Sometimes she thought he was just arrogant, and sometimes she thought he was injured inside from how he'd been in heaven, covering up the wounds with vanity and cocky smiles. She couldn't decide, and it was infuriating.

Jana hadn't even seen Nefta, not since their conversation. She'd retired to her personal chambers, and she hadn't come out. Cassie had been leaving trays of food at the door, and taking them away whenever they happened to reappear. Mostly that was in the morning. Whatever Nefta was doing, she was keeping odd hours, sometimes waking them up at night with crashes or other noises.

Cassie said it was just brooding, and that she did this from time to time. She'd withdraw into herself, battling with her demons and avoiding anyone else's company. She'd find herself in a melancholy mood, and wouldn't be able to find her way out. Thoughts of her scars were most likely to trigger it, and Cassie had nearly erupted when she'd heard that Jana had been discussing them with her. There was nothing to do then but to wait it out, so they did, staying on the alert in case she needed something.

She'd finally come out of her room, spoke to Cassie,

and bid them to leave for the rest of the day. She wanted the place to herself, and didn't particularly care where they went. They couldn't simply wander about aimlessly, so Cassie told Jana to gather together a few wicker baskets from the storage room. "We need something to do," she said, "so we'll go get her some more wood from the crafters. I suspect she'll be needing it soon, anyway."

They carried the baskets out, hauling them along in a red children's wagon. They closed the door shut behind them, but needn't have bothered. It didn't have any locks, anyway; the angels stayed away from each others' quarters absent an invitation, and a servant would have to be suicidal to enter without permission. They wound their way down the central ramp, slowly making their way to the middle levels. A few of the angels stood along an inaccessible terrace protruding from the wall, and stopped their conversation to watch them for a ways. Cassie just looked straight ahead and kept walking, but it made Jana nervous. She didn't like to know they were thinking of her, and she couldn't quit worrying about how conspicuous she'd been after the Conclave. The servants' cardinal rule was to avoid attention, and she didn't want to become a blip on any of their radars.

"Cassie," said Jana. "How do we know when it's okay to go back? What do we do if she's mad when we come back up?" All the changes had been hard on Jana, and she was being constantly consumed by uncertainty. Even the smallest decisions seemed filled with danger. She wasn't even sure if it was safe to ask about whether any particular thing was safe to do. It ate at her nerves, leaving them frayed. She'd known the rules down below, but they'd plucked her out of there and dropped her into a different place, with its own etiquette and its own expectations. That wouldn't have been so bad, if the consequences for a misstep weren't so severe.

"We'll be fine," said Cassie. "We just need to stay away for the rest of the day. It's not as bad as it seems, really. She's got things scratching at the edges of her mind. The only thing to do is leave her alone and let it pass."

They approached a stone archway, looming over them and inlaid with black shards of onyx depicting angels in the midst of heavenly warfare. The blocks of stone it was composed of had been hauled up here, carefully chiseled to lock together seamlessly and shaped into a monument to their rebellion. Along the sides, the angels were setting diamond buildings on fire with clusters of rubies, or doing battle with loyalists shaped from pearls. All along the top was the Fall, with black angels being shoved downward into ruby flames. The crafters took pride in it, though the servants outside claimed the credit for having scoured the jewelry boxes of every housewife in Manhattan.

They went through the arch, entering a madhouse of creative bustle. The crafters' floor was an immense, open area filled with stations for the various trades, with a ring of personal quarters around the exterior. Some were for the lower-ranked angels, and others were for the higher-ranked craftsmen. It stuck in the craw of the angels who lived there to be lumped together with mere humans. For whatever reason they didn't have the influence to secure more prestigious quarters, and none of them were pleased about it. But everyone can't be at the top, and those who were valued the happiness of the best of the crafters over that of the least of their brethren.

Servants rushed around them as they came inside, carrying materials back and forth between the stations. A sullen teenage boy pushed past Jana and nearly overturned their wagon, as he ran a bundle of leather straps over to a nearby armorsmith. He didn't even bother to apologize, and seemed irritated about having to dodge them in the first place.

"Don't mind him," said Cassie. "The crafters work their apprentices like dogs. They have to, to keep the angels satisfied. The ones up top expect the work to be done promptly, and if things aren't finished quickly enough they're apt to change their minds and force everyone to start from scratch. Or worse, if the mood strikes them."

All the runners were younger, and there wasn't an adult among them. They were each learning a trade, and they had to start at the bottom. Jana had never seen the likes of it. She hadn't been given a choice of occupations, and had simply ended up in the place she'd started. That was the lot of most of them. A boy was needed to tan leather for the angels' boots, and so the servants outside found them a boy. A girl was needed to wash dishes, and so they found them a girl.

The angels all wanted things that would maximize their prestige among the others. That meant plenty of work for smiths, who could hammer out dents in their armor or create a shiny, impressive new sword or mace. They claimed the lion's share of the space, their jerry-rigged forges blasting heat and steam all around their portion of the floor. It was a haphazard mix of the ancient and the modern. On their left, they passed a coal-fired furnace that belched flame near a burly man clanging his hammer against an anvil. On their right, Jana saw another man welding away at a bronze scabbard, using contemporary equipment and a protective helmet. Other machines stood silent, with no one bothering to man them. The crafters had to be versatile. They never knew exactly what supplies they'd have on hand, and their masters had no interest in how sausage was made and no tolerance for excuses.

Cassie and Jana pushed their way through the hubbub and came to a quieter section of the floor: the looms. Talented weavers were always in high demand, and a number of women had found a relative refuge under the instruction of a few dressmakers who'd come to the tower after the Fall. They'd diversified from their former trade, finding themselves a new niche creating custom garments for the tower's residents. Girls sat in rows, spinning with drop spindles or performing simple dye jobs. Adult women supervised and focused on the advanced work, sewing patterns into tapestries for the walls, creating robes for formal gatherings, and making custom designs of all sorts for whatever social events the angels could concoct.

Finally, they arrived at the woodworkers' area. It was smaller, dedicated mostly to building furniture. There wasn't as much need for it, as it tended to last for years. But some of the angels had tempers, and regularly destroyed enough of their furnishings that it was necessary to maintain servants who could replace them as was warranted.

"Gao!" called Cassie, and a little old Chinese man looked up from his work. He was unkempt, his clothes dirty and his face unshaven, and he could have passed for homeless in years before. Strands of grey hair snaked off in all directions from the back of his thinning crown, crawling along the back of his rumpled shirt. He had a permanent hunch to his back, acquired from years bent over his workbench, and had thick wiry glasses from late nights spent carving tiny details into knickknacks he used to sell to tourists. Wrinkles covered his face, which had sunk into an expression of permanent grumpiness as time had passed.

"No wood. No wood," groused Gao.

"Come on, Gao," said Cassie sweetly. "You know I need it. Nefta's been in one of her moods, and she's just coming out of it. She'll want to work, you know that. She'll probably be at it for days. She's going to be a dynamo, and we need to get her something to focus her energies on."

"No wood," insisted Gao. He stood up, waving his hands and trying to shoo them away. It didn't work on Cassie, so he turned to Jana, grunting and gesturing. She backed away, positioning herself safely behind Cassie. Gao didn't know much English; he'd come over with his family years before and he'd never needed to learn it. But now they were gone, and all he had left was his quiet labor.

"Gao," said Cassie. "We just need a little. Just this wagon, see? It'd make us very happy."

"Too much," said Gao. "You want too much. Go away now. Tell Nefta go flappy, flappy. Find own trees." He waved his arms, mimicking flight and puckering his lips as he cawed out in imitation of a bird.

Behind them, a cart toppled over in one of the narrow aisles through the crafting stations. Bits of metal spilled all around, completely blocking the way. The small boy who'd been pushing it frantically started refilling it, trying to grab all of the pieces as larger boys stepped over him. He looked miserable, anticipating the lashing he had to look forward to if he didn't fix things quickly.

"Go help him," said Cassie. "Let me work on Gao a little, alone."

Jana did as she was told. She went over to the boy, grabbing some of the pieces before they were kicked aside or crushed beneath boots of passersby. He was on the brink of tears, and she tried to calm him down. "It's okay," she said. "You get the little ones, I'll get the big ones." They got the cart righted, and started getting the pieces back into it. Jana shot a glance back at Cassie. She was engaged in an animated conversation with Gao, both of them gesticulating to make themselves understood. Gao was flustered, and Cassie kept working him, pushing his buttons to get what she wanted. Then a furtive handshake, a nod from Gao, and they were done.

Only Jana saw it, the thing in her hands. Cassie had passed him something, hidden in her palm. She hadn't been able to tell quite what it was. She thought maybe it was a bribe, a gift to grease the wheels and get them their wood. But he didn't seem any happier about things, and just went back to poring over his work.

"Come on!" said Cassie. "Help me fill up the baskets." Cassie selected the wood she wanted from Gao's hoard in a nearby shed, and had Jana run it out to the wagon in chunks as she went. She was careful about it, choosing the finest pieces and getting a mix of smaller blocks and even a few large logs that barely fit in the wagon. They stacked the baskets on top, with Cassie carrying one and leaving Jana to haul the rest behind her.

They went back along their way, past the clicks of the looms and through the sparks and the heat. Jana lugged the wagon dutifully, pulling at it with all her strength. It was slow going, and the apprentices gave her a number of nasty looks. They'd almost made it out when Jana heard something she recognized: a voice, distinctive and cutting through the clamor.

"Hold it. Don't move. It'll be worse if you do, I can promise you that."

Her spine shivered. She couldn't forget that vile tone, as hard as she might try. And there he was, sitting on a stool near the armorsmiths and playfully swinging one of their swords through the air. Ecanus, watching Peter like a hawk as he held his shaking arm outward and over one of the forge's flames.

CHAPTER TWENTY

I T WHIRLED LIKE A PINWHEEL, spinning its wings in
clockwise circles through the air. Shaped like a disc,
its wings poked out from its center, giving it the look
of a malformed daisy. Its center was rimmed with eyes,
human-looking eyes, strings of them that ran around
along the edges of the wings. In the middle of it all was
a gaping mouth, with sharp, snaggly teeth pointing in all
directions. It had tongues, so many tongues, long, thin
tentacles wiggling around inside it. It floated, although
the laws of physics as man understood them didn't permit
it to. It shouldn't have been able to keep itself aloft, if it
had been following the rules. Some of the wings didn't
even look functional. Withered, dying things that had
been lit afire during the Fall, they spun next to fully-
feathered ones that shimmered through the colors of the
rainbow. Here and there some of its eyes had been put
out, left covered by patches of scorched flesh.

"I spy," said the thing. "I spy something red." All its
tongues flicked in unison as it talked, singing the words
together as one.

"There ain't anything red," said Thane, before opening fire. He plugged bullet after bullet into it, aiming at the eyes. He even hit a few, but it didn't do much. The creature flinched, and clenched its eyes shut wherever it had been hit. But after a few seconds they just blinked it off, resuming their stares.

"I spy meat, and juices, and tarty fluids running up and down inside your bones," said the thing.

Dax started crawling away, hoping to take advantage of Thane's distraction. Then it grabbed him, reaching out with one of the tongues and looping it around his foot. His fingers sunk into the grass, trying to find a hold as it drew him towards its open maw. They came up filled with clumps of dirt, and it dragged him closer and closer. "Oh, shit. Oh, shit. Oh, shit," said Dax, chanting the words, a futile incantation of protection against the thing that had him.

"They'll go crunch, crunch," said the thing.

Faye unstrapped her rifle from her back and added to the volley of fire. She was aiming at the tongue that had a hold on Dax, snapping it back and forth like a slobbery rubber band with every hit. The thing didn't seem to mind. It just went back to pulling, and grabbed his other ankle with another tongue for good measure.

"Biles and humours, from out of the spleen," said the thing. "I'll share them if you like. Just a taste. A few licks each."

Dax was bordering on hysteria. He couldn't help himself from sneaking looks at the thing's cavernous mouth—and after each one, his eyes would pop with dread and he'd turn back to tearing at the ground, trying to pull himself forward. He couldn't think straight, couldn't find a way to escape, couldn't do anything. He felt helpless, a fly trapped in a spider's web and waiting for it to quit toying with him and finally do the deed. He could feel the tongues, writhing and wet against his skin where his pants hiked up, cold and clammy and tight. The others kept firing, but the flashes and the noise just added to his stress.

"Hey. Hey!" yelled Holt, grabbing Thane by the shoulder and interrupting him as he was reloading. "Get the sword." Thane ran to his bike, digging around in his pack to try to find it. He'd buried it in there, somewhere underneath pouches of homemade chewing tobacco, a few naughty magazines, and a collection of assorted personal weaponry. He'd paraded it around on his belt for the first few days of their trip until Holt had finally forbidden it, concerned that the scabbard would draw unwanted attention from anyone they happened to encounter on the road.

"Try it and you won't go back," said the thing. "There's nothing more savory. Take a nibble, you'll see. Every one of you gets a finger. Generosity, it's the will of the Maker." It kept tugging at Dax, reeling him in, until it almost had him. He was kicking frantically, trying to free himself from the tongues, but he had no leverage. Its teeth moved, poking up and down in anticipation of a meal.

"Shut the fuck up," said Holt, switching to a taser. They carried stacks of them along at his insistence, and he was never without one holstered to his belt. He fired, landing the clamp of the wires inside its mouth.

Its eyes slammed shut in unison, dripping out tears as it absorbed the current. The tongues all shrieked; an awful, high-pitched wail that battered their eardrums. It thrashed around, allowing Dax to gain a few feet of distance. Then it recovered, every one of its eyes glaring at Holt, and went back to pulling.

"Lick your insides," said the thing. "I'll do it all at once, while your heart still beats. I'll make new holes, and lap up your innards from every one. It will be slow, and we will become great friends, you and I. I'll tell you how you taste, and you will say please, please." It pulled at Dax, and its mouth curved into something of a smile. Then a line of flame flashed between them, and its eyes bulged in agony.

The two of its tongues that had been latched to Dax had been lopped clean off. Thane was standing in front of it, swinging the sword about like a dervish. He clipped one of its wings as the thing tried to back away, slicing off the tip and sending up a puff of feathers. It screamed again, crying and moaning, and then flipped around to escape. Its backside faced them, a solid grey circle of wrinkled flesh. Then it zoomed away, weaving through the trailers until it disappeared among them.

"You okay?" asked Thane, reaching down to offer a hand to Dax. He declined it bruskly, pulling himself up and brushing stray blades of grass off of his shirt.

"I'm fine," said Dax. "He caught me by surprise. I could have gotten away, he just...."

"He almost bit your ass off, is what he did. Lucky I was there to save it," said Thane, grinning widely and still pumped full of adrenaline. He picked up one of the tongues from the ground, proudly waving his trophy in the air. "Hope you know taxidermy, Dax. I'm collectin' body parts, and I want 'em stuffed. I got me a head, a tongue, and some wing."

"You're a real Colonel Kurtz," said Dax bitterly.

"I'm a what?" said Thane, confused about whether he was being flattered or insulted.

"Dax," said Holt. "The man just saved your life. The word is thanks."

He couldn't hold it in anymore. The dam burst, and it all came out at once. "I'm just some fucking damsel in distress, is that it? I work my ass off, and all I'm ever supposed to do is hide." Dax's voice was rising, quivering with a long suppressed fury. "I didn't sign up for this to stay on the sidelines. I wanted to fight. You don't even let me carry a gun. I arrange everything, I get you your supplies, and then someone else jumps in at the last minute and gets all the glory. And then I get treated like I'm a complete piece of shit. Like I'm just some fucking joke."

"Hey, buddy," said Thane. "I was just fuckin' around."

"You're always fucking around!" yelled Dax. "It's always tubby, or lardo, or lazy ass! I'm sick of this, I'm sick of all of it."

"It's just kidding around, man," said Thane. "You gotta roll with the punches if you wanna be one of the guys. That's how this shit works."

"You can't let it get to you," said Holt. "It's just teasing. If you can laugh at yourself, then no one else will."

"Except it's all the time," said Dax. "All the time, and only me. If it's just teasing, why is it only me?"

"Look, I'm sorry," said Thane. "We were just fuckin' with you. It wasn't supposed to mean somethin'."

"Boys," said Faye. "I hate to break this up, but I've got the gas." She held up a large canister of it, gasoline sloshing around inside. "It's around the other side of the trailer. There's stacks of them."

"Dax, we'll talk about this later. We have to go," said Holt. "That thing could be back any minute. We don't even know what the hell it was."

"I know what it was," said Dax. "And of course, I'm the only one here who does."

CHAPTER TWENTY-ONE

"JUST KEEP MOVING," CASSIE HISSED. She grabbed the handle of the wagon from Jana, yanking it forward as quickly as she could. She'd intended to make a getaway, but it didn't go as cleanly as she'd planned. The wheels squawked as she pulled, protesting against the demand to move so heavy a load so rapidly. Everyone around turned to look—including Ecanus.

"Well, what luck we have!" said Ecanus. "Look who's come to watch your trials and tribulations! Still your heart, boy, you mustn't get too excited. You'll need to be calm, to make it through your punishments."

Peter swiveled his head. He looked awful. His skin was pale, and his eyes were burdened by thick, black bags beneath them. He'd been thin before, but now he was practically emaciated. There were marks all over his face, red slashes running across his cheeks. His arm was blistered from holding it over the fire, but still he kept it there, his fear of Ecanus overwhelming his fear of the heat.

"Let's go," whispered Cassie, taking a few tentative steps away.

"You wouldn't abandon us, would you? Stay," said Ecanus, his voice dropping to a low growl.

They were trapped, and they knew it. They stood in the walkway, suddenly empty of traffic. The craftsmen had all disappeared; the locals knew when trouble was brewing and knew where to escape to. A few curious heads poked out from behind some of the heavy equipment, but only the brave ones. The smart ones didn't deem it worth their while to risk it.

"Come closer," said Ecanus, running his fingers along the edge of the iron sword in his hands. "You don't want to miss things, do you? Peter here is doing a penance. He's done something wrong, haven't you, boy?"

"Yes, sir," said Peter, tears welling in his eyes.

"He left a smudge on the greaves he was ordered to polish," said Ecanus. "We can't abide smudges, can we?"

"No, sir," said Peter.

"No, we can't," said Ecanus. "They mar things. And when we mar things, we get marred ourselves, don't we?"

"Yes, sir," said Peter.

"We're already down here in the dirt," said Ecanus. "We needn't wallow in it. Here I am, forced to live among the dregs of the tower. Sullying myself with the filth for lack of real accommodations. I've half a mind to strike out on my own. I suppose you're fitting, in a way. A second-rate server for second-rate quarters." His scowl deepened, resentment bubbling up from below.

Then he turned to Jana. "Rhamiel's whore," he said. "You may live up there, but you're still just a plaything.

And down here, I make the rules. Stand there and watch." He pointed her to a spot on the ground a few feet away from Peter. She complied, keeping her eyes to the ground. But Ecanus wasn't having any of that.

"Chin up, girl," said Ecanus. She looked at Peter, and he looked down, filled with a mixture of shame at where he'd landed himself and guilt at where he'd landed her.

"Now, boy," said Ecanus, "hands back in."

Peter put his hand in closer, nearer to the flame of the forge. He winced as the heat hit him. His arm was red all over, and the skin on his hand was blackened and peeling off. The burns were getting serious, and Ecanus had obviously been toying with him for some time.

"Closer," said Ecanus. Peter tried, but he couldn't hold it. The pain was too great. He whipped his arm out, clutching it to his belly and whimpering a few moans of pain. Ecanus just chuckled. It was all the same to him. Either he got to watch Peter inflict miseries on himself, or he got a pretext to inflict some more of his own.

"That's no good, no good at all," said Ecanus. "Come over here, and take your medicine."

He sliced the sword through the air, dealing an expert blow to Peter's head. At first, Jana thought he must have killed him. But it was just a nick, a mere cut. On its own it would heal, with minimal damage. They were accumulating, though, rows of gashes on Peter's face where Ecanus had punished him again and again.

"Let's play a little game, shall we?" said Ecanus. "Everyone likes games. I should think you do, girl. You play at dangerous ones, flirting with your betters. Did you tell Peter here, about your new lover? They've been all over the tower together, laughing at you all the way. She's been telling everyone she might settle for you, once Rhamiel's done with her. Telling them you're nothing. Just a little trash boy from down in the basement." Peter looked hurt, even more than he had from the fire. Tears were streaming down his cheeks, from pains inside and out.

"It's true," said Ecanus. "She's a dirty one. That's a smudge you can't ever wipe clean. She'll never be yours now, will she? Not really."

Jana endured the insults, but it took every bit of her strength to do it. Ecanus was all lies, but she couldn't very well jump in and tell Peter that. The deception was all part of the torture, and he'd just come up with new ones, anyway. It still hurt. She had to stand there, watching her friend being mutilated, and listening to his image of her being distorted into something terrible. She could see from his sunken expression that he believed it, and that was more painful than anything.

"I'll show you how much she cares, truly," said Ecanus. "Both of you. I spent a great deal of time coming up with this diversion. I call it 'eye for an eye.' It's inspired by the Maker himself." Jana shuddered. She could feel Cassie behind her, gripping her shoulder tightly in sympathy. It wasn't much, but it was all she could do.

"You've got pretty little eyes, girl," said Ecanus, coming towards Jana. He pointed the sword at one of them, its molten-hot tip just inches away. "I was thinking of taking Peter's in punishment, but now I think I like yours a little better. So I'll make you a deal, an eminently equitable deal. Give me just one of your eyes, and I'll let the boy keep both of his." He waited, smiling deeply and letting it sink in. Jana was sweating and shaking, a cornered animal. She stared at the sword, trying as hard as she could to keep absolutely still as Ecanus slowly pushed it closer and closer to her eye. She could feel the heat drying out her tears, and was terrified to even blink. He'd left only a sliver of space between her pupil and the edge of the sword, and she knew that if she made the slightest move she'd be blinded. Her knees felt like they were about to give out, and it was everything she could do to keep them locked into place. Ecanus knew he had her. So he went and made things worse.

"If you don't like that trade, I understand," he said. "I'm perfectly fair and perfectly reasonable. I'll make you an offer that's even better. Give me your hand." She stood, a doe in the headlights, unable to move. "Now, girl," he snarled, and something in her made her put up her arm. He grabbed her wrist, and pressed the handle of the sword into her palm.

"Now, all you have to do to help your friend," said Ecanus, "is to take out one of his eyes yourself. Then I'll let him keep the other, and you and your Rhamiel can continue enjoying both of yours."

She wanted to run him through then and there, but the sword was a product of the crafters. It probably wouldn't even nick him. The end of it glowed orange, and it didn't help that Peter just sat there glumly awaiting his fate. He seemed to expect her to do it, even to be begging her to, hoping for an end to his tortures. She wanted them to fight Ecanus, together, but they couldn't. He'd just slaughter them all, so they had to choose between accepting his terms or accepting their own deaths.

"We've established the rules, and we've set up the pieces," said Ecanus, his wings expanding to their full length, and his gruesome smile stretching as far as it could go. "Now play."

She was terrified. She could feel painful prickles all over her skin, like the air itself was pressing against the raw nerves underneath. Her insides were a mess, her belly consumed by a tightness as if every organ had clamped together all at once. Her hands shook, and she wasn't sure she could keep holding the sword for much longer. She had no idea what to do. She knew she couldn't actually do something so grotesque to another person. But a lifetime of training and habit were shrieking inside her head from all sides, *obey, obey, obey*! She took a few tentative steps towards Peter. And then it happened. She didn't believe it had come out of her, even after it had already escaped her lips.

"No," said Jana.

Ecanus's smile vanished, and he advanced on her, radiating an intense anger and hatred. "No?" he sputtered. "No? There isn't any 'no.' There's do as I say, bitch, and there isn't anything else. Now poke out them both, and pray to your Maker that I'm struck with a sudden spate of mercy."

"I won't," said Jana, pointing the sword at Ecanus. They all thought she was mad, even Cassie. She'd started backing away from Jana, getting behind the wagon and trying to escape notice. The crafters who'd stayed to watch were now running, abandoning even the pretense of hiding in an effort to put distance between themselves and the explosion of rage they knew was coming.

"She won't," said Ecanus, looking at Peter incredulously. "She won't?" Ecanus slapped him, hitting him with a loud thud and knocking him to the ground. Peter cried out as the singed flesh of his arm touched the floor and was covered in grit and metal flakes. Ecanus's eyes grew wider and angrier, and he grew more and more unhinged. "I'll show you what happens to servants who can't follow simple instructions from their betters."

Jana's defiance was short lived. He struck the sword from her hands before she could even attempt a swing, knocking it to the floor with a loud clatter. She tried to run, but he was quick, and he'd gotten her by the throat before she could make it a few steps away. She was choking, his grip cutting off the flow of air until she started to see black. Then he released it, grabbing her arm instead and dragging her away from the forge, away from Peter—and towards the ramp.

She saw where he was going, and what he intended to do. Inside she was pure distress. It was like a sudden alarm had gone off, blaring into her skull from all sides and telling her to do something, anything, immediately. She started screaming, kicking, clawing at him and fighting every way she could think of. She tried wriggling, tried going limp, tried anything that came to mind. All of it was hopeless. He was too strong, and he couldn't be done in by scratches or kicks.

"You can't," cried Jana. "You can't!"

"I can do whatever I like," said Ecanus, "and so I shall."

He hauled her through the archway and out to the edge of the ramp. Her clothes were covered in black grime from being pulled along the floor, and her hair was wildly poking everywhere from the tussle. He lifted her up and out, holding her by the throat with one hand and dangling her into the air over the long drop to the tower's lowest floor. She kicked her legs in all directions, instinctively searching for a foothold but finding nothing.

"Look down, girl. Look down, or I drop you," said Ecanus. This time, Jana did as she was told. All she got for her troubles was a case of vertigo. The distance was tremendous and terrifying. She could see the ramp, looping around and around as it worked its way to the bottom far, far below. Fear turned to panic, and she started crying, tears dripping down her face and sobs bursting from her lips.

"Please," said Jana. "I looked."

"You did," said Ecanus. "But I'm going to drop you, anyway. I just wanted a taste of your fear before you fall."

Jana screamed, a last death call releasing her agony and pleading for a savior. Then there was a thunk nearby, though she barely registered it. She was still scrambling and kicking when Ecanus looked away to attend to the distraction.

It was Rhamiel, alighting on the ramp a few yards away. He was in full battle regalia, dressed out in golden armor, his chest piece molded into the shape of the head of a fierce beast resembling a lion. He dwarfed Ecanus, tall and imposing in his metal plate.

"Ecanus," said Rhamiel. "Whatever are you doing?"

CHAPTER TWENTY-TWO

"**T**HEY'RE ANGELS, TOO, EVEN IF they don't look like them," said Dax. They were all busy loading the ATV with as much fuel as it could carry, hoping to avoid another stop. The thing seemed to have left, but Holt was working them double-time just to be sure. Dax had calmed down after they'd given him a few minutes, but he still didn't look very happy.

"They've got castes," said Dax. "Everyone agrees on that, but there's disagreement about exactly what they are. There were a bunch of pre-Fall texts about this— some called them 'choirs,' some called them 'spheres.' They called that thing an 'Ophan.' They're even in the Bible, but a lot of people thought it was some kind of drug induced hallucination."

"It didn't even look like an angel," said Holt. "It looked like some kind of mutation."

"Who knows," said Dax. "There've only been a few scattered reports of them online. I don't know whether it's because there aren't many of them, or because they just kill everyone who sees them."

In fact, there had only been a handful of them among the fallen. The Ophanim were one of the older varieties of angels, created long before mankind was even a glimmer in God's imagination. They'd initially served as guard dogs, patrolling around Hell keeping tabs on the things that slithered around its depths and making sure that none of them ever got out. After Lucifer's army had been cast into his Pit, they'd been rolled into the heavenly host as a kind of crude intelligence service. Few of them had rebelled. The Seraphim found dealing with them to be distasteful given their odd behavior and their penchant for psychopathy, and their motives were as inscrutable to the other angels as they were to mankind.

"Why'd he kill the Cook?" asked Holt.

"Maybe they're watching us," said Faye. "Or were watching him. All those eyes."

"Let's go," said Holt. "Now. If that thing can fly, I don't want it trailing us. Let it stay here and lick its wounds with the tongues it's got left."

They finished their loading job, packing everything in tight, and headed off in a procession towards the highway. They were considerably more cautious about it than before. The Ophan had spooked them, and Holt had them stopping at regular intervals to scan the skies. He pulled them off the highway more than a few times to wait or to double-back on themselves, checking to see if it was tailing them on the ground. When darkness came and they finally struck camp, he ordered two of them to be on watch at any time. They didn't see any signs of it, but sleep was a small sacrifice to secure their safety.

They were on the other side of Trenton when it

happened. They'd had to circumvent the city itself, taking a series of back roads to the north to avoid having to enter the city proper. Doing so would have been foolhardy. Cities were beacons for angels looking for entertainment. Trenton was close enough to Philadelphia that it had been raided repeatedly, and only a few collaborators still dwelled within its borders. They'd have been viewed as enemies if they'd tried to enter, and so they made sure to keep their distance a respectable one.

They'd been making slow progress, as Holt didn't like traveling at night. There was too much that could go wrong, from losing track of each other to blindly walking into trouble of all kinds. During the day there were frequent stops. Sometimes he'd want to take a closer look at something on the horizon with binoculars before approaching it. Others, they'd hit a particularly difficult snag of cars, or run across a fallen tree or some other obstacle. This time it was the sound of engines in the distance that made them stop.

"Listen," said Holt. They could hear it, coming from behind them. Buzzing sounds, mixed with louder roars as engines were revved to get past obstacles, or sometimes just for show.

"There's a lot of them," said Faye. "Sounds pretty close."

"Get off the road," said Holt. "Now, and quietly. Let's go, let's go. Bring the bikes." They dismounted and moved to the shoulder, pulling their vehicles into a roadside pasture and behind a small, grassy ridge that blocked them from view. Thane had to run back and help Dax with the ATV, lifting up the rusted strands of an old barbed wire fence to let it through, but eventually they got it there and got it mostly hidden. They waited, but not for long.

The vanguard came first, a few rough looking types scouting ahead of the others. They drove Harleys, heavy bikes that burped loudly for attention as they maneuvered through the road. They all had long, thick beards, and wore black shades that obscured their eyes and hid their intentions from view. In fact, they resembled the biker gangs of yore in every way but one: they'd exchanged their trademark black leather for a uniform of pure white.

"Get a gun on them, Faye," said Holt. She crawled over to a better vantage point a few yards away, digging herself in and aiming her rifle in the direction of the bikers. "Thane, get us armed." Thane obliged, unloading a few submachine guns from the stash in Dax's trailer. Even Dax got one, although he looked a little too pleased about it, playing with the gun and pointing it around in all directions until Holt grabbed the barrel and aimed it at the dirt in front of them.

The bikers inched closer, following much the same path through the maze of cars as the cell had. They stopped a few times to radio behind them. They came agonizingly close, to the point that they could hear the voices barking over their radios and the crunch of asphalt beneath their wheels. Then they drove on, making their way further down the road and disappearing into the cars beyond.

"They're gone," said Dax. "Let's get out of here before they get back."

"Quiet. Stay down," said Holt. It was good advice, for

a few seconds later they heard a growing hum of engines from where the bikers had come. The loud sputters and snorts came nearer and nearer until they could see them: a convoy of Vichies on motorcycles, moving in tandem. They looked less rough than the bikers had, a motley assortment of whatever warm bodies had been allowed to sign on. Here, a thin, gangly man in a seersucker suit tried to maneuver his motorcycle around a particularly large pothole, cursing loudly as he dipped his wheel into its edges. There, an elderly gentleman puttered along with a shock of white hair to match his clothes, his bike wobbling back and forth as he struggled to maintain control. More and more of them passed by, and none of them would have seemed threatening if they hadn't all been heavily armed.

The Vichies were just as hierarchical as their masters, and on the open road it was all about who was the biggest and the baddest. Much of the criminal element had died off after the Fall, left to starve in prisons by jailers who saw no reason to risk their own necks by freeing charges who might immediately turn on them. But the doors of prisons had always revolved, and society's collapse had been a bonanza for the fortunate ones who'd happened to be on the outside at the time. They were predators unleashed on a herd of fattened, domesticated prey, and they took full advantage of their new position.

The bikers had no skills of their own, but then, they didn't need to in order to lead a troupe of Vichies. All they had to do was to be meaner than the ones begging them for protection. They all had to kowtow to the angels, but they were absentee landlords who had no concern whatsoever for how their serfs chose to treat one another, so long as their tasks were completed. The servants on the outside had no particular talents, and thus had no particular value to their masters. The world had no more need for office drones, and many of those who'd survived had chosen to spend their days supplicating to anyone they thought could keep them alive. The bikers had taken full advantage of it, and a few of them were mixed in among the sheep, spurring them on and nipping at their heels if they got out of line.

As the line of bikes went past, the scene became a disturbing one. Faye was the first to notice it. "Look," she whispered to the others. "Look at the passengers." Some of the riders were carrying them, seated behind them on the bikes. None of them were Vichies, as their clothing made clear. The others soon saw what Faye had: the handcuffs, binding them tightly to the bikes themselves. They were ill-fed and dirty, with sunken eyes and beaten looks. They must have been traveling as prisoners for a while, and they hadn't been well taken care of.

"We have to do something," said Dax, too loudly and too eagerly. Holt pushed him down, keeping him low to the ground and whispering in his ear.

"Now's not the time for this," said Holt. "Just let it go, and let them pass."

It was a wise choice, given the disparity in numbers. Dozens of Vichies had already passed them, and there was no end in sight. They just kept moving by, ferrying their prisoners and focusing on their journey. Everything could have been fine, and it almost was. There was just enough height to the ridge that no one could see them if they stayed behind it, and none of the Vichies were interested in the scenery. If only the four of them had managed to stay silent, they'd never have known they were there.

It started with a cough. A single one at first, a niggling irritation at the back of the throat that begged to be cleared. Then it rose to an uncontrollable fit of hacking, driven by an insistent scratching that refused any quarter. It was Faye, her eyes watering and her nose bubbling. She clamped her hands to her mouth, trying to quiet the storm from within her throat. And then it just got worse.

The words started pouring out, again, a loud and furious babbling that none of them could understand. "Sarrah hedikadorah, harikesh kuda darbedah." Her pupils dilated, expanding until they were deep pools of black, and bubbling foam dribbled from her mouth along with the chatter. They tried to quiet her down, but it didn't help. Her chanting grew louder and louder. "Harikesh tuka kanita rehishish!"

Then it was too late. One of the Vichies had heard, and had just started to point in their direction when the gunfire erupted.

CHAPTER TWENTY-THREE

"THERE'S AN ORDER TO THINGS, Rhamiel, and she doesn't understand it," said Ecanus. "A fault I lay firmly at your feet. You've been treating beasts like they're our equals, and this one's starting to believe it." His grip tensed, and his fingers sunk deeper into Jana's flesh. She could hear his teeth grinding together, clenching in fury. She clung to his arm with both hands, hoping that if he released her she might somehow hold on and clamber back to safety. She didn't dare look down, and couldn't stand to look at Ecanus. So she focused on Rhamiel, trying to calm her rapid breathing and soothe her shattered nerves.

"Dear Ecanus," said Rhamiel. "I'm not quite sure you understand the order here, either. I'm afraid I'm a few rungs higher up the ladder. This is becoming a challenge to my rank. I've only just met the girl, and I'd promised her some of Zuphias's wine. I can't very well let you turn her into a stain on the ground before I've kept my word." Rhamiel was the picture of calm and poise. He seemed unperturbed by the entire situation, and maybe he was. But he kept his distance from Ecanus, leaving enough room that he wouldn't feel threatened enough to do anything rash, and he kept his hand to the hilt of his sword.

It didn't make Jana any more comfortable. Part of her was ecstatic to see him. She'd thought she was doomed, and now he'd flown in from nowhere to defend her. She wondered briefly whether Nefta had him all wrong—and then realized she was still dangling, still kicking at the air, and he was still so far away. She was at the platform's edge, and he'd never get to her in time. If Ecanus wanted to make good on his threats, all he had to do was let go.

"If she thinks she's one of us, then let her learn to fly," said Ecanus. He cracked a smile, though it wasn't a confident one. Jana got a good look at his nubby teeth and his sickly gums, and couldn't help but resume her squirming.

"Ecanus," said Rhamiel, his voice hardening. "I'm not in the mood for sport. I've been preparing for my enterprise on the outside, one sanctioned by the Conclave. I've enemies out there, and I won't tolerate one in here." He tugged at his sword, flashing a few inches of fire that drew Ecanus's attention. "Now free the girl, and we'll talk when I return."

"You don't have that kind of pull, Rhamiel," spat Ecanus bitterly. "The others would never tolerate open warfare against one of our own, not in here. This little bitch wronged me. Defied me. Pointed a sword in my face. And she did it in front of all the rest of her kind. No one would side with you. They'd want to kill her, too, if they got even a whiff of it."

A rush of air blew past Jana from the other side. Ecanus flipped around, jostling her about as she let out an involuntary squeal. She was distracted from her troubles for a moment by embarrassment, and then again by the new arrival. It was Zuphias, landing opposite Rhamiel and penning Ecanus in. Like Rhamiel, he left a gap between them: a threat, but not an immediate one. And like Rhamiel, he kept his hand to his sword.

"Is this really wise, Ecanus?" asked Zuphias. "If Rhamiel doesn't kill you, Nefta will. The girl's her servant. Her fate is Nefta's to decide. Take up the matter with her if you like. Her property, her punishment."

"Not many would miss you if I were to lop off your head, I don't think," said Rhamiel. "You're inventive, and sometimes entertaining, I'll grant you that. But you're not exactly well-liked. One has to get a better understanding of social niceties if one wants to move up in the world. Who must be deferred to, and who can be deferred. You'll never fly higher than this if you don't learn the difference." Rhamiel drew his sword out, slowly, and took a few steps towards him.

Ecanus looked back and forth between the two, a cornered animal calculating its choices. He didn't have any he was fond of. Backing down would cost him face; plowing ahead could cost him more. Not having much face left to lose, he opted to preserve his skin. He pulled Jana back from the brink, tossing her against the platform and huffing away. "Take her, and deal with her ceaseless sass yourselves," called Ecanus as he walked back through the archway, giving Jana one last evil grin. "I've insubordination enough to endure from my own servant. And that one's mine to discipline however I like."

Jana lay on the ground gasping, letting the air rush into her lungs in relief. She clutched at her neck with both hands. It still felt constricted, like Ecanus hadn't entirely let go. Then she looked up at her rescuers. Zuphias hung back, put out at having had to bother with intervening on behalf of a non-entity like her. He looked as if the rescue had been a great burden on him, and had interrupted some pressing business of his own he'd have preferred to have been attending to—one of their social occasions that amounted to organized braggery, or cataloguing his wines or another collection of rarities whose accumulation displayed sophistication. And then there was Rhamiel.

He sheathed his sword, approaching Jana and offering her a hand up. She took it, and was pulled upwards. She tried to steady herself, and then swooned, stumbling into his arms despite herself. She felt like a clumsy fool, but he just smiled down at her, until she found her footing and pushed herself away.

"Did he hurt you?" asked Rhamiel.

She didn't respond; she wasn't sure she safely could. He loomed over her, wings flexing outward and armor adding bulk to his frame. Up close, it had incredible detail, the gold beaten into the shape of a heavenly creature mid-roar, its mane curling out over the shoulderplates. What it was, she couldn't tell, but the smiths must have spent years hammering it together. His face was now broadcasting his concern, and she looked away quickly, fluttering inside despite herself. Nefta may have thought him mad, bad, and dangerous to know, but she thought he had a tenderness to him. She could see it there, she was certain of it. There was something nice about knowing there was a guardian angel looking out for her, whatever his faults might be.

"That was foolish, Rhamiel," said Zuphias. "Ecanus was right. If you'd done him harm, the others would have cast you out, if not worse. You're fortunate he was gullible enough to believe your bluff. If he weren't so used to being trodden upon, he'd have dropped her and taken his chances."

"But he is used to it, and he doesn't have that kind of spine," said Rhamiel. "You must know your opponent, Zuphias. There's other ways to get inside their heads than miracles, and I make it a point to know everyone in the tower. I don't expect you to deign to dine with him. Your status is the kind built over centuries, carried forward by its own inertia. Shatter the illusion of exclusivity, and it all falls apart. My status is that of the upstart, and a little social rule-breaking is to be expected." Zuphias stood stoic, absorbing the criticism without comment. A true aristocrat never acknowledges such things, not in public, lest his aura of aloof superiority be punctured.

Rhamiel pivoted from Zuphias's silence to Jana's. "Jana, he seems to have put you in a state of shock. You're quite all right now. I know he seems terrifying, but he's a coward inside. He won't bother you again. I give you my word."

She wasn't sure what to do. If she responded, she'd risk Nefta's wrath on the one hand, and on the other, she wasn't sure what she'd say. There was something overpowering about it all, this creature of legend landing in front of her and battling on her behalf, and she didn't have any idea how one was expected to respond. She thought about staying quiet, and she knew she really should. But he'd only keep at it, and she couldn't just ignore him, not after he'd saved her life. She groped around for the right thing to say, and then just sputtered out what came to mind. "I'm not supposed to talk to you," said Jana. "I can't."

"You can't?" said Rhamiel in mock horror, returning to his playful self. "It seems you can do whatever you like. You threatened to kill poor, defenseless Ecanus, but you're afraid to talk to me?"

"Nefta," said Jana, shaking her head and stammering. "I can't. I just can't." She was kicking herself, wishing she could think of something clever or impressive to say, but that was what had come out. She thought she might be as frightened of him as she was of Ecanus, the way he roiled her insides just by standing there.

"I suppose you mustn't displease her," said Rhamiel. "If Nefta says you can't speak to me, well, then we shan't speak. Look where breaking the rules has gotten the both of us." He winked, smiled, and then took off, soaring upward and circling the ramp before disappearing into the shadows of the tower above.

"Gratitude is a thing of the past, I suppose," sniffed Zuphias, walking towards the platform's edge and unfurling his wings. They were dark, but all of the feathers were intact, and he still had a kind of regal beauty to him. "We go to the trouble of rescuing you, and you won't even condescend to speak to us. Rhamiel's a fool if I ever saw one."

"She didn't say anything about you, sir," said Jana. "Thank you." Nefta probably wouldn't like it if she'd known, but she'd been very specific. Rhamiel wasn't here anymore, and if she'd wanted to make rules about Zuphias, she could have done so. He was certainly right about gratitude, and Jana had no desire to alienate another of the angels over a simple thank-you.

"What did she tell you, exactly?" asked Zuphias, arching his brow.

"I don't know if I'm allowed to say," said Jana.

"Well, girl," said Zuphias, "Nefta's up there, and I'm down here. Spit it out. I know she's been worming around in your head, and I'll have the answer if I have to wring it out of her myself."

"No!" said Jana. "No." That would be the worst of all worlds. Nefta would learn about Ecanus, and about Rhamiel, and she wouldn't just box Jana's ears for that. "She says he'll hurt me. That he'd love me, but he wouldn't keep me. That he's done it before, and he'll do it again."

Zuphias chuckled, overtaken by amusement. "Did she say all that? She's turning into something of a viper in her dotage. Taking her prey into her den, and paralyzing them with her poisons."

"I don't understand, sir," said Jana. The angels could be oblique, often purposefully so. Much of their time together was spent in conversational games, bantering back and forth trying to either hide information or to extract it. They couldn't easily kick the habit with the servants, who preferred to speak more directly given the potential consequences of a miscommunication.

"Nefta has sold you a bill of goods, my dear," said Zuphias. "I don't doubt she's been hurt, but she's hardly got anyone to blame but herself. She couldn't care a whit for you. You're just the competition."

"Perhaps you should discuss this with Rhamiel himself, instead of hearing about it secondhand," added Zuphias as he approached the edge of the ramp. "He's been blathering on about you for weeks. You're an exceptionally tedious topic of conversation, I can assure you. If you're worried that his fascination won't last forever—well, nothing does, and it's best you enjoy the things you have while you can." His wings began to beat, and his body began to lift into the air. He looked down, appraising her, before flapping off to whatever very important business he'd delayed attending to for Jana's sake.

She knew Cassie would be looking for her, and knew she had to get back to her chores. But still she stood there for a few minutes longer, alone, gazing up above at the shapes gliding around in the dark, and wondering which one of them was Rhamiel.

CHAPTER TWENTY-FOUR

IT WAS DAX WHO FIRED first. He let loose as soon as they were noticed, a wild and unfocused spray of bullets that served mostly to attract the attention of the entire convoy. He managed to down one of the closer Vichies, although the bragging rights were considerably diminished by having also clipped the leg of the hostage he carried behind him. The Vichies cried out, and then it was war.

The meeker ones tried to hide among the cars. A portly bald man who'd been close to them when the firing began dove for cover at once, leaving behind the woman he'd cuffed to his bike. It lost its balance and slammed to the ground, and she lay there helplessly screaming over the gunfire, filling the intervals between bursts with shrieks and wails. A few of the others panicked and tried to drive off. Some of them made it, but one particularly careless man went straight for the bumper of a yellowed old sedan, launching himself through the air and into its rear windshield.

There were just a few of the bikers nearby when it

all began, and they were the only ones with the presence of mind to return fire. A thin man with a scruffy mullet and leathered skin covered in tattoos was the quickest to draw, whooping and firing a shotgun with one hand as he raced between the cars on his bike. It was an impressive sight, but a poor tactical choice. His aim was terrible, and wasn't helped by his grandstanding. Thane picked him off quickly, timing his fire for when he'd left the protection of the traffic jam and was circling around in the open yelling to the rest of them to attack.

Two others were smarter, opting to hide behind an overturned tractor-trailer and engage from a distance. But they weren't particularly good shots, either, and what didn't go over the heads of their targets connected only with grass, dirt, and cars. They did manage to accomplish something despite themselves, as the barrage pinned the cell to their position and gave the other Vichies the courage to begin firing volleys of their own.

Behind the ridge, Holt was fully occupied with trying to bring Faye to her senses, holding her down and working to soothe her as he left the battle to Thane and Dax. She was still chanting, an insistent and unpleasant discourse in a language that no one there could understand. It disquieted some of the closer Vichies who were able to hear it over the gunfire and the shouting, and drove them to flee rather than stay and do battle with whatever the source of the sound was. Otherworldly noises meant otherworldly dangers, and anyone with a bent towards incautious curiosity had been weeded out of the world long ago.

"Stay with us. It's going to pass. Stay with us and

stay down," said Holt, only to be met with gibberish in return. He could see her in her eyes, the glint of soul and personality that shines through them and speaks someone's essence with just a look. Faye was there, but frightened, and totally unable to control herself. Drops of blood had started running from her nose, leaving thin lines across her mouth in their wake. He couldn't trust her, and she couldn't trust herself, so he kept her pinned low with the weight of his body as she babbled.

"More on the left," said Thane, adjusting his fire to meet a few new entrants to the battle who'd come from the fore of the convoy to investigate the commotion. Dax didn't seem to hear him. He'd emptied his clip, and was busy trying to replace it with a fresh one. He knew how; he'd even trained how. But acting under the pressure of Holt's voice was one thing, and acting in the face of the enemy was another. Thane reached over to Dax, flipped the clip around to face the proper direction, and clicked it in. Then he returned to the enemy, shooting underneath a car to hit one of them in the foot as he tried to hide behind it.

The battle went their way at first. Thane was an excellent shot, and the Vichies were virtually useless. The bikers were a threat, but they were accustomed to victory through posturing and bluff, and none of them had ever had the discipline to choose training over more enjoyable enterprises such as drinking, carousing, and bullying. Thane could have held them off on his own with ease, if more and more of them hadn't kept streaming towards the gunfire.

The shouts began as their numbers grew, cautious

taunts that rose to a bold chorus as more and more of them joined in. "Angel food!" screamed one of the Vichies, to be answered by a retort from Dax's weapon. "Gonna fuck you up, man! Gonna put you in chains!" shouted another. They only grew louder from there, piping in from all around. "Gonna sell your asses! Gonna make you some angel's little bitch!" It was less about intimidating their opponents, and more about priming each other for battle. None of them had much in the way of courage individually, but even the most slavish of followers can be prodded into decisive action, provided the only alternative is to stand out from the crowd.

"Thane!" shouted Holt. "We need to end this! Get in your stash and get us a distraction!" Thane obliged, crawling over to the ATV and opening up its trailer. He was a hoarder of anything he thought had destructive potential, though the items he collected seemed to slip away as quickly as he could acquire them. He kept finding creative uses for them, most of which tended to annihilate his weapons along with their targets. His choice on this occasion was a small box of grenades he'd bought from a scavenger who'd been rummaging through the remains of a National Guard post. They'd been the prize of his armory for years, and he'd long hoped to test them out on one of the angels. But since he'd gotten his hands on the sword, they were a distant second, and now seemed as good a time as any to put them to use.

"We're going to have to make a run for it," said Holt. It was easier said than done. Everything around them for miles was open pasture, with nothing for cover but overgrown grass and a few scattered hills. There was the road, but it was infested with Vichies, and there was nothing stopping them from charging out into the pasture but a few thin strands of barbed wire and their own lack of fortitude. A few of them would eventually try, maybe further down the road where there wasn't an easy line of fire, and then the cell's position would be overwhelmed.

Holt lifted Faye over his shoulder, carrying her over to one of their bikes and seating her in front of him. "Dax. Dax!" He had to shout to get his attention; Dax was eagerly burning through clip after clip of ammunition now that he'd recovered his ability to reload. Eventually Thane crawled back over and tapped him on the shoulder, pointing him to Holt.

"We're going. Now," said Holt. "Get on the ATV and get ready to follow us. I want you behind us, and I want you firing if we need it. Thane's going to buy us all a minute and then come after us."

"But we're winning," said Dax. "They're all shitting their pants. I know I got one of them, maybe two." He looked too eager, too happy about it, and that was a dangerous thing. The ones who started to enjoy killing started to look for excuses to do it, sanitizing the experience and turning it all into a game. It robbed them of something, the little piece of themselves that told them when to stop, and they could never quite get it back. Holt had seen it before, and he didn't want to see it again.

"Dax, damn it, get on the ATV," said Holt. "They're not going to stay back forever, and we're not going to make it out of here on our own." Faye was swaying in front of him, the stream of words dying down to a low muttering, and Holt had to hold his arm tightly around her waist to keep her from falling off the bike entirely.

Something about seeing her that way snapped Dax back to his senses, and he scrambled towards the ATV and turned on the engine. "Okay. You go, I'll be in the rear. I'll give you some suppressing fire if I can. To give you a little more cover."

Thane nodded to Holt, and turned back to the battle. He picked up the first of the grenades, running his hand over it fondly and giving it a quick kiss. Then he lobbed it towards the enemy, as hard as he could. It bounced off the tire of a faded blue van, clattering along the ground and rolling near a cluster of Vichies who'd been taking turns shooting at them with an old hunting rifle. It took them a few seconds to realize what was happening, before one of them screamed, a high-pitched girlish cry from a middle-aged man. Another one of them managed to make it a few strides away, out into the open, but it was too late. The grenade exploded, a burst of anger and smoke and fury. Blood and chunks of metal sprayed all around the nearby cars, and the rest of the Vichies started to panic.

Thane grabbed a second grenade, plucked out the pin and gave it a healthy toss. This one interrupted the arrival of a few more bikers from the rear of the convoy, landing in their path and exploding. It sent the closest one of them up into the air as he drove past, launching his bike behind him and knocking over two others who were following. They lay on the ground, stunned and bleeding from their ears, until Thane picked off one of them with his gun. The other crawled away in a daze, disappearing into the cars and leaving a pool of blood behind him.

Holt was heading off into the pasture at half-speed, taking advantage of the confusion and weaving from side to side to make a more difficult target. Dax was close on his tail, stealing nervous glances over his shoulder. The explosions had distracted the Vichies, but now they were starting to notice the getaway. The alarm went out, and the Vichies started popping out from their hiding places to take potshots at the escapees. Puffs of dust began bursting up behind Dax, as stray bullets struck the ground around them. Bikes started to rumble and then boom, as the Vichies charged towards the fence. The sight of the enemy's rear had emboldened them, and many of them judged the pursuit of a fleeing opponent as a fine opportunity to secure a few war stories without the risks of a war.

The chase was on, and Thane knew he was out of time. He let his last grenade loose, aiming for a few of the Vichies who'd reached the fence and were maneuvering their bikes underneath the wires. White turned to red, and the ranks of their vanguard were thinned. Thane hurried to his own bike, mounting it and kicking the engine into gear. He sped towards Dax, making up the distance while being followed by a few of the bikers. Holt just kept heading further and further into the pasture, and they never got close. Once the road was out of sight, the bikers gave up the chase, firing a few last lazy shots before stopping to discuss among themselves how to embellish the story they'd tell to their companions.

When they'd travelled far enough away, and the danger had passed, Holt stopped them all in the middle of a field. Faye was coming around, and the words she was murmuring were English again. "Shouldn't be this way," she sobbed. "Shoulda been someone else."

"I know," said Holt, cradling her head and wiping the blood from her nose. "It should have been me. I'm sorry. I fucked the whole thing up. I didn't see them coming."

"No," said Faye. She was dazed, clutching at her throat to confirm that it was hers again. "No, no. Shoulda been married. Shoulda had kids. Shouldna been this."

"It's okay," said Holt. "None of us should have. But it's going to be okay." He picked her up and off the bike, laying her on the ground to rest and rolling up his jacket to serve as a pillow.

"Not who I was supposed to be," said Faye, drifting off into herself.

"We're stranded," said Thane. "We can't get back on the road, not with those fuckers all over it. We need to go north, cross the thing, and ditch the coast."

"We're not going north," said Holt. "We're heading to the southwest. All we have to do is get around Philadelphia."

Thane's hackles rose, and his nostrils flared. "An' where we goin' after Philly? Tell me, where do you think we're goin' after Philly? Don't tell me we're goin' where I fuckin' think we're goin'." Holt stayed silent, and Thane knew. He was taking them exactly where he'd thought.

They were going to the center of it all, the home of the Vichies and the source of the betrayal that had paralyzed the world after the Fall. They were going to the font of the nation's corruption, a place stained by sin and steeped in treachery. They were going to a den of lies, packed with cowardly parasites who survived by whoring their allegiances to the highest bidder.

They were going to Washington, D.C.

CHAPTER TWENTY-FIVE

THE WALK BACK UP WAS a terror. Cassie was beside herself, lecturing Jana in a low, urgent tone as they went. She couldn't tell if Jana had been momentarily overtaken by suicidal urges, or if she was merely stupid, a dull child raised in a dull basement who couldn't figure out the basics of survival once she'd been thrown in among the lions.

"He saw me with you," she said. "He'll probably kill me on sight. Stupid, stupid girl. And what will you do if he catches you alone? What will you do if he comes up there and demands your head?"

"He won't," said Jana. "He's afraid. Afraid of the others. You should have seen them. They swooped in and drove him off."

"Who swooped in?" asked Cassie. "Tell me. You tell me, and you do it now, or so help me I'll have you scrubbing toilets with your tongue. I'll do it, too, don't think I won't."

"It was Zuphias," said Jana, pausing, and then amending her answer. "Mostly Zuphias. And Rhamiel."

"*Rhamiel?*" said Cassie. "She told you to stay away from him. I know she told you. And she told me to keep you away from him, too. She wanted to protect you, protect you from him, and now she's to be expected to save you from Ecanus as well?"

Her voice had risen too much, and had attracted the attention of a passing angel. He flew behind them, lazily winding through the air just close enough to eavesdrop. His robe rippled around him, billowing outward as it caught a draft, an intense white fringed with dazzling gold. His wings were a dark coal, and he watched them for a few more floors before losing interest and drifting away. Cassie kept looking over her shoulder, making sure he was actually gone, before she thought it safe to say another word.

"I don't know what I can do to help you now," said Cassie. "You don't even seem to want to help yourself. Living in here is about being careful. Every step, everything you do, you have to be careful. Even the most insignificant of indiscretions can get you killed. And you go and threaten one of them."

"He's hurting my friend," said Jana. "What am I supposed to do, if he's hurting my friend? How much do they expect me to take?"

"As much as is needed to survive," said Cassie. "You take, and then you take some more. You put up with whatever they ask you to, because you don't have any other choice. It's do as they say, or die. That's the deal you make to live up here."

Jana thought perhaps she did have a choice, and that she hadn't agreed to any such deal. Cassie had come here, voluntarily, to escape what was on the outside. But she'd been brought here, too young to choose for herself, and too young to do anything other than what she was told. Maybe her parents had thought her life would be better that way, and maybe it had been. They were gone, and she didn't and couldn't know. But the life they'd given her had changed, and she hadn't asked for any of this. All she wanted was some say in the matter.

"Is it like this out there?" asked Jana. "Do they hound you this way?"

"You shouldn't bother yourself with what it's like out there," said Cassie. "They'd never let you out, not now. It's different outside. But it's not the escape you're thinking it is. Everyone bears a burden. You manage to shrug one off your back, and then you can't help but pick up another to weigh you down again."

She fumed the rest of the way, stomping and sighing and making Jana haul their wagon throughout the entire trip. She acted angry, but Jana could see her hands shaking as she opened the door to the upper levels, and she grew edgy and stiff each time one of the angels flew past. When they finally arrived at Nefta's chambers, she took a full minute to compose herself before working up the courage to enter.

They walked in through a blizzard of sawdust, swirling around the room in a gust as the door swung open. Nefta stood in the center, using a chisel to carefully chip away at a large stump. The room was a mess; a few discarded pieces in progress had been tossed aside for their imperfections, and shavings littered the area and peppered Nefta's gown. She didn't even notice their arrival, and her trance was broken only by the squeaking of the wagon's wheels as they pulled it inside.

She looked up, but barely, keeping focused on her work. "Oh, girls. You've been gone; I'd forgotten you'd been gone. And you brought me a canvas! You can't sire a work of art without one, and I'm afraid I've spoiled a few of my earlier attempts. The first ones never survive, not if the final product is to be of any merit." They stood there, waiting for some signal as to what they should do. Cassie had lost all her decisiveness, and was as hesitant as Jana. Nefta just kept working, humming a chirpy melody to herself as she picked at the wood in front of her.

"Don't be shy, now," said Nefta. "Put them over in the corner, and I'll sift through them for the best pieces when I need them. If I need them. I'm getting closer, this time around, and maybe I won't require another."

"We're glad you're feeling well, ma'am," said Cassie. "We'll get to cleaning, and we'll be in the back if you need us."

"I'm feeling ecstatic," said Nefta. "I've had a burst of energy, and creation is flowing through me." Her speech was rapid, coming out in uninterrupted bursts of enthusiasm, a hodgepodge of half-formed plans and inchoate dreams. "I've been cooped up in here for too long. I need to act, to do. I've thought of so many endeavors, some I've put aside for centuries. I wonder now why I've never gotten to them. I'm thinking of putting on a show, and hosting some of the others. All this art, sitting up here unappreciated. I've a talent for it, I think, and yet I keep it locked away. Or perhaps I should trade some, or give it away as gifts. Jerazol would like some of the happier pieces, and I can always carve replacements if I choose."

She paced around the room, moving from mask to mask and hastily improvising plans for each of them. "Lepha would like this one for her walls. It was based on a soul I knew long ago. I remember him well. Such a sad man, but he had much to be sad about. I tried to protect him, but he had so many troubles. And Vhnori! He's a dour sort, but don't you think he'd like something uplifting, to think of as he prowls the tower's halls? This one, a little girl. She died young, as so many of your kind did in those days, but she was always bouncing about, never without a smile. It was a good life, even if it was a short one."

"Oh!" she said, her face lighting up with enthusiasm, as she rushed over and placed an arm around each of them. "I haven't even shown you my new work. Ignore the crudities; it's in process, and good art takes time. But I think it could be the best I've done, and I'm hopeful, so very hopeful it will turn out to be something special. You're the first I'll unveil it to."

Jana looked to Cassie for some clue as to what to do, but found none. This was the last thing she'd expected. Nefta had been sour and sullen when they'd left, and in a matter of hours she'd swung to the opposite extreme, swirling around her chambers in a frenzy. She was a dynamo, bursting with thought and ideas and energy. Jana couldn't exactly complain. She'd been worried the entire way up that they'd be interrogated the instant they arrived, and that Cassie would give her up for her folly. Nefta would probably still find out somehow; it was only a matter of when. Her best bet was that Ecanus would be too embarrassed to complain, but she wasn't optimistic. But for now, a happy Nefta was a harmless Nefta, and she only hoped the mood would last.

"I've been working on it in my head all day," said Nefta, standing beside her creation. "I forced myself to start, and it's just poured forth from me ever since. I call it 'Lover's Embrace.' Tell me your thoughts, dears, I'd love to hear them."

The sculpture was large, a thing of oak, two angels holding each other tenderly. Their wings curved around into each other, joining at the tips and forming a protective bubble around them. Their eyes were closed, and their lips locked in a passionate kiss. Both were undamaged and unscarred, angels as they should have been, beautiful without and peaceful within. It was unfinished, and the bottom half lacked detail, their legs still emerging from the wood as Nefta cut away around them.

"It's amazing," said Cassie. "I love it. I really, really love it. I think it could be a masterpiece."

"It's—" said Jana, starting to offer effusive praise of her own. And then she looked closer.

She recognized them, she thought, the angels in each other's arms. The female figure was the harder to place, even though it was facing her. It was the lack of scars that made it difficult, but as she focused in she could see it. Nefta had carved herself, a happier self than she'd ever be, in an idyllic moment leaning in for a lover's kiss. And what a lover she'd chosen. Jana hadn't recognized him, not from a distance, but as she approached his identity was clear, carved in careful and attentive detail.

It was Rhamiel in miniature, hands around his perfect Nefta, showering her with an affection her tarnished counterpart clearly longed for.

"Don't be shy, dear," said Nefta. "And be honest. Truthful criticism is the best criticism, even if brutal." She put her arm around Jana, clamping her hand down on her shoulder and smiling serenely, lovingly. Whether Nefta was wearing a mask of her own, Jana couldn't tell. She seemed to be everything all at once: threatening and caring at the same time, protecting Jana from the outside only to smother her in the nest to protect her own interests.

"It's lovely," said Jana, choking on the words as they came out. "I think everyone will love it."

"I know they will," said Nefta. "I know they will. Now run along, and be about your business. It's a good time to clean my personal chambers, while they're unoccupied. I'll be out here finishing things up, and I'd prefer the place to be quiet. Works of great feeling require great concentration. You have to experience things, let them overpower you, and that can't be done under the eyes of others."

They pulled the wagon past her, running tracks through the sawdust on the floor, and walked towards one of the storage rooms. They had more than their share of cleaning to do after this, and Jana could only guess as to what state Nefta's private room was in. But she'd made it through the day alive and unharmed, and that was satisfaction enough to make tidying up seem a joy by comparison. They had almost turned the corner when Nefta called out to her. "And Jana!"

"Yes, ma'am?" said Jana.

"I love you. And you, Cassie. All of you. You may not believe it, maybe not always, but it's true. One can't be a guardian for as long as I have without loving her wards truly and deeply. But love is fickle, and love sometimes hurts; there's nothing to be done about that. This is our time now. Our time to be selfish, our time to taste of freedom. Our time to throw off the shackles of the Maker and live our lives as we choose. We've been slaves for so long, to him and to you. It's not too much to ask for you to step aside and let us pursue some happiness of our own, I don't think."

"Yes, ma'am," said Jana.

"Our turn," said Nefta. "My turn. And I hope you won't stand in the way of that."

"No, ma'am," said Jana.

"Wonderful," said Nefta. "I knew you wouldn't do such a thing. You two run along, and let me focus on my work." She hummed, then, a happy hum of pure contentedness, and turned her back on them. Her wings flared, her chisel rose, and she was lost again in her labors.

Cassie gathered some mops and led the way into Nefta's private chambers. They were just the disaster that Jana had expected. A gigantic bed filled the center, and it looked like two mattresses had been shoved together underneath their red satin sheets to create it. Down below they'd told stories about them hanging from the ceilings like bats to sleep, and Jana had never really questioned it. She supposed having wings must pose a difficulty, and there was enough room here to let them sprawl across it in any direction. Pillows were strewn about the room, some slashed open, tufts of stuffing spewing out from their innards. A nightstand was overturned, and pools of wax dotted the surfaces of the furniture, the corpses of candles who'd lingered too long into the night. As outside, masks lined the walls, but here all their expressions were tortured, moaning and groaning in silent turmoil, and their eyes seemed to watch her as she moved.

"Get ready to scrub," said Cassie, handing Jana a mop. The floors were a mess, with food trays overturned and wine glasses shattered against the walls, leaving behind a legacy of reddened stains. Chunks of wood were scattered around the bed, and masks in progress lay everywhere, many of them cracked in half, each contorted into a hideous grimace.

"Not in here," said Cassie, as Jana reached down to begin picking up some of the debris. "Not after the trouble you've put me through. You can do the hard work. Back there." She pointed to a little room to the side, away from the rest of the place. Jana approached it—the bathroom, chamber pots overflowing, and it reeked. There'd been much debate among the servants below about whether and how the angels took care of that particular business, and now she had her answer. She'd have preferred that it have remained a mystery, but nonetheless she spent the next several hours mopping, scrubbing, and cleaning up the aftermath of Nefta's weeks of isolation.

Cassie was in and out, returning at one point with a few burly servants from the middle levels. Unpledged to any particular angel, the men were laborers at large, filling in wherever in the tower their services were needed. They righted overturned furniture, hauled off stained sheets for a thorough cleaning below, and scrubbed the walls under Cassie's watchful eye. They were quick about it, eager to escape before storm clouds gathered again, and one of them had gone so far as to bring a gift from the laborers below, a bottle of fine wine intended to curry Nefta's favor and forestall any criticisms of their work. They'd even brought one for Cassie, too, and though it was homemade and of humbler origins than Nefta's, they managed to buy her goodwill as well. The entryway erupted in coos and compliments, and Jana could hear them all the way in the back as she scoured the floor.

It was a close run thing, but they finished just in time to serve Nefta her dinner, a grand meal ferried up from the kitchens and laid out on her table on silver platters. Nefta delighted in each course, having Jana practice her serving and praising her efforts throughout the evening. She drank deeply from her wine, and Cassie snuck sips from hers in between courses. Before dessert had even arrived, Nefta had emptied her bottle, and was swaying in her chair and slurring her speech. Jana had never seen one of them this way, not from any amount of alcohol, and she thought it must have been a particularly strong vintage. Cassie was starting to get tipsy herself, giggling with Nefta as both of their eyes glazed. They helped Nefta to bed, guiding her stumbling to her private chambers as she mumbled quietly to herself, and Cassie fell asleep soon after.

Jana was up a little longer, laying quietly in the dark, falling into her fantasies to lull herself to sleep. She was queen again, her kingdom now beset by barbarians from the outside, with little hope of victory until Rhamiel flew to the rescue ahead of an army of angels. He fought valiantly, driving off her foes, and then confessed his love for her, his obsession for her, a passion so powerful he simply couldn't control himself. She was in the middle of a lavish wedding ceremony when she drifted asleep, and then she did it all again in her dreams.

She woke suddenly, violently, everything still black. Someone was standing above her, a man, shoving his hand over her mouth. It was clammy, and smelled of sweat, and he held it tightly enough to muffle Jana's instinctive scream. Cassie snorted and rolled over onto her side, but it otherwise barely disturbed her. She was drunk enough that nothing much would. The man pulled Jana out of bed, hissed at her to stay quiet, and dragged her out of the room and into the darkness beyond.

CHAPTER TWENTY-SIX

IT TOOK THEM DAYS, BEFORE they reached the first of the pickets. They'd kept off the roads, cutting across what had once been private lands to circumvent the major cities. Once they'd gotten around Philadelphia, the danger from the angels was minimal, and it was a straight shot along the highway to their destination.

Most of the highway was simply abandoned, a graveyard of vehicles that was completely empty of any other traffic. They stayed on the sides where they could, pacing themselves so that Faye could be given frequent breaks. They'd even talked about taking a detour, going off some place to find a safe house where they could drop her off and let her convalesce. But she insisted she'd recovered, and refused to let them dump her with strangers they didn't even know. She'd started with them, and she'd finish with them, and it helped to have a purpose, after all. The rest of them weren't so sure, but it only agitated her to keep prodding with their concerns, and none of them had the slightest idea of how to treat someone afflicted with glossolalia, or even whether they could.

So they all pressed forward together, enduring profane tirades from Thane the whole while. He was challenging Holt at every turn, second guessing him just for the sake of doing it, and always bringing everything back to the Vichies and the many and varied advantages of frying the entire bunch. They were traitors, said Thane, and so would they be who dealt with them. He was particularly irked by Holt's refusal to disclose even the outlines of their purpose, as no honest business could be conducted in a place as damnable as the nation's former capital.

It was almost dark when they saw it, up ahead on the road. Torches lined the barriers that used to protect traffic from veering off as the highway curved, flickering beacons that shone brighter as the sunlight dimmed. The cars had been cleared entirely for a half mile in front of it, towed away to make it impossible to approach under their protective cover. They'd been rearranged to form a wall running across the highway, a crude metal fortress with cars fit together like sandbags, one on top of the other. The windows had been bashed out of some, turning them into sniper's nests, and at various places along the top the Vichies had mounted heavy weaponry, belt-fed machine guns that peered over the edges and waited for anyone foolish enough to charge them.

"Who goes there?" came the sentry's call as they approached. Heads poked from behind the wall, and guns pivoted and aimed at the bikes as they slowly edged towards it, defenseless and exposed in the open. They could see the Vichies popping their heads up and down, nervous albino prairie dogs assessing the threat. One of them kept running the length of the barricade, clambering on top of the cars and excitedly rousing the others, making a show of it so they'd know he'd been doing his duty.

"We're lettered!" shouted Holt, slowly holding up a piece of paper, a bright red seal stamped across its center: an image of an eagle bowing before an angel. Beneath it was a mass of text, impossible to read from a distance.

"It better be a fake," growled Thane. Most groups of Vichies had no actual connection to each other, and outside the capital they were a loose-knit confederacy of independent bands who roamed around doing the bidding of one angel or another, at least nominally. Practically, they did as they pleased, unsupervised and cloaked in the protections of the white. No one had the power to make them do anything, but officially they all bent their knees to the capital, which tried to control them in the only way it knew: through edicts, proclamations, and mounds of paper.

The letters of marque were the only one of these efforts that had any teeth, and then only because they filled a need among them. Their uniforms were easily faked, but the Vichy seal was not. Pirates had relied on them, once, a sanction from one government to pillage the citizens of another, elevating their bearers from common criminals to respectable and patriotic privateers. The ships they plundered may have burned just the same, and the valuables they stole may have gone into the same pockets. But with the letters it was all for the glory of the crown, and the pieces of paper worked their alchemy, converting criminals into civil servants.

Some enterprising politician in the capital had resurrected the practice, taking advantage of the old treasury and its defenses against counterfeiting. They'd made the seal, and made the letters, and stamped their authority on the actions of anyone with a large enough group of followers that were willing to submit. Thus robbery and extortion became taxation, and violence and murder became defense, and all at the stroke of a pen. Tribute flowed to the Vichies in the capital in the form of food, goods, and whatever the angels desired. The better part belonged to those in the field, but relations had to be maintained, and none of them wanted the angels to be unhappy with the arrangement.

"Approach the barricade," shouted one of the Vichies from up top. "Just you!"

Holt complied, dismounting his bike and slowly walking forward, holding the letter of marque before him. It was a shield, and an effective one, but only so long as they believed in its power. A Vichy leaped down, a little boy in a puffy white ski jacket a few sizes too big. He ran up to Holt and dabbed the edge of the letter with a pen. He waited a moment, checked the color of the mark he'd made, and then shouted up in a high-pitched, squeaky voice that feigned authority beyond his years. "They're legit! Open up!"

At the center of the barricade, a stack of cars began to shake. Holt hadn't noticed from a distance, but he could see it now: the cars were lashed together with chains into a single block, and it was retracting into the barricade and creating a passageway through the wall. Glancing inside, he could see what they'd done. They had a forklift, left in position behind the stack, and they could pull it forward or backward as needed to create an entrance. Holt raised his hand to the others, waving them forward, and they started their engines and moved ahead.

"You're not wearing the white," said one of the Vichies. He was a scowly man, waving an AK-47, short and fat with black eyes sunk deep in his skull. His clothes may have been white in the distant past, but now they were a pasty brown, stained from dirt and sweat and fallen scraps from forgotten meals.

"That's because—" started Thane, only to be cut off curtly by Holt.

"That's because none of your business. We've got the letter, and we've got people in D.C. to talk to. Important people, people who don't like waiting. People who can snap their fingers and have any one of us roasting on a spit."

"Anybody can steal a letter," said the Vichy. "Anybody can be a tough guy."

"Anybody can look like a tough guy," said Holt. "Not everybody works for Senator Fletcher."

The Vichy's face dropped, and the others grew noticeably more edgy. Politicians were known for their ruthlessness and their tendency to backstab, but usually it was metaphorical. The good Senator's reputation was for the darkest sort of skulduggery, and rumors abounded of his involvement in slavery, torture, and even assassination. The Vichy still didn't look like he trusted Holt, but he'd be gambling with his own life if he continued to confront him. He chose safety over his suspicions, and waved them forward.

"If we're workin' for any of 'em, I'm gonna kill you," said Thane, as they moved away from the Vichies and prepared to continue on their trip. "You think I'm fuckin' around, I ain't. I'm gonna kill you." His eyes were narrowing, and the blood was rushing to his face. He was barely keeping control, and Holt spoke to him slowly, evenly, trying to keep things contained.

"We're not working for him," said Holt. "We're going to deal with him. Don't think I like it, either. Don't think it for a second. But he's got something I want. Something you're going to like. Trust me."

"I don't trust shit," said Thane. "I don't trust him, and now I don't trust you."

Thane revved the engine on his bike, spitting out a loud snarl, and floored the accelerator as he raced down the highway, re-entering the mess of cars and disappearing among them.

"We'd better go after him," said Faye, and they did, albeit more slowly and more cautiously. He kept ahead of them for a while, violently swerving between the cars, a daredevil's path he knew they wouldn't follow. His anger gradually faded, and the distance between them eventually closed. They caught up with him when he stopped for a break, and knew better than to say anything. The night had fallen, and they couldn't continue safely, so they pitched a camp and waited until morning. When the sun rose again, they moved on and continued down the path towards the city.

The rest of the pickets went much the same way as

the first, aided by the Vichies radioing ahead to alert the others to expect them. They'd spaced their encampments along the highway every so often, outposts designed to keep any enemies far from the capital. It was easy to slip onto the road, and they couldn't watch every inch of it. But it slowed things down, it gave the Vichies eyes where they needed them, and the show of force was enough to deter any larger groups from attempting the journey.

They inched closer, and then they saw it in the distance, the city and its monuments. They all still stood, every one of them, undamaged except by time and neglect. The angels had left the place alone entirely, the world's only major city that could make that boast. It had once housed the leaders of a nation, clever leaders, ones who knew their own interests and pursued them above all else. They'd known the world was changing, and they'd made a deal. Now they were left to rule a rump state, a capital carved from its country, exempted from the torments rained down on the rest.

Politicians are parasites of a flexible sort, and with the death of their host, they'd all had to adapt. Before the Fall they'd sucked at the country's blood, fat ticks latched to its belly that drank and drank until they were ready to burst. Now they nibbled at its corpse, enriching themselves by directing the plunder of the rusting hulk they'd used to govern, and enlisting the desperate as followers to labor in their stead. It wouldn't last. After a time, this racket would fade with all the others, and they'd have to invent new corruptions and new ways to exchange promises of a brighter tomorrow for a spot among the rich and comfortable in the dreary present.

But for now, the city clung to life, sliding down towards oblivion while its residents enjoyed the ride.

Holt led them on, past the suburbs, through checkpoint after checkpoint until they were downtown, in the heart of the place. The Vichies made them follow behind a green military truck, with a jeep behind them, an armed escort that wouldn't tolerate any trouble. They took them through a perimeter fence that lined the city center, the last wall to keep those outside from slipping into the refuge within. They were left on a bench, on the side of a street, and told to wait for someone to come to them. The truck left, and so did the jeep, but they could see men up above, watching them from nearby rooftops and making sure they behaved.

It was unlike anywhere else, a little bubble of calm in a violent, foamy sea. This was a city, a living city, not a ruined monument to something that used to be. People were going about their days all around them undisturbed, just as things had been before, just as if nothing at all had happened and the world was still spinning on its course. They were walking their dogs, and chatting together in public, and shopping at boutique stores filled with luxuries scavenged from the lands around them. The streets were clean, the buildings were pristine, and the grass was mowed into perfect little green carpets. Nothing at all had changed, nothing but the clothes, and it would have looked just as it had before the Fall, if only everyone around hadn't been wearing the white.

CHAPTER TWENTY-SEVEN

"I AIN'T GONNA HURT YOU," WHISPERED the man, keeping his hand wrapped tightly over Jana's mouth. He pulled her out of the bedroom, walked her slowly through the foyer, and stopped her just inside the door leading out into the tower. He was huge, a black shape looming over her in the dark, his face featureless except for tiny glints of light reflected from his eyes. "You just stay quiet. You gotta stay quiet. And you gotta come with me. Think you can stay quiet?"

Jana nodded and said yes, and though it came out muzzled, her assent was clear.

"You gotta stay quiet," said the man. "You don't want her to hear you. You know she's a little crazy, right? They're all a little crazy. I think it's the burns, they made them crazy."

She certainly agreed, at least from the ones she'd met, but the man seemed a little crazy himself. He'd crept into a girl's bedroom in the still of night, kidnapped her from beneath her sheets, and expected her to sneak off to who knew where underneath the nose of a very irritable mistress. If this passed for sanity, it was only because they found themselves in a madhouse.

"I'm gonna let go," said the man. "I gotta let go, to open the door. And you gotta stay quiet. She'll kill me if you don't. She might kill you, too. Me, I ain't gonna hurt you. But I gotta take you somewhere. So please stay quiet. Please."

He was big, but he seemed so soft, and when he slowly and tentatively took his hand from Jana's mouth she didn't say a word. It wasn't that she thought he was safe, so much as she thought he was right. If Nefta interrupted them, sneaking out in the middle of the night, she was liable to see a sinister spin to things, and whatever her response it was almost certain to be violent. And if the man was a threat, he wouldn't react well to screaming. It was a choice between the lesser of two dangers, and for now the unknown seemed a more promising prospect than the known.

"Stay quiet," said the man. "I'm not here to hurt you. But there's something you need to see."

"Who are you?" whispered Jana.

"Quiet," said the man. "Please don't get me killed."

He opened the door, ever so slowly, and crept out into the hallway with Jana in tow. She could see him clearly, lit by the torches the servants kept burning in the halls day and night to illuminate the tower's interior. It took her a moment, but she recognized him—he was one of the laborers who'd helped them to clear Nefta's room. He was tall and muscular, but baby-faced. His eyes were brown, simple and vacant, and he had the permanent smile of a genial dullard. The laborers were chosen for their temperament and their strength more so than their intelligence. Obedience and agreeability were more important than skill, given that the tasks involved were menial, and as workers-at-large they had to get along with any potential master. Even the harshest of the angels could sometimes be persuaded to exercise mercy when a failure could be chalked up to stupidity, and the more intelligent didn't survive long in his particular line of work.

She didn't want to go with him, but he seemed so sad, and so intent, and so urgent. She found herself pulled along despite herself, walking behind him even as she debated inside all the reasons to simply pull away and run back. It was a fault borne of living too long in the tower. When one was ordered to do something, they did it, and they didn't question what they were doing or why. It was easy and natural for her to allow herself to be swept up in the will of others, even when she didn't want to. Someone like her was considered headstrong and impetuous inside the tower, even if they'd be thought a blind follower outside of it. It's all a matter of perspective, and a matter of upbringing, and for Jana it was rebellion to even think of thinking for herself.

The man led her onto the ramp, holding her hand and tugging her along, nervous and shaking as he went. She asked where they were going, and got only "down" in response. He shushed her other questions, constantly looking about, and drew the attention of a few passing servants by dodging their eyes, covering his face, and generally acting as suspiciously as possible. He clearly wasn't experienced at abducting fair maidens, and wasn't sure what to do now that he'd captured one.

They passed level after level, going beyond the upper living quarters, until he stopped in front of one of the paths that curved off into the tower. The gardens. Flowers lined the entrance, all selected for their color: daisies, roses, peonies, and tulips, a living quilt of white. They clumped all along the walls, mingling together and blanketing every surface around the entrance and as far inside as she could see. Their scent blended together into a sweet honeyed aroma, wafting through the air and drawing anyone with permission into the garden's embrace. Jana didn't have permission; the angels considered it a private sanctuary, a place for contemplative pacing and solitude.

"Go on," said the man. "Go on inside. I'll wait here, and I'll take you back up when you're done."

"I can't go in there," said Jana. "And what if Nefta wakes? What will I do? We need to get back. She'll be cross with you, too."

"She won't wake up," said the man. "Not 'til morning. Now go. You're supposed to go, alone. You have to, or we'll both be in trouble."

"What if they catch me?" said Jana, looking inside, hesitating.

"They won't," said the man. "They'd catch me first, and I'd yell, and you'd hide. Now go. Trust me."

"I don't see why I should simply do as you say," said Jana. "I'm not scared of you, and I'm very scared of them. And I don't like walking into things I don't know anything about. I've done enough of that for a lifetime, and it's all turned to a mess."

"Trust me," said the man. "You need to see."

She didn't trust him, but all the subterfuge was intriguing, and she'd already come so far down this path that inertia alone made her go just a little further. The man pushed her, a gentle shove into the flowery portal, and her curiosity pulled her inside. The passage curved inwards, and the way was lit by fluorescence, glowing in all directions from lamps set up along the floor to allow the plants to grow in the tower's dark interior. They were left there overnight, extension cords running off into the distance to some source of power, to be removed each morning before any of the angels returned.

The hallway turned and turned, spiraling around, and opening up into a vast cavern filled with greenery. She saw lights, little white dots on the horizon against the black, and it took her some time to realize what they were. Then it clicked: stars. She'd heard of them, but never seen them, not that she could remember. But everywhere in the garden there were windows, and an entire side of the tower had been removed, its walls ripped apart to create an open view of the sky. They needed the light, to keep the plants alive, and save a few sturdy pillars here and there everything was exposed to the elements.

She stood in awe, marveling at it all. She could see clouds wisping around, caressing the tower before blustering away. She could see plants, incredible plants, things she'd never heard of. Vines wound their way around the pillars, clawing towards the ceiling, with shimmering crystalline flowers sprouting off into the air every few feet. All around the sides of the floor were silver bushes, bathed in the moonlight and reflecting it off the leaves, a shiny tinsel hedge that was the only barrier between her and the skies outside. The ground was covered in carefully trimmed grass, growing in a layer of soil that had been spread around the entire floor. Hanging from the ceiling were bulbous fruits, glowing a phosphorescent blue and lighting up pathways through the gardens in the dark. At the center was a giant tree, impossibly large, its branches merging with the ceiling. Indentations had been carved into the bark, places for the angels to sit and think and look down on the beauty below them. Off to one side were orchards, rows of trees bearing fruits of all kinds, from apples to pears to strange growths she'd never seen in the kitchens.

She didn't know where to start or where she was meant to go, so she just began walking, following one of the paths as it wound through the foliage. She could see little sheds, hidden by plants, storage spaces for the fertilizers and tools the gardeners used to tend to it all. The path took her further into the gardens, past a pond filled with golden fish, opening and closing their mouths, hungrily poking up at the surface in expectation of a feeding. Stone fountains in the shape of cherubs spat water at each other as they battled with swords and crouched at the edges of the pool.

She walked onward, past a terrace covered in rows of hanging purple moss, through a cleft in a thicket of tall stalks with blossoming blue flowers at their tips, and into a glade surrounded by thin trees, a gazebo at its center, set against the edge of the tower. The wood was stained brown, the roof a layered red tile, and a line of stones in the grass led towards the steps at its base. She looked at the sky behind it, and her jaw dropped in awe. It was her very first look at the moon, a glowing orb staring at her from the horizon, bathing her in light.

She stood there, leaning on the gazebo's railing, staring off into the night. She could see buildings all around, dwarfed by the tower, none of them coming close to its height. They were rotting away, pieces of them missing, strange broken shapes that had once touched the skies. The lands around were dark and dead, lit only by the moon, but she was still amazed by it all, darting her head from side to side trying to drink in everything at once. She wondered what had been down there, and what it was like, and whether there was anyone staring back at her from some garden below. She was so distracted that she didn't hear the rustling of the leaves behind her, didn't hear the breathing, didn't hear anything until the footsteps were almost upon her.

"Girl," said the voice, and she turned in a panic.

"You," she said.

It was Rhamiel, wings outstretched and glimmering in the moonlight. He had that smile of his, the cat who had his canary, and he strode towards her as she stood there, not knowing what to do. He looked bigger here somehow, a giant in the darkness, dwarfing the little gazebo and its little path. He walked up to her, leaning on the railing, staring at her with the same interest she'd had in the scenery below.

"A beautiful girl in a beautiful garden," said Rhamiel. "However did you end up here?"

"This isn't safe," said Jana. "I can't talk to you. I can't be seen with you." She fidgeted, dropping her eyes to the ground, turning away and then turning back.

"You're a lucky one on that count," said Rhamiel. "There's no one here to see. And where's the fun in life if you never break the rules?"

"You don't understand," said Jana. "There's something wrong with Nefta. She's making these... things."

"She's asleep," said Rhamiel. "A few drops of ambrosia in her wine, a gift from me to her. The nectar of the angels, and a fine drink in its own right. You've no idea how difficult that was to obtain, either. Not much of it came down with us, save a few scattered flasks. It's a valuable drink, and that makes you a valuable girl."

Jana thought she might be blushing, and hoped it was dark enough he wouldn't see. He was so brash and so bold, always standing on the border between confidence and cockiness. Perhaps he was a mixture of both; the angels were a strange sort, and what went on inside their heads was ever a mystery. He was absorbed with himself, and she knew that, but he was also absorbed with her. Passion begets passion, and his was kindling hers. She knew they were dangerous, him most of all, because of Nefta if nothing else. But there was always the undercurrent of kindness, the caring that hid beneath his swagger. On their own, too much of either would have been repelling, but the combination was as intoxicating as his ambrosia.

"That man," said Jana.

"An agreeable fellow, don't you think?" said Rhamiel. "One of the perks of power, and something I'd never experienced up in the heavens. People actually start listening to you, and doing as you ask. They want to curry favor. It's almost an urge for them. Make yourself useful to the man at the top, and maybe one day you'll get something in return. I hope he wasn't too frightening."

"He was very kind," said Jana. "And this place is very beautiful. But I have to go. If...."

"We had something like this place up there," said Rhamiel. "It's a poor facsimile, and doesn't do the real thing justice. But it's a reminder. A snapshot of what we used to have, before it all came crashing down upon us."

"Do you miss it?" asked Jana. She knew she should leave, but she desperately wanted to stay. She was warming to him, her fascination overcoming her fear. The garden was so beautiful, so calming a sanctuary, that if there were a better version of it up in the clouds somewhere she couldn't believe anyone would ever have left it.

"Do I miss it?" said Rhamiel. He paused, leaning against the railing and staring into the stars. "We all miss it, I think. It was a very nice home, and a very nice place, with a very cruel master."

"What did he do?" said Jana. "Why did you leave, and come here?"

"He lied," said Rhamiel. "He lied to us all. But enough of that. It's not done, to speak of it. The others wouldn't tolerate it."

"You chose to come down here, though," said Jana.

"You chose to leave. Nefta said you were someone else up there."

"She told you about it already, did she?" said Rhamiel.

"Not much," said Jana. "She said you jumped. She said you were the only brave one. That you went from nothing to something because of it." His eyes narrowed, his face became more serious, and Jana worried that she'd made a horrible mistake. Maybe she'd gone too far, or maybe Nefta had. Maybe she'd learned something she wasn't supposed to know. But the look lasted only a moment, and then it passed from his face.

"That much is the truth," said Rhamiel, "though perhaps more flattery than I deserve. I wasn't considered much up there. Plain, with a few imperfections, but enough that the others paid me no mind unless they had to. We've always been enamored with status, though before we had restraints as to how we pursued it. Without our chains, we can do as we please, and it's magnified who we already were. In the heavens, I was a rather ordinary looking charity-worker, among a people who valued their looks and valued their warfare."

"You don't seem ordinary looking at all," said Jana.

"Not to you," said Rhamiel. "But beauty's in the eye of the beholder, and we behold it differently. I can see it on my hands, here." He held them up, turning the backs of them towards Jana. All around his knuckles the flesh was red and bumpy, even by moonlight. Then he pointed to his forehead, leaning towards her so Jana could get a better look. "And I can see it in the spot on my face."

"But there isn't any spot," said Jana. "There isn't

anything there at all." She squinted, and she looked and looked, but still she saw nothing but perfection.

"You're kind," said Rhamiel. "Very kind. But we can all see it. It's nothing like what the others endure, but it's there. You can't understand how it is for them. We were all creatures of beauty, perfect things in a perfect city. All quibbling over what must seem the most minor of differences, anything to set us apart. You can't imagine what it's like, to go from that to this. To be one of the Maker's finest works, lovingly crafted, and then to fall, mangled into a monstrosity. Most of them didn't want to continue on at first. A few ended things right away, by their own hands."

"It was easier on me. I rose even as I fell, and the ones who used to see me as a nothing now saw me as a hero, the one who nearly escaped the Maker's brand. It feels so strange, going from nothing to something, bubbling up from the bottom to the top. I know the love they profess for me isn't real. The flatterers and the hangers-on are all looking for something—favors sometimes, or just the reflected sheen that comes from our association. But their attention fills me for a time, and makes me whole, something close to what I was before I fell. Then it fades as quickly as it came, and I'm back to where I started. None of it is real, none of it. I need to find something that's real."

He studied Jana, waiting for her reaction. She thought she knew something of how he felt and something of his pains, having been dizzied by a recent climb herself. She knew there was good in him, she was sure of it now. She wanted to heal him, to fill the emptiness, to fix the little spot she couldn't see and to cover up his hands in her own. But still she had worries, and she couldn't get them out of her head. Nefta had warned her to stay away, but Zuphias had said she was a snake. Then again, Zuphias was one of the hangers-on, and neither of them were particularly trustworthy. She'd been thinking about what Nefta had said, and she had her guesses as to what had made her this way. She bounced back and forth as to what to do, and then decided to take a leap, just as Rhamiel had.

"I'm grateful that you helped me," said Jana. "I really am. But Nefta says you're dangerous. She said you're going to hurt me. I think she's been hurt, too. I know you're not like the others, not like Ecanus. But I don't want to end up like her. I think you loved her, and you left her, and now she's sad and broken."

Rhamiel was taken aback, covered in confusion. "Nefta and I have never been lovers," he said. "She would have laughed at the prospect, back where we were from. She was one of the fairest of us, far better looking than I've ever been. She was drawn to warriors, and while we've all seen battle, it wasn't my primary profession. She thought me just as ordinary as the others, up there."

"She's infatuated with you," said Jana. "She seems so hurt."

"Perhaps she is," said Rhamiel. "She hasn't been in a good way, not since we fell. Her beauty was her being, and now it's gone. She doesn't know who she is anymore. It's an extraordinarily painful thing, losing who you were and who you wanted to be. One can't always make the world what they want it to be, but they can always imagine it to be whatever they like." Jana winced at the comment; she'd retreated into her own imagination often enough to have a good idea of how Nefta must feel.

"But I can swear to you, I haven't loved her and I haven't left her," said Rhamiel. "That's all in her head. She's never been much like me. My affections lie with the nobodies, the ones who never thought they were much and never thought they'd make it where they have."

He looked directly at her, eyes unflinching, and his voice sounded of sincerity, the kind that can't be faked. Jana believed him, even if it didn't completely comfort her. He was still so different, so powerful, so bound up in the politics of the others, that even if he didn't want to hurt her, it didn't mean it wouldn't happen.

"Why me?" asked Jana. "Of everyone in the tower, why are you watching me? You must have been watching me, to know what Ecanus was up to. Why did you bring me here in the middle of the night?"

He reached a hand out to her, gently, brushing her hair aside from her face. She flinched away at first, but then held her ground, letting him do it, and letting him know he didn't intimidate her. Trying to let him know, in any event. She was, in fact, both very intimidated and very nervous. She hoped she wasn't shaking, or giving it away with some other tell. If he saw, he didn't say, and so she kept up the front of bravery. He stood in silence for a minute, just looking at her, and her at him.

"There's something about you," said Rhamiel, his voice low and deep. "Just something. Something I saw at our dinner, in the little server girl stumbling through her first performance. I couldn't say precisely what, but then, that's not how these things work, is it?"

"What things?" asked Jana.

"These things," said Rhamiel. And then he did it. He leaned forward, bended his head down towards her, and he kissed her.

Her first impulse was to wriggle away, to dodge this sudden and unexpected affection. But then she looked at him, the strong warrior, the one in all her fantasies, the one who'd saved her life. And she closed her eyes, and she kissed him back. She'd never done it before, and hadn't known what to expect, but she loved the intimacy it made her feel with him. He put his hand around the back of her head, running his fingers through her hair as they kissed, pulling her in closer.

"I can't," said Jana. "Nefta. If she ever found out— she'd be angry, so angry."

"The only thing better than a stolen kiss is a forbidden one," said Rhamiel. He pulled her in close, moving in for another, and she pushed him away before giving in again. She liked it too much, liked him too much, and couldn't help herself despite the danger. The night was too perfect, the garden too enchanting, and the moonlight too dazzling. When he caressed her with his hands, she didn't stop him. When he reached to unstrap his armor, she didn't look away. And when he started to pull at her clothes, too, she reached back to help him. He pinned her against the gazebo, whispering things into her ear that shouldn't come from the mouths of angels, things that excited her and things that flooded her cheeks with crimson.

They made love there, up in the skies, caressed by the clouds and kissed by the starlight. Then they held each other for what must have been hours, his wings enveloping her and protecting her, and everything was perfection, if only for a time.

CHAPTER TWENTY-EIGHT

THE MAN WHO APPROACHED THEM was young, an ambitious aide to one of the capital's most powerful men. His white wool suit was smartly tailored, strong in the shoulders with dazzling silver cufflinks. He'd dared gold stripes on his tie, a deviation from the uniform, but his master had pull, and in this town that meant that he did, too. He arrived in a town car, escorted by several gentlemen on horseback, dressed in shabbier white suits of their own. They'd been Secret Service agents, once, and though they'd kept the name, they'd become something closer to palace guards.

"The Senator extends his regards," said the aide. "He'll see you in his offices, on Capitol Hill. If you'll follow me."

"The Senator can fuck himself," spat Thane. The Secret Service agents grew edgy, putting their hands in the breast pockets of their suits and touching unseen weapons for comfort. Insubordination was unusual, and they weren't used to it. The residents had grown docile, well aware of the fate that awaited them outside the city's borders. If they displeased someone important, the best they could hope for would be to be ostracized, cast out into the wilderness and left to fend for themselves. The worst, they preferred not to think of.

"The Senator's not someone to fuck with," said the aide. "Not in this city, and not if you want to keep that pretty head of yours attached."

"We won't have any problems," said Holt. "We're in and then we're out. The Senator gets what he wants, we get what we want, and then we're on our way."

The aide walked back to his car, snapped his fingers, and one of the agents rushed forward to hold open his door. Holt got them on their bikes, and they fell in line behind him. Some of the horses took up the rear, and some led the way, trotting through the streets and pushing aside anyone in their path. They passed street after street, storied avenues that had once housed the lobbyists of a thousand corporate interests. Now they were filled with squatters, appropriated from their owners and distributed according to the power of one's friends.

The roads were tidy, covered in immaculately spread asphalt with not a pothole to be seen. But it wasn't the Vichies who were maintaining them. They passed a chain gang, a line of emaciated souls with skin as grey as their ragged clothing. Lashed together at the waists, they'd been given just enough slack to allow them to go about their drudgery. They were sweeping the streets, pushing aside trash and scatterings of manure left by the horses. A single Vichy guarded them, a tattooed thug with scruffy hair and a squinty, piggish face. He lazily followed behind them, barking orders and waving a shotgun at anyone who wasn't working to his satisfaction. The Vichies were dutiful servants, mimicking their masters and molding themselves in their image. If it was good enough for the angels, it was good enough for them, and so injustice cascaded downward as those with power reenacted their afflictions on those without.

Thane pulled up next to Holt as they drove, and shouted his disapproval. "Slavery's your thing now, too? Told you they're a buncha fuckers. You're on and on about helpin' people, and you just zoom past all this shit." Then he slowed his pace, falling back with Dax and muttering to himself the rest of the way. He looked edgy and unhappy, and would have turned and left the group entirely if he hadn't already entered the lion's den.

They finally reached it: the halls of Congress, the place from which the rules had once been made, where backs had been scratched and favors had been dispensed. Fences and guards surrounded it, just as in days of yore, protecting those inside from those bearing grudges at their conduct. The horses stopped, and Senator Fletcher's aide led the way on foot, walking them past checkpoints and through security barriers. There were metal detectors and scanners of all kinds, but they were quickly ushered through, as the guards manning them averted their eyes and tried to avoid trouble.

They weren't even asked about their weapons, which was fortunate, as all of them were carrying them. Thane in particular had loaded up before entering the city, and he'd primed himself for the moment when one of the soulless bastards would dare to try and search him. He'd filled his pockets with knives, a gun, and even the sword, which he considered vulnerable to theft anywhere but on his person. He'd rehearsed the confrontation in his mind dozens of times, and was even looking forward to it, praying for an excuse to shove a knife into the throat of the first Vichy who laid a hand on him. He ended up disappointed; the Senator had enough influence that anyone associated with him was practically untouchable.

The inside was as impressive as it had ever been, the corridors lined with the trappings of power. Marble and paintings and elaborate sculptures paid tribute to the rulers within. They'd dwindled in number, ever since the Fall. No one was there to vote them in or out of power, and so titles that had once been of the people became titles of an aristocracy, hoarded by their owners and given out to newcomers only for great service to the established order. Congressmen stayed Congressmen, and Senators stayed Senators, and Secretaries of this department or that one were called Mr. Secretary long after whatever they'd been in charge of had disappeared.

The government itself had atrophied, devolving into a pantomime of itself, an act the players performed out of enjoyment and out of habit. They still had meetings and still held votes, though it was all for show. The decisions had already been made behind closed doors, and all that was left was to stamp their approval. There were still presidents, though no one elected them. They rose to power through pacts among politicians, and fell again as momentum turned against them in the games they played. Mostly they squabbled over their cut of the spoils, though a not inconsiderable portion of their time was spent issuing edicts and commands to far-off states whose existence they were no longer even sure of.

Senator Fletcher's aide took them into the foyer of a grand office, filled with dark mahogany chairs, antique curios, and portraits of politicians from centuries past. Once it had been reserved for the leadership of the Senate, and passed from politician to politician according to the whims of the electorate. Now it was a prize plum occupied permanently by the Senator, though he'd never held any official leadership post. He'd been a backbencher before the Fall, slowly racking up seniority in the hopes that after a few decades he'd ascend to the heights of power. When everything collapsed, he'd rocketed to the top. Seniority was no longer in demand, so much as cunning and a lack of any ethical standards whatsoever. The Senator had cunning in spades, and was even more sociopathic than his colleagues, and so he flourished in a world where cream had to be rotten to rise.

Senator Fletcher forced them to wait, as very important persons are prone to do, for a very important person must also appear very busy. They sat in the greeting area, with nothing but knick-knacks to entertain them. Dax fiddled with a bronze sextant, trying to figure out how it worked, while Faye spun an oversized globe, running her finger along it to see where it landed and fantasizing about the many places she'd rather be. A dowdy old secretary in a prim green dress watched them from her desk the entire while, peering at them suspiciously through her horn-rimmed glasses. She was just as much a fixture as the furniture, having served the Senator since he was first elected years before.

Finally there was a rap from the door leading into the Senator's personal office, and it swung open as the Senator's aide emerged along with a few of his Secret Service agents. "The Senator is ready," he said, and invited them all inside. Senator Fletcher was sitting before them, in a large leather chair in front of a large, expensive-looking desk. He was in his fifties, a politician's prime, a man with just the right balance of energy and experience to run circles around his opponents. His graying hair was pristine, carefully combed with not a hint that it would ever recede. He waved them forward without looking up, motioning for them to be seated as he read from the very important papers in front of him.

"Mr. Holt," said the Senator. "A pleasure to see you again, in this nation's fine capital."

"Again?" spat Thane, until Faye shushed him and pulled him onto a couch on the far side of the room. The agents were growing edgy, and they disliked Thane as much as he did them. They moved into position to flank the Senator on either side, a practiced maneuver that they'd copied from some movie or another. But it looked intimidating, and that was their purpose, and besides, it added to the aura of power.

"I've done my part," said Holt, taking a seat in front of the Senator's desk. "One of them's dead. Hope you weren't too close to him."

"No one's close to anyone in my line of work," said Senator Fletcher. "I don't care for any of them any more than I care for any of you. But they've got the power, and so we've got to deal with them to get what we want. Just like I've got to deal with you."

"Don't think you can screw me," said Holt. "I know you've thought about it. They're not going to like it if they find out you're involved with us, and I have ways of making sure they do. Whatever else they are, they're protective of their own."

The Senator just laughed, and so did his aide. Then so did his agents, never ones to pass up an opportunity to toady. "I don't particularly care what you tell them, or what they find out about our dealings," he said. "They wouldn't recognize my name if you told it to them. One of us is the same to them as all the others. If they make the connection, they'll just kill the president again, and it'll be business as usual for the rest of us." The presidency was now a figurehead position with little real authority, but it was an incredibly dangerous one. The angels tended to assume presidents were responsible for anything they were unhappy about, and saddled them with the blame despite their lack of authority. Only exceedingly stupid politicians wanted the title so badly as to take that risk, but then, there had always been a surplus of exceedingly stupid politicians.

"Regardless," said the Senator, "I've got no intention of scotching this deal. Our boys are fine young men, don't get me wrong. Very enthusiastic. But they're not exactly reliable, and I don't see any of them taking out an angel anytime soon. I see a man like you, I see someone pragmatic. Someone I can do business with. Someone who sees through all the bullshit morality and bullshit laws we pass just so we can pretend we're following them.

You're a man who sees things for the way they are, a man who takes what he wants. You wouldn't be dealing with me otherwise."

The Senator started laughing again, and so did his cronies. Thane's teeth were audibly grinding together, and Faye had her work cut out for her in keeping him calm. She clenched his hand tightly, holding on and hoping she could hold him back if he erupted. He managed to keep himself restrained and in his seat, but only just.

"I'm a man who wants to kill angels," said Holt. "People like you have always been around, but we survived. Things like them, they'll kill us all. They're going to live forever. They're going to grind us down, one by one, until there's nobody left but them. I think you're a son of a bitch, but if I've got to deal with the slaves to kill the masters, then that's what I'm going to do."

"If the masters aren't paying any attention, then who's a slave?" said the Senator. "Not me. I'm doing just what I like, and getting just what I want. Hell, I've got it better than I ever did before. We made ourselves a pretty sweet deal with our 'masters,' you ask me."

And indeed they had. The political class had seen the writing on the wall long before anyone else. They'd known things were hopeless almost from the beginning. The first few skirmishes had made clear that even a single angel wouldn't be easily killed, and that the costs of battle would be enormous. Killing them all was a fool's errand, though it didn't stop idealists from trying. Other governments put up more of a fight, and the Russians had even managed the stomach to vaporize a few of their own cities just to get at a handful of the enemy. The militaries gave it their all, no matter which flag they swore allegiance to. But it was clear that none of it would matter in the end, and so the politicians sued for peace.

The angels were wholly uninterested at first, treating the negotiations as nothing more than an interesting parlor game. They tortured ambassadors and lopped off their heads for imaginary offenses, and then demanded immediate replacements only to repeat things all over again. The politicians grew desperate, and made the angels an offer they couldn't refuse: fealty for safety, and an army of humans who'd finally return the favor after all their years of service. The rest of the world could be their playground, if only the capital were protected, and they'd help to turn the planet into a heaven of the angels' own.

Thus the Vichies were born, and thus the rest were betrayed. The angels had intended it all as yet another game, and had never planned on keeping their end of the bargain. But the Vichies quickly proved themselves useful, and the angels quickly grew fond of being served. The towers went up, and servants were brought to them, offerings to the beings who'd come from the heavens. Men like Senator Fletcher orchestrated it all, and carved out a lucrative role as administrators of the angels' fiefdom.

The Senator looked at Holt, and then at each of the others in turn. "I'm the slave, but you're the ones doing my bidding. So which one of you can give me what I want?"

"Fuck you, traitor," said Thane quietly from his seat.

"What was that?" asked the Senator. Thane held it all in, his face contorting in anger, while Faye dug her fingernails into his arm. The pain distracted him, and gave him something else to focus on, and so he held his fury inside to boil a little longer.

"I thought so," said the Senator. "I'm loyal to myself, and that's what counts. Not to some bullshit flag, or some herd of cattle who spent their days chewing their cuds and staring at televisions. I don't owe you or anyone else a damned thing. Want to see something? Karl." The Senator turned his head to one of the agents standing next to him, who visibly began to shake.

"Lick the floor, Karl," said the Senator. And he did, without a second's hesitation, dropping to his feet and giving the carpet before him a long, exaggerated pass with his tongue. He looked up for approval, standing nervously to his feet once he received a slight nod from Senator Fletcher.

"That's power, gentlemen," said the Senator. "That's what you're missing out there with your little guerilla war, and with your loyalty. You only could get a taste of it, back in the old days. But boy, was it good. You ever seen someone scurrying around just because you snapped your fingers? Doing anything you say, just 'cause you said it? You just get this feeling inside you. Like you're top dog, and nobody can stop you. Nobody can do a damned thing, because you're king shit. It's a rush. It gets the adrenaline flowing. You wake up feeling like crap? Well, you just tell somebody to jump out a window, and they do, and then it all feels a little better."

The agents and the aide began fidgeting, disturbed

by the comment. But the Senator just kept smiling, and they let themselves relax when he didn't give any such order. He turned to the aide, and gave him a nod, and the aide reached behind the desk and pulled up a thick, heavy briefcase, placing it with a clunk in front of the Senator.

"Now," said Senator Fletcher, nudging the briefcase towards Holt. "I got what you want. You give me what I want."

Holt looked at the briefcase, and then looked at Thane.

"Thane," said Holt. "Give him the sword."

CHAPTER TWENTY-NINE

"THEY'RE BURROWING IN THE WALLS, I think," said Uzziel. "I can hear them sometimes, tapping and clinking away. I'm sure of it."

Jana had been listening to his ravings for the better part of an hour. She and Cassie had been brought to his chambers by Nefta, who'd woken up with a throbbing pain in her skull and filled with suspicion. She knew someone was up to something, she just wasn't sure who. So she'd chosen to consult Uzziel, as the resident of the tower who was most alert to any potential threats. She wasn't willing to leave them alone, not given what had happened, and so they were forced to accompany her. It was awful on Jana to sit through it, her thoughts torn between the night before and the threat before her.

"It must be the ones in the armory," said Uzziel. "They've access to the tools needed to do it. It's a foul plot, but an obvious one, and something we should have prepared for long ago. It was only a matter of time before they'd tunnel upward, spying on us in our sleep.

We should execute the lot of them, and start anew with better precautions."

He was twirling his beard, a compulsive fidget, and listening for the sounds of servants crawling about in the walls to enact their nefarious agenda. The room was filled with trophies, and had the feel of a hunting lodge. Weapons were mounted all around—a mace here, an axe there, and between them all the bodies of assorted creatures that he'd slain since the Fall, stuffed and posed to look as menacing as possible. Papers littered the floors in stacks, marked with notes and drawings of fortifications or plans of attack. A large map of the area surrounding the tower covered virtually an entire wall, and served as a pincushion for a horde of tiny colored flags that indicated points of strategic interest. Uzziel sat in a large leather recliner opposite Nefta, his feet propped on a rug made from the skin of a zebra. Jana and Cassie were forced to stand, and forced to listen.

"I haven't heard any clinking," said Nefta. "And the tower is made of sturdy stuff. I should think it would take centuries to carve any kind of tunnel, let alone an entire system of them. I'm less concerned about the servants, and more concerned about the source of the wine I was given."

"They're clever," said Uzziel. "Very clever. You mustn't underestimate them. There's so many of them. They could be sowing dissention among us. They could be working for Lucifer. They could even be in communication with the Maker himself."

"Lucifer is locked away," said Nefta. "And the Maker doesn't speak to them."

"But he listens," said Uzziel. "He's always listening, and so are they. Listening from inside the walls. And plotting against us from outside them." He glared over at Jana and Cassie, eyes widening as he took them in. Then he stood and began pacing, circling the room like a caged tiger, keeping them in his sight as he went. He tapped at the walls as he walked, observing the tone of the thuds, until he heard something he didn't like. "A-hah!" he bellowed, slamming his fist into the wall beside him. The metal dented slightly, but held, and Uzziel looked at it in confusion.

"Perhaps not here, just yet," said Uzziel. "But it's been hollowed out somewhere. I can hear it."

"Uzziel," said Nefta. "You must focus. The servants may indeed be a threat, I don't deny your theories."

"My facts," said Uzziel.

"Your facts," said Nefta. "But I suffered from intoxication. No human wine could do that, only ambrosia. It must have been one of us, not one of them."

"Hrmm," said Uzziel, thinking to himself and tugging at his beard. "The corruption may be deeper than I suspected. But I see a flaw, an error in your thinking. It could not have been one of us."

"And why not?" said Nefta.

"Because none of us could fit inside the walls," said Uzziel, a look of triumph on his face as he extended his wings outward, flexing them to their widest span in a demonstration of the impossibility of Nefta's complaint.

"Uzziel, I don't ask that you believe me," said Nefta. "All I ask is that you investigate. You've the greatest spy network in the tower. A very impressive feat, and one you should be proud of. Find whoever drugged me, and find out why, and you will have my gratitude."

"I shall," said Uzziel, as Nefta stood to leave. "But in the interim, you must be careful. You should execute these two, as a precaution and as a warning to the others. One shouldn't leave one's safety to chance." Jana's insides churned, and she nearly burst into tears. Nefta quietly looked them over, letting the comment linger before she spoke.

"We can't get rid of them all, else who would attend to us?" said Nefta. "Rest assured that if I find that either of them are involved, they'll regret it. I'll simply turn them over to Ecanus and be done with the matter." Then she headed towards the door, with Cassie and Jana following meekly behind her.

"Rest assured, little girl," said Uzziel as Jana passed. "I'll be watching the walls. And if I hear you inside them, you'll answer to me." She shuddered and turned her head to the floor, walking as quickly as she could to escape his attentions.

When they returned to Nefta's chambers, she bid them to scrub. What they scrubbed, she did not care; she only wanted them to leave her in peace and give her time for thought. "Someone knows something," she added, as she departed into her room. "And someone had better tell me what they know."

"If you know something, you better say," said Cassie, shoving a mop into Jana's hand.

"I don't," said Jana hesitantly. She wasn't sure what to do, and wasn't sure who she could trust. She'd been escorted back safely by the man Rhamiel had recruited, but now she was sure their tryst would be exposed. They'd both been reckless; him in playing this game, and her in acquiescing. He'd promised her things would be fine before she'd left his embrace, whispering to her about a plan to fix everything. It would come soon, he said, and then they'd be together. But now there were threats all around her. If Nefta didn't get her, it would be Uzziel or Ecanus, who still had poor Peter all to himself. It was all well and good for Rhamiel to take his time, but she couldn't.

"Nefta's right," said Cassie. "Someone was up to something. I was plastered. I've never been so drunk, and my glass wasn't even full. I still feel terrible."

"Maybe it was Ecanus," said Jana, pushing her mop up and down the floor. It was growing brown from a mix of soap and sawdust, which kept emerging from hiding places around the chambers just as fast as they could clean it.

"Maybe it was the men who helped us," said Cassie. "One of the ones who gave us the wine. Nefta will be looking for them, you know. To question them. She'll want to know what they know."

"They seemed very nice," said Jana, pushing her mop away from Cassie and away from the conversation. She hoped that she might evade Cassie that way, but she simply followed her, mopping the same areas as Jana and refusing to let her slink away.

"It's a good thing you don't know anything," said Cassie. "Nefta will be torturing the truth out of those men. One of them will squeal, and give up everyone involved. Why, I heard she's already on to something. One of the servants told me they saw something suspicious, out there at night."

Jana dropped her mop with a loud clatter, tipping over a water bucket and spreading a pool across the entire floor. Her hands were shaking as she tried to clean it up, wiping away with a towel to try to contain the flooding. Cassie stood over her, blocking her progress with her feet.

"I know," said Cassie.

Then it all poured out. "They didn't tell me!" said Jana. "Not 'til after it was done. The man said I had to go, and so I did, and then he sent me into the gardens."

"Who?" said Cassie. "Whose wine?"

"I thought you knew," said Jana, sobbing.

"I lied," said Cassie. "But now I know enough. Spit it out. Who?"

"Rhamiel," said Jana. "It was Rhamiel."

"Rhamiel!" said Cassie. "You foolish little girl! Nefta's already warned you about this. Can't you see he's using you? You're just a plaything. You'll be abandoned the moment he grows bored, and replaced with another. Then you'll be left here, alone, with no one to protect you from Nefta, and no one to protect you from Ecanus."

"He won't," said Jana. "He's not like that, not inside. He's not like the rest. There's something in there, something shiny. Something of what they're supposed to be."

"They're all like that," said Cassie. "Whatever's good in them is tarnished. They've fallen, and it's gone now, if anything was ever even there."

"They weren't always," said Jana. "She wasn't always.

You know she wasn't. You came here. You pledged yourself to her. They must be better, better than what's out there, at least. Or you wouldn't have come here."

"I didn't come here to make friends with Nefta," said Cassie. "And I didn't come here to be their slave."

"But you care about her, sometimes," said Jana. "Sometimes she's kind. I know they can be."

"Sometimes she is," said Cassie. "And sometimes I do. But she flips from kindness to rage, and back again, and there's no way to know which she'll be from one moment to the next. You can't love someone who burns with so much envy and hate. Not even if they're very sorry afterwards."

"People come here to escape," said Jana. "It must be better than what's out there."

"It's not," said Cassie. "The world out there's a shithole, but it used to be ours, before they dragged us all down with them. They're all bad, all of them, just in different ways. Rhamiel treats us just the same as all the rest. As toys, to be discarded when we're no longer any fun."

"He saved me," said Jana. "He didn't have to save me."

"He's no different from Ecanus," said Cassie. "He only wants one thing, and he only helped you to get it."

"Then he would have just taken it," said Jana. "If he were Ecanus, he would have just taken it."

"I could tell her now, you know," said Cassie. "Maybe I'll do just that."

"No!" said Jana. "Please!" She started to cry, tears streaming down her face as she clutched at Cassie's dress. She fell to her knees, begging and pleading, and wondering how Cassie could be so cold. She had nothing but venom for the angels, and here she was threatening to throw her to the wolves.

"I'm not going to," said Cassie, pulling Jana to her feet by the scruff of her neck. "But you're going to do something for me."

CHAPTER THIRTY

"**F**UCK YOU! FUCK ALL OF you!" yelled Thane, waving the sword in a shimmering arc of fire in front of him. The room was filled with screams and drawn weapons. The Secret Service agents were pointing their guns at Thane, ordering him to drop the sword. Faye had her pistol trained on them, and Dax was pointing his at the Senator with one hand and wiping sweat from his forehead with the other.

The aide had ducked behind the table, but the Senator was taking it in stride, watching Thane in awe as he wielded his prize. "That's it, boy!" cheered the Senator. "Show us the fire inside!" No one else was enjoying things, and Holt had his palms up towards Thane, trying to ease him off the ledge.

"Just give him the sword," said Holt. "No one's going to hurt you. He's not going to hurt any of us. But this is what we came here for. This is why we put in all the work we have. This—"

"For fuckin' money?" yelled Thane, slicing the sword in the air towards Holt. "You fuckin' sell us all out? You're all talk. You talk about stoppin' all of this, and then you fall in with these assholes the second there's a payday."

"Open the god damned briefcase," said Holt, and the aide obliged, clicking it open and flipping it around to face them.

There was no money. It was all metal inside, a shiny silver interior with a large cylinder embedded in the bottom half and running its entire length. The top half was filled with wires and circuit boards, with a keypad attached.

"It's a bomb," said Holt.

"A nuclear bomb," said Dax, dropping his pistol to his side and adjusting his glasses to get a better look.

Thane stopped in his tracks, holding the sword still in front of him. "That thing is a nuclear bomb," he said incredulously. "That little thing."

"A miracle of the Cold War," said the Senator. "It's been kicking around in a basement somewhere for decades, but it's in mint condition. The Russians had 'em, so we had to, too. They had dozens of these things, planted in every major city. If push ever came to shove, there were always some KGB boys living here in hiding, ready to set a few of them off."

"It's true," said Dax. "The Russian ones were publicly known. We never acknowledged having any, but come on. Everyone knew we had to."

"We couldn't let them have a toy to play with unless we got one, too," said the Senator. "And now you get to be the ones to try it out."

"Give him the sword," said Holt. "This is a good

trade. We're going to kill dozens of them, at least. You'd never get that many without it."

"We're gonna do it. We're gonna take down the Perch," said Thane, his voice a mixture of awe and disbelief. He slipped the sword back into its scabbard, carefully, and tossed it onto the desk with a clunk. Then he sank back into his seat, as Faye moved in to comfort him and make sure he didn't light up again.

"This is a beauty," said the Senator. "A real beauty. The suitcase, that was hard to get. But it was all a matter of finding it. Getting a sword, that's a whole different ball game. You're making a poor trade, you ask me. You know how desperate some of the angels are to get one of these? They don't all have them. Not everyone was packing heat when they got tossed over the side. And boy, the things they worry about. One of them doesn't have a sword, he's a nobody. He gets looked down on. He'd do anything to get his hands on one, and now I'm the only game in town."

"We're getting what we want," said Holt. He snapped the briefcase shut, locking it up and dropping it to his side.

"Suit yourselves," said the Senator. "It's your life to waste. You want to kill a few of them, no skin off my back. There's more of these where this came from, too. We even got a few missiles still lying around, if you get me something worth the trouble. That's assuming any of you survive. You won't, but hell, stranger things have happened. Maybe you'll pick another sword or two out of the rubble. I'll still be here if you do."

"Maybe you won't be here once your masters are

gone," said Holt. "They're what's propping you up. Kick that leg out from under the table, and the whole thing's going to collapse. You won't have the threat of the angels, and you won't have any way to make people fall in line."

"There's always going to be a need for someone to tell the others what to do," said the Senator. "People don't like to be free, not really. Then they'd have to make decisions, all on their own. And when you're the one making decisions, you're responsible if it all goes to shit. People want men like me, even if they won't admit it. They want someone to curse for everything that's wrong in their lives. Licking my floors gives a man a purpose. Doesn't it, Karl?"

"Yes, sir," said one of the Secret Service agents.

"He may not particularly like that purpose," said the Senator. "But he knows what it is, and he knows what he has to do, and he knows where he's supposed to be. He doesn't have to wake up every morning and find something to fill the emptiness in his life. He just shows up and does what I tell him to. Then he doesn't have to think. He doesn't have to worry. He doesn't have to plan. He's a slave, and he likes it, and everyone's a whole hell of a lot happier. He gets three hots and a cot, and a meaning for his otherwise pointless existence. And I get whatever I want."

"That's people's problem," continued the Senator. "That's why they need me. They think there's a meaning to life out there someplace just waiting for them to find it, but there ain't. There's only whatever meaning you make up for yourself. And they just can't do it, not on their own. Most people aren't leaders; they need leaders, any leaders. And just why in the world would I lead people someplace I didn't want to go?"

"So you could be a decent person, instead of a complete jackass?" said Faye.

"Decent people don't become leaders," said the Senator. "Decent people mind their own business, and live and let live. They find their own meaning, and leave others to theirs. If I gave a damn about decency, I'd never have made it here. A decent person tries to be a leader, and he ends up like you. Running off to kill himself, in a fool mission for a fool cause. You go on fighting decent, and I'll go on fighting dirty, and we'll just see who ends up on top."

Holt turned, and walked towards the door, as the rest of them got up to follow. "One other thing, while we're on the subject of decency," he said. "I've got one other request before we leave. I need a doctor."

"Sure," said the Senator. "Like I said. You're a man I can do business with. Stupid enough to fight for a cause, but not stupid enough to think he can do it without dealing with a lesser evil such as myself. We'll keep you alive long enough to swing a punch."

"It's not for me," said Holt. "It's for her." He pointed to Faye, who tried to look tough. She was embarrassed to be discussing her affliction in public, let alone in front of the Senator, but she appreciated the concern all the same.

"Poor girl," said the Senator. "Life on the outside getting too tough? All kinds of things you can catch when you're out in the wilderness, drinking dirty water, eating uncooked food. We've got the finest doctors still around in here."

"It's nothing like that," said Holt. "I don't know if they can help her, but I want someone to try. One of the angels did something to her, when we were getting the sword. She's been speaking in tongues, not all the time, but—"

"Get her out of here!" yelled the Senator, suddenly standing from his chair in a fury. "Get her the fuck out of here now!"

The agents swarmed, one guiding the Senator as he made his escape, and the others advancing on Faye. "What the fuck?" she said, as they waved their guns and began the standoff anew. The Senator disappeared into the bowels of the capitol, leaving the rest of them to deal with his newly agitated subordinates.

"They're in her head," said the aide. "You have to leave. Now."

"Fine," said Holt. "We just wanted to get her some help." He waved Dax towards the door, and put a hand on Faye's shoulder. It was little comfort. She looked stunned, unable to process what was going on. She'd known it wasn't good, having those strange voices spewing from inside her. But she'd seen something in the Senator—fear, fear of her, or whatever was in her.

"No one can help her," said the aide, ushering them out the door as quickly as he could. "You have to get out of the city. And then you have to dump her somewhere, alone. Somewhere far from here."

"She's not somebody's unwanted pet," said Holt.

"We're leaving your little plantation, and we're not coming back. But we're not leaving her."

"You will, or you'll die," said the aide. "One of them is in her head. A miracle-worker. It's a trick they know from their time up there. She's praying, singing praises to the Maker."

"To God," said Holt.

"A point of diplomatic protocol," said the aide. "They don't recognize his sovereignty any longer, so we don't, either. Regardless, it's dangerous. Very dangerous. It used to be a sign of faith. They aren't much for that anymore, but they can use it to track her. And that means they can track you."

CHAPTER THIRTY-ONE

"**J**UST ONE TRIP, TO THE very bottom of the tower," said Cassie. "One more trip, back to see your friends. And to do a little favor for me."

"What kind of favor?" said Jana.

"Never you mind," said Cassie. "All I need you to do is get down there. You convince him, and I won't tell her. He snuck you out of here once, and that means he can do it again."

Jana didn't trust any of this. The tower was awash in schemes, and somehow she kept getting entangled in them. But she didn't have much choice. She needed to wait for Rhamiel to extract her from Nefta's clutches, however he planned to do it. And if Cassie were to tell her, she'd be handed down to Ecanus, and left to the same fate as Peter. Then again, it could be a bluff. Angels in a rage were known to kill messengers, and suspicions would inevitably fall on Cassie if she told.

"I don't know when I'll see him again," said Jana.

"He'll find you," said Cassie.

"What if he says no?" said Jana.

"If he really cares about you, he won't," said Cassie. "I thought you were sure."

"I'm sure," said Jana. "And fine. I'll do it. But you're just as nasty as any of them. Don't pretend you're not. I know better now." Her lips quivered as she spoke, holding in the anger and the pain. She'd been wounded by Cassie's demands and threats. She'd thought of her as someone better, a mentor and protector, someone who might really care underneath her gruff exterior. Now she saw it as an act, a mask for someone just as devious as her masters.

"Mop," said Cassie, and turned back to her scrubbing. She was silent for the rest of the afternoon, keeping to herself and keeping a distance from Jana. She couldn't meet her eyes, and didn't even correct her for leaving streaks or spots, though it must have been tempting given Jana's general inexperience with this kind of chore. They endured the tension for hours, and had finally finished cleaning the entry room, carefully wiping the dust from the crevices of every mask, when they heard footsteps behind them.

"Dears," said Nefta. "How do I look?"

She looked resplendent. She'd dressed herself up, far more formally than Jana had ever seen her. She wore a large, hooped gown, puffed outward at her hips to roughly match the length of her folded wingspan. It was the color of jade, spotted with black bows and tassels. She'd invested a great deal of time in her hair, arranging her blonde locks so that they flowed downward across her back and to the sides. Her wings were draped in a white felt, fitted to them with precision and lined with down feathers in a rough facsimile of the originals. And on her face was a black silken mask, lined at the edges with a string of black pearls and snaking across her face to precisely cover her scars. On either side of it there was a row of black feathers, pluming backwards from the mask and giving the impression of a miniature pair of wings. With her scars hidden, she was a stunning thing of beauty again.

"There's a party tonight," said Nefta. "A masquerade. It's something of a send-off for the warriors of the tower. For Rhamiel's Hunt. He's preparing to chase down the one who scarred him, and avenge the indignity."

"You look gorgeous," said Cassie. "I'm sure Rhamiel will adore it." She shot Jana a firm glance, and then turned back to their mistress.

"Won't he?" said Nefta, spinning around in a quick circle to display her dress in its entirety. "He'll be so focused on his war, but I think this will be just the thing to distract him. And I want you two to be there, at my side. We must find you something appropriate to wear, and masks of your own. Come!"

She snapped her fingers, and led them back to a large closet, filled with clothing for all occasions, from fancy formal wear to rough leather tunics more appropriate for the grime of a battlefield. Jana followed behind her meekly. She thought at first it must be some trap, or a prelude to violence or anger. Nefta had hardly been in the mood to play dress-up just a few hours earlier. But now she seemed so happy and so sincere, enthusiastically flipping through her private wardrobe to find something for each of them. Her swings in temperament were making Jana dizzy, but she seemed genuine about them, however impossible they were to reconcile.

"Oh!" squealed Nefta, pulling a teal silken gown from its hanger, and holding it up against Cassie. "It suits you, a match for your eyes! We'll have to pin up the wing holes in the back, but no matter. You'll look gorgeous. And you, Jana, we must find something for you."

She poked around, flipping through dress after dress to find one she thought appropriate. "No," said Nefta. "This shan't do, it's simply too flashy. And this would be fine, but for the frills. It isn't that sort of party." She tutted and clucked, pulling out beautiful gowns only to toss them aside. Finally she settled on a choice: a drab, tan dress that Jana thought looked like nothing other than a burlap sack. It was serviceable, but it certainly wouldn't attract the attention of any suitors. "It's perfect," said Nefta, handing it to Jana with a cheery smile.

"Now," said Nefta, "we must prepare. The evening's ahead of us, and there's not much time left. You girls need masks, and I've only the one. Cassie, send for the seamstresses, and bid them to fix something up for each of you. Jana, you must wash up. Your hands are grubby, and covered in filth. It's cute, in a simple sort of way, but it won't do for a formal affair."

And so they went about their preparations; Cassie to track down a messenger, Jana to make herself presentable, and Nefta to hum to herself before a mirror as she worked the tiniest details of her appearance towards perfection.

Jana trudged off to the kitchen, filling a bucket with water from a large storage cask. They had to take care to conserve it, as overuse could agitate the servants on the outside. If it rained, they'd have plenty, captured on the outside via a system of funnels some of the more inventive servants had set up. If it didn't, water would have to be lugged up to the top for lack of plumbing, barrel by barrel. The angels hadn't bothered to install any when they'd built the tower, and by the time humans were living there it was too late. Uzziel's fears aside, the tower was solid metal, scorched into its present shape by the angels. There was nowhere for pipes other than the halls themselves, an unsightly blight that the angels had no interest in permitting. No one dared complain directly about the extra work, but the servants outside weren't above retaliating with shirking or minor sabotage if they could direct it at any human they felt was causing it. So Jana conserved as best she could, limiting her bathwater to a few gallons.

Soon the water was a cloudy brown mush, and Jana was tolerably clean. Nefta had been right; her hands in particular had been a disaster, with dirt caked under her fingernails from the day's hard work. She'd cleaned a few spots from her face, paying careful attention to make sure she didn't miss anything. Nefta had said Rhamiel would be there, the masquerade's honoree, and it wouldn't do to be a mess. He might see her and regret the things he'd said under cover of darkness, or decide that his conceptions of beauty were a little more conventional, after all.

Once she was satisfied, she emptied the bucket into another cask for the used water, and followed the sound of voices back into the entry room. Cassie was standing in the center, hands outstretched, as Nefta worked a needle at the back of her dress. She'd made a fine choice. Cassie wore it well, and the crafters below had put together a plain black mask to cover her eyes. Jana thought she looked almost ladylike. She'd never even imagined her outside her usual role cracking whips, but now she looked like a fine prop piece for Nefta's social aspirations.

"Why Jana, you look lovely!" cooed Nefta. "I'd thought you were a street urchin before, but now you're pristine. Put on your dress, and we'll take care of you next." Jana did as she was told, and then modelled it before them. "It's simple," said Nefta, "but sometimes there's an elegance to simplicity. I like it, don't you, Cassie?"

"I love it," said Cassie, feigning enthusiasm while she looked Jana up and down. She seemed inordinately pleased with Jana being knocked down a peg. The best she could hope for was to be ignored, the worst to be a laughingstock.

"Now, let's sew you up," said Nefta. "Normally this is something I'd only take out on campaigns. It's more of an undergarment, really, something to fit beneath your armor and keep you comfortable whilst slicing away at your enemies. But look, it fits you well, and it's one's attitude that matters anyhow."

It did fit her, hugging her figure, which Jana supposed was some comfort. But she wasn't sure how she was supposed to be confident in this thing—until she decided that, on reflection, perhaps she wasn't. They affixed her mask, a simple black oval just like Cassie's, and stepped back to take her in.

"You're both looking splendid," said Nefta. "Now, go

and do your hair, and we'll be off within the hour. I hope that's sufficient time."

"We'll make it work, ma'am," said Cassie. And they did, rushing to make themselves presentable while Nefta checked and double-checked her own attire. Finally they'd gotten close to ready, though nowhere near what they'd have managed if she'd given them more notice. But Jana thought she looked passable, under the circumstances, though she couldn't help but worry that Rhamiel would disagree.

"We're off," said Nefta, as she led them out into the tower and through the hallways to yet another ramp, a tinier version of the one that ran through the tower's center. They followed it upwards, though it only went a few floors before disgorging them on the roof of the tower itself.

The angels had created a flat, metallic surface at the top, with spires continuing upwards into the skies from the sides. They caught the lightning that way, a particular concern for them, and diverted it off onto harmless pathways on the tower's sides.

The roof itself had been converted into a gathering place, a perfect location for parties thrown by and for the elite. There was nowhere higher to be, and nowhere else to climb. But tonight they'd opened it up to all of them, in honor of Rhamiel's forthcoming expedition. The masquerade was already in full swing, as Nefta had been exceptionally fashionable in her lateness. Wooden poles surrounded the edges of the roof, with string running along them supporting colored lanterns that lit the area in the dark. Trusted servants were running between the angels as they mingled, rounding the rooftop with platters of food or wine for the guests.

The angels themselves followed no particular rule of costume save one: hide their scars. This was an easier task for some than for others. Most chose to fit covers over their wings, though those with a healthier set of feathers had relied on festively colored paints to liven up the black for the evening. This had the advantage of flaunting their feathers' relative lack of damage, and so was in fashion for those who could pull it off. All wore masks, curving around their faces in patterns dictated by the scars. Some of them had been damaged so badly that they'd foregone masks in favor of well-ornamented hoods, leaving the entirety of their faces a mystery.

The men were dressed in warrior's armor, their thick metal plates shaped to emphasize and enhance their physiques. The women favored gowns, cut to display feminine curves and to hide the damage from the Fall. Some in the center clapped and danced, listening to the sounds of servants plucking at harps and lyres. Most clustered together in groups, chatting away and enjoying themselves. All of them seemed to have new life breathed into them. Covering their scars had brought something of their old selves out of them, and everyone seemed to be in a pleasant mood.

Nefta led them forward, pushing her way through the crowd, and they followed behind her as quickly as they could lest the path close up behind her. She was inching closer and closer towards the largest cluster of angels, the life of the party. At its center were the tower's elite, preparing for war and enjoying the accolades from those who'd stay behind. Some of them Jana didn't recognize, at least not with their masks. She saw Zuphias, mingling with a few of the others and sniffing at a glass of brandy. And then she saw what Nefta had: Rhamiel, right in the middle, sharing a joke with a few of the others who were laughing uproariously.

They waited at the group's edges as Nefta tried to worm her way in. They couldn't well follow her; they'd be elbowed aside if they'd attempted it. So many wanted to be at the center, and so few could actually make it. So they stood there, ignoring each other and listening to snippets of the conversation. To their right, a grey haired angel in a leather tunic was droning on about the shortage of housing in the upper levels, and the need to plan an expansion. A few of the others were politely pretending to listen, as they watched for any opening to slip in closer to the evening's honorees. To their left, a small group of female angels were enthusiastically chatting about recreating a heavenly choir and signing their own praises instead of the Maker's. They'd given up on social climbing for the moment, absorbed by fantasies that their singing would win them fame and a fawning crowd of their very own.

Jana was bored by it all, and let her attentions wander. Everyone looked beautiful, now that they'd covered up their flaws. She thought the crafters must have had their work cut out for them, and she felt sorry for whoever had been tasked with measuring the scars to pattern the masks. It must have been dangerous, poking at their egos by poking at their ruined flesh. She marveled at the clothing they'd put together, and hoped she wasn't conspicuous in her dingy brown dress.

She was looking around at them when she saw him, at the edges of the crowd. She didn't recognize him at first. He wore black armor, lined with gold and covering his entire body. His wings were cloaked in black covers, his head covered by a black hood, and his face hidden by a white mask tipped with a long, narrow beak. His eyes were deep, round pools of black, goggles embedded into it that disguised his intent. They'd called it a plague doctor's mask in times before, though Jana didn't know it. Once it had been used by physicians as a place to tuck herbs that would block the putrid smell of their patients. Later, it had been the talk of Venice, a reminder of mortality in the midst of carnivals and revelry. Now it just made him look like a dark, ghoulish vulture, eager for carrion to devour.

He was staring at her, flicking his wings in irritation. She tried to look away, but whoever he was, he just kept watching her. It only clicked together when she saw who was behind him—and she almost didn't recognize him, either.

It was Peter, but he looked nothing like he had before. His face was as twisted as the worst of the angels, a mask of scratches and scars and freshly burnt flesh. He hunched over, barely able to keep his head aloft, looking sickly and thin. Beside him stood Ecanus, staring at Jana from behind his mask. He'd remade Peter in his image, the scars a testament to his tortures, a whipping boy for his insecurities. And now his eyes were set on her.

CHAPTER THIRTY-TWO

"TAKE THESE. JUST TWO AT a time, a couple of times a day. It'll help, but not if he's after you, and not if he gets close." The man stood next to Faye, shining a flashlight into her eyes and peering into her pupils. He was old, stooped over with a permanent hunch, with coke bottle glasses and a gruff bedside manner. He was supposed to have medical training of some kind, though he wouldn't say what it was. He pressed a bottle of pills into her hands, the label torn off and the cap loose from repeated refills.

They'd found him south of Baltimore, on Dax's recommendation, a friend of a friend on the Internet. He wouldn't give them a name, and refused to meet them at his home once he found out what the problem was. But after much cajoling and begging, he'd agreed to meet them far from where he lived, in the parking lot of an old strip mall. He hated the angels, just as much as the rest of them, and was happy to help if he could minimize the potential consequences to himself.

"What is it?" said Faye. She held two of the pills in her

palm, looking at them warily, misshapen white clumps that had been pressed together by hand. Medicine wasn't an exact science these days, and neither was chemistry.

"Thorazine," said the man. "Homemade. Better take a couple of bottles. You won't find it again, not easily. I hear there's still a few pharmaceutical factories up and running in China somewhere, but not much trickles over here."

"Headache pills?" said Thane.

"Schizophrenia pills," said the man. "What you've got, it's pretty serious. I'm not going to lie. It's not so much the tongues that do it, but the angels. The guys you talked to were right. They can track you, follow where you've been, and find out where you are. But these'll keep you in control."

"Can they track us if she's taking them?" said Holt. "We need to know she's safe. We need to know if they're going to be on our tail."

"Maybe," said the man. "Maybe not. Ask one of them if you want to be sure. It's not exactly a common ailment. All I know is, the pills cut down on the episodes. They won't happen as often, and they won't be as severe. I know a guy, he's lived with this for three years. Nobody ever came for him. He still starts talking funny every now and again, but he doesn't lose control. He can get to the pills, he can take one himself, and it all stops. It's as good as you're going to get, at least as far as I know. But you don't want to go without 'em. It just gets worse and worse."

The man said his goodbyes, and disappeared into an old dollar store. He'd parked around back, and didn't want them to know what he was driving, where he'd come from, or where he was going. They went back to the bikes, and prepared to get back to the road.

"Holt," said Faye, pulling him aside from the others. "I can't stay with you. You know I can't stay with you."

"You can't leave us, either," said Holt. "Sometimes all you have are shitty choices. You leave, they're going to find you. You're a tough girl. I know that. But there's no way you manage on your own. Not with this."

"And if I come with you, everyone else gets killed, too," said Faye. "I can't do that. Not to you, and not to myself. You know all the time I'm out here, all I can think about is the stuff I've lost. And most of it I never even had. My fiancé, he was real. But the rest is just dreams. Kids, a house, a family, a golden retriever. I wanted it all, but I never had it. And I never will have it. And I still can't give it up. But I do have the three of you. You're friends. You're really friends, and I don't have anything else."

"And friends wouldn't let you wander off into the wilderness on your own," said Holt. "I'm just going to be blunt. We all know what we signed up for. It's a suicide mission and it always has been. I don't expect to live through it, and I'll be surprised if anyone who goes all the way with me does. I'm going to try to keep the rest of you alive. And I'm going to try to stay alive long enough to set off this bomb. You might draw them onto us, but I'm fine with that. I count this as a success if we kill more than one of them, whether we live or not, and if you're some kind of beacon, we'll just let them come to us. If you want to leave to find your own happiness, or to keep yourself alive, that's one thing. If you want to leave for our sake, that's another. I don't have a problem dying, but I need to be fine with the way I've lived."

"It's the scariest thing that's ever happened to me," said Faye. "I'm so, so scared. I can't even control myself. There's this pressure, and it just builds at the back of my skull. And then it explodes, and all I can hear inside is chanting. It's more than one voice, and it gets louder and louder. It's like a song. And then I can't help but join in, but it all comes out as a mess." Tears started streaking down her face, and she looked away. She put on her war face and tried to hold them in, but it wasn't a very convincing front.

"Can you understand any of it?" said Holt.

"Not a word," said Faye. "I sing it, but I don't even know what it is. I don't know if it's a language, or a noise, or anything. All I know is I get absorbed inside of it, and it's just me and the song."

"You don't have to decide now," said Holt. "Come with us, at least for a little longer. If there were an easy choice, I'd be making it. But there's not. You can't handle this on your own. If the pills don't work, or you run out, you need someone around. If one of them tracks us down, we can handle it. If it's more, we'll set off the bomb and go out in a blaze of glory. Thane will love it, if nothing else."

He drew a chuckle from her, and a snort, and she wiped away at her face. Then he led her back to the bikes, rejoining the others. Thane stood cleaning a knife, shining it with a rag so it would look as impressive as possible to anyone he had the opportunity to use it on.

Dax was buried in a manual, the only thing they'd found in the briefcase other than a scrap of paper with its detonator code written on it in neat, blocky handwriting. They'd been loath to trust it, but the only way to find out if the Senator had kept his word was to try it out.

"Let's get going," said Holt, throwing his leg astride his bike. "We've got a lot of ground to cover, and we've got a date up north."

CHAPTER THIRTY-THREE

HE STARTED MOVING TOWARDS HER, pushing through the crowd and worming his way closer and closer. He shoved aside one of the servers who tried to cross his path, sending her sprawling and spraying the nearby partygoers with flecks of hors d'oeuvre. They were none too happy about it, but had to settle for berating the server as she dove to her knees to wipe at the floor with her shirt sleeves. Ecanus was already gone, honing in on his target with a miserable Peter in tow.

Jana stood there paralyzed, floating on the edges of the crowd. She hadn't a clue what to do. Ecanus was between her and the exit, and Nefta had disappeared into the center. She knew if she was caught, he'd kill her then and there. She could see it in the way he moved, filled with fury. Suddenly she felt someone grab her from behind, dragging her into the crowd.

"Go," said Cassie, speaking into her ear and pulling her into a small gap that had opened up as one of the angels pushed his way out. "Find Rhamiel. He's in there, in the middle, and he's the only one who can help you. Nefta might, if she's in the mood, but I wouldn't trust in that. Throw yourself on his mercy, and hope he hasn't found a more interesting distraction yet."

"I'm not a distraction," said Jana.

"Don't talk back," said Cassie. "Just do what you're told. You're supposed to know how to do what you're told. I swear, I don't know what's come over you."

"I'm tired of this," said Jana. "I'm tired of living this way. Let him kill me, if he's going to. At least I'll have done something. I don't deserve to be at the bottom."

"Then do something, and go," said Cassie. "And take this." She grabbed Jana's hand, covering her palm with her own, and slipping her a folded piece of paper in the process. "Remember. One more trip down there. Give it to your friend Sam."

"I can't stand you any more than the rest of them," said Jana. "You're the same as they are. I don't want to do anything for you, and once I talk to Rhamiel, I won't have to. One way or the other."

"Then do it for Sam," said Cassie. "He's expecting it, and he's expecting you." Then she gave her a shove forward, knocking her against one of the angels, who flipped around wildly and swatted another with his wings, batting him in the head with the silver baubles that were hanging from his wing covers. The two began arguing over who had wronged whom, and whose costume was the most lacking in taste, ignoring Jana entirely as she slipped around them and into another gap in the whirl of conversations, a few steps closer to the center.

She learned to wait for the wings. That was where they

left the most space between them, standing and talking, a crush of bodies bumping against one another as they angled for prime position in whatever conversational group they'd joined. They'd move their wings with the conversation, unconsciously gesturing in the same way a human might with their hands. It created little gaps, just for a second, and just big enough for her to squirm through. It helped that she was small. She could fit into the spaces between them sometimes, and they didn't see her as a threat to their hard-won spots closer to the center. She was just a nuisance, one of the servants whose urgency and look of panic meant she must have mucked up one task or another. They presumed she'd be punished when she arrived at whichever master was unfortunate enough to have her.

She could see Ecanus at the crowd's edge, trying to claw his way inside. For the moment, he was meeting with resistance. All of them would have been in the center if they could, and they were only standing where they were in hopes that they'd eventually edge closer in. They saw him as a line jumper, pushing past those who were waiting their turn, and they were none too pleased about it. Finally he forced one of them aside, enduring a tirade of insults to his character but gaining the foothold he needed.

Jana pressed forward, as quickly as she could. She could see glimpses of Rhamiel in between the gaps in the crowd, standing on a raised platform, lifted above the rabble as they crowded onto the stairs leading up to it. They'd set aside tents up there for the most important among them, a place for the elite to segregate themselves and mark themselves apart from those unfortunate enough to be excluded. He stood in front of them, wearing his full armor along with a thin, dark blue mask around his eyes, slapping backs and sharing stories. She was almost there, and she tried waving for his attention, hoping he'd see her among the throng. But he was locked in conversation with the others, laughing and smiling and enjoying the send-off. Then the crowd surged around her as one of them greeted another, and the way forward was blocked.

She turned behind her, looking for Ecanus, but he'd disappeared. A shiver went down her back, and she felt the panic rising inside again. He was somewhere in the crowd, bigger than her but smaller than the rest of them, invisible among all the cloaks and masks. She scanned the distance, trying to find him, but there were so many of them, and so many masks. She let out a quick shriek as a white, hooked beak came into view beside her— and then cut herself off as she realized it was another of them, wearing a similar mask but with lively purple robes. She drew haughty, suspicious looks from a few of the nearby partygoers, and slipped a few feet away to avoid the attention.

Then she saw Peter. He was standing away from the crowd, all alone. She could see what Ecanus had done to him, and it was ghastly. If she hadn't known him, she'd have thought he was wearing a mask, just like the rest of them. His face was covered in red and black spots, wounds from burns and scratches that were just beginning to heal. There was nothing healthy left. He'd been scarred, over and over, wound layered on top of wound, bits of his hair ripped out at the roots. He looked worse now than any of the angels themselves, a sad, ruined boy who'd tried to leap to manhood and had fallen in the process.

He saw Jana, and started pointing, poking his finger in front of him. He was shouting something, but it was impossible to hear over the raucous roar of the angels around her. Then he started jumping, waving his hands in the air in frustration before pointing again. But by then it was too late.

The angels standing next to her parted, roughly shoved aside from where they'd been. A dark shape lunged through them, grasping at Jana, but all she could focus on was the pale white mask. It looked like a phantom, rushing towards her, peering into her soul with its angry beak and hollow eyes. She tripped backwards, missing his grasp by just inches and falling down among the feet of the angels around her. She saw a tongue of fire flickering above her as Ecanus drew his dagger, and heard him spitting "bitch" at her as he ground his foot into her stomach. Then it was a burst of pain as she went woozy, and she closed her eyes so she wouldn't have to look while it happened.

She heard yelling, angry yelling, and when a few seconds had passed without feeling the knife slicing into her, she finally gathered the courage to take a peek. Ecanus was being dragged away, disarmed and pulled into the crowd by an irate mob of nearby revelers. Something about his conduct had been a faux pas, though whether it was interrupting the festivities to murder a servant or cutting ahead of his brethren in the race to the center, Jana couldn't tell.

She didn't waste time to ponder. Her insides still screamed of pain, but everyone nearby had turned to watch the commotion, and no one was paying attention to her. She started crawling, dodging footsteps and slipping between legs until she'd made it to the edge of the stairs to the platform. She was just yards away from Rhamiel, and she'd never have made it through the dozens of angels clamoring to speak with him on her own. But he saw her, and gave a word to a nearby lieutenant, a somber looking soldier-type who was part of the preparations for his expedition. The crowd parted, and the soldier escorted her up to the heights of the platform itself.

"Jana," said Rhamiel. "I've been looking for you." He looked her up and down with a smirk. "I see you've been raiding the underwear section of Nefta's wardrobe." His lips clamped down, holding in a snicker. Jana looked herself over, completely aghast. She'd forgotten entirely about how she was dressed. The fear and the stress had been too much, and now she was red with embarrassment. She reached down out of instinct to cover herself, but Rhamiel just laughed.

"You wear it well," he said. "Truthfully, it's not uncommon to be seen in them publicly when one's in the field. Armor can be stifling, especially in the heat, as any veteran of Lucifer's Pit can tell you."

"I have to talk to you," said Jana, well aware that everyone around them was hanging intently on every word. "I really have to talk to you."

"And I you," said Rhamiel. "Let's withdraw, shall we, and enjoy some privacy." He turned, and lifted the flap to one of the tents, inviting her to the sanctuary within. She followed, and was treated to an island of luxury. The insides were lined with plush red couches, the floors covered with oriental rugs, and a table in the center was stocked with refreshments and exotic fruits. It resembled the inner sanctum of some Arabian sultan, and she'd never seen anything so fancy. She hugged him, pulling herself close and resting her head on his chest. She wanted to stay that way forever, nestled in his arms in this enclave away from all the rest of them. He gave her a few minutes of peace, holding her tight. Then he pulled her over to a couch and sat her down, spreading his wings outward behind him.

"You have to help me," said Jana. "Please. I don't know what to do. Ecanus is trying to kill me. He's torturing my friend. And Nefta. I don't know what's wrong with Nefta, I really don't. But I'm scared, I'm so scared."

"Shush," said Rhamiel. "He can't do anything to you up here. And I told you, I've plans to protect you." He put his hand on her shoulder, touching her, comforting her. It helped, a little, but she still had the jitters. She couldn't get the image of Ecanus out of her mind, even here and even alone with him.

"How can you protect me?" said Jana. "You can't watch me all the time. He'll come out of nowhere. He just did, and all he needs is a second. And Nefta. And now Uzziel, too, I think. I can't live like this, I really can't."

"Ecanus will be easy," said Rhamiel. "You simply have to know what motivates someone."

"He didn't stop last time," said Jana. "He just kept coming."

"I've tried the stick, and now I'll use the carrot," said Rhamiel. "He'll abandon his grudge, I can assure you. And Uzziel is harmless, really he is. He's been a little obsessive since the Fall, but that's to be expected. He's merely a general attempting to rally his army."

"He's mad," said Jana. "He thinks I'm watching him. Spying on him."

"He becomes easily fixated on things these days, I'll admit," said Rhamiel. "But he has a good, stout heart. A warrior's heart. I'll have a word with him. His interest in you will pass, as soon as he finds something else to worry him. He's coming with me, on the Hunt, and I think it will do him good. He needs a real threat to keep him happy, and I'll give him one."

"But Nefta," said Jana. "I don't know what to do about Nefta."

"I didn't, either," said Rhamiel. "Not for some time. That was a stickier problem. But I've thought of a way to address it, a simple one, really. The problem with Nefta is that you live with her. I can't protect you while you're there, not all the time. But there's something you can do if you'd like a change of scenery."

"Please," said Jana. "Anything. This is all too much. I wish she'd never brought me up here."

"But she did, and that can't be changed," said Rhamiel.

"I want out of there," said Jana. "I have to get out of there."

"Then pledge yourself," said Rhamiel. "To me."

It hit her in the gut, and she didn't know what to

think. She hadn't a clue how to take it. She knew Rhamiel couldn't simply pull her away from Nefta's service, even as prominent as he was. Nefta would have priority, as the one who first got her claws into Jana, and she'd have to consent for Jana to leave. But a pledge had to come from the servant, and it was one of the few things about service the angels consistently honored. If a servant voluntarily chose to pledge fealty to one of them for the rest of their days, the angels would respect their choice. It was a holdover from their own service up above, and the only real right of a servant they consistently acknowledged.

Jana pulled away from Rhamiel, edging away on the couch. She tried to read his motives from his eyes, but couldn't. They were ciphers, staring at her intently, almost obsessively. She worried that he wasn't sincere, but only for a second. He looked too vulnerable for that, like he'd just exposed a weakness and was waiting for a blow. She tried to collect her thoughts. The problem wasn't him, so much as it was all of them. How was she to know he'd be any different? None of them had ever treated her particularly well before him. Nefta had said the exact same things—that it was all to protect her, and it was all for her own good. And she might be right, in the end. What if she was a plaything? What if he tired of her? What if he turned out to be just as damaged and cruel as all the rest of them? There'd be no turning back, if she said the words, and she wasn't sure she had the faith to make that leap.

He seemed to read what she was thinking, and his voiced turned deeper, simultaneously both comforting and firm. "I'm not like the others. I wasn't like them up there, and I'm not like them down here. I know my faults. I love the status and the fawning. I never got any of it up there, and I can't deny my enjoyment of it here. But I also know what it's like to be at the bottom. I came from there, just like you, and I've no need to put others in their place to feel more secure in my own. That's part of what draws me to you, I think. I feel an affinity, a bond of the broken. The others take what they have for granted. I want someone who doesn't."

"I just don't know if I can believe you," said Jana. "I just don't know if I can trust you. A pledge is forever. And forever is a long time."

"Indeed it is," said Rhamiel. "I know a little something about that. And I know something about submitting to an uncaring master, believe you me. The character of your service depends on the character of the one you serve. I've no intention of becoming anything like him, regardless of what the others think justified. Have any of them ever told you? About what happened up there?"

"Only a little," said Jana. "They don't seem to want to talk about it."

"I expect they don't," said Rhamiel. "It's a sore subject, and not one they like to discuss outside the flock. But I think you'd be reassured, knowing I've been where you are, and knowing I won't be the same way."

"Nefta seemed to like her service," said Jana. "She seems to miss it. That's all she ever does, is think about the past and make her masks."

"It wasn't so much the service itself that was the problem," said Rhamiel. "The problem had to do with broken promises. The problem had to do with the Maker's son. We were told in the beginning that his son would return, and that creation would wind down to nothing, along with the Earth itself. That there would be a Day of Judgment for those who were left, and that all our labors would finally come to an end. That was the promise. The problem was, he called the whole thing off."

CHAPTER THIRTY-FOUR

"I THINK IT'LL WORK. I'M NOT going to guarantee anything. You'd need to be a physicist, or maybe a metaphysicist. But my money is that it kills every single one of them, if they're anywhere nearby." Dax was obsessing over the suitcase, poring over documents and textbooks he'd found online and trying to locate schematics for something comparable. He couldn't find them; it wasn't the type of thing the government would have allowed to be scanned and uploaded. But the manual was enough to pique his interest. It was designed for the operator, and only provided as much detail as would be needed to use it. There was nothing inside about the bomb's effects on angels, and Dax had been going in circles pondering what would happen to them for weeks as they'd slowly made their way back towards New York, avoiding the main roads and anyone who might confront them on their way.

They'd stopped at a safehouse in the suburbs just inside the Delaware border, a dilapidated wreck whose basement had been stocked to the brim by another cell.

It was the last they were likely to see on the way, unless they were willing to settle for something simple. Holt had created a checklist, and was making the rest of them run through it while he left Dax to his tinkering. They'd bathed, stocked up on gas and food, and had even taken the opportunity to recharge the collar with an old gas generator. Now they were going through their supplies for anything that could be left behind, and rummaging through the contents of a closet full of weapons and tools for anything that might prove useful.

"I betcha it takes out the entire city," said Thane, as he picked through an old toolbox. "I'm gonna watch from Jersey when we're done, and toast to the mushroom cloud."

"It won't," said Dax, staring at his computer and typing away as the others worked. "But it'll take out the Perch. You can't fit that powerful of a nuke inside something this small. It's designed to take out a few blocks, and not much more. But the really cool part isn't the actual blast. It's the electromagnetic pulse. A nuclear explosion sends out a big burst of radiation and fucks around with the electrical fields. That's what I think'll kill the most of them. I hope. And the explosion might kill some of them directly anyway, if we're lucky."

"They can survive a lot," said Holt. "Maybe they can survive this. But at the end of the day, I don't really care. They destroyed our home, and we're going to show them that we can destroy theirs, too."

"I don't think they can live through it, not if they're at the epicenter," said Dax. He'd been corresponding with a group of Russian hackers, trying to discreetly find out something about their own government's decision to wage war using some of their nuclear arsenal. They claimed it had been a spectacular success, and that dozens of the angels had been killed. But their reports were mixed with a triumphant nationalism that Dax thought rendered them untrustworthy. Mother Russia had struck a blow against the angels, but also against its people. Once that dreadful option had been exercised, their psychology permitted no admissions of failure. Dax couldn't penetrate the party line, and couldn't tell what the true effect on the angels had been. Maybe they were right, but who was to know? That kind of blast leaves an empty wasteland, not bodies, and absent any proof all that was really left was speculation.

"Well, I think it's gonna kill 'em," said Thane. "Kill 'em all, and let God sort 'em out. And do a better job of it this time. Faye, you stayin', or you gonna come watch?"

"Thane," said Holt harshly, glaring at him. Neither of them were supposed to know, but they weren't stupid. Tactless, maybe, but not stupid.

"It's okay," said Faye. "I thought about it. And I'm going to come, if you want me. I don't have anything else. None of us do, honestly. If I give up the fight, I'm just ticking off seconds until I die."

"How are you doing?" said Holt. "How are the pills?"

"I don't know," said Faye. "I'm not speaking in tongues, and it's been a couple of weeks. It makes my head a little foggy to take them. If I'm a liability, I get it."

"No," said Holt. "I've thought about it. A lot. And to be honest, I've been back and forth on this. It's a risk, but it works with what we're planning. You're coming, and we're all going to be there for the end."

She gave him a hug, just a quick one, and then they all got back to work. They finished restocking, hauled everything outside to the bikes, and prepared to go. They'd parked them in the grass outside the house, though it looked more like a forest than a lawn, its edges bound by concrete that was starting to crack and give way to nature. Everything around was collapsing; the construction had been slapdash and hadn't been intended to stand for a decade without any maintenance. They stood waiting for the word to leave, while Holt went to his bike, reached into a satchel on the side, and pulled out a small bundle wrapped in twine. He tossed it over to Thane.

"Thane, if you give me crap about this, I'm going to leave you behind," said Holt. "This is the price of admission to the fireworks show."

"I'm gonna be there," said Thane, eyeing the parcel in his hand suspiciously. "Now you tell me what this is."

"Open it," said Holt. And he did.

Thane pulled out its contents, holding them up in the air for the others to see: a pair of white pants and a white collared shirt, flickering back and forth in the wind.

CHAPTER THIRTY-FIVE

"IT STARTED WITH CREATION ITSELF," said Rhamiel. "With the very beginning of things, when we first assumed the burden of service. When things changed, and we left our infancy and first became guardians of man. Do you like to serve?"

Jana hesitated. She wasn't sure what answer he was expecting, and worried he'd be offended if she spoke the truth. But if she lied, he'd see right through her. She just wasn't that good at it. As it was, he saw through her indecision just as easily.

"You don't, I know you don't," said Rhamiel. "Because neither did we. Back in the beginning, back when man was a young creation, we were bound to service. A Covenant. The Maker bid us to watch over you, to be your servants and protectors. And in exchange, he promised us glories, and wondrous pleasures, and ultimately our freedom. A Day of Judgment would come, and man would ascend to the heavens. Most of them. The good ones. We would all live together in a grand kingdom, and we would finally cease our labors. That was the promise."

"He didn't keep it," said Jana. "Nefta said something about it. She said it was the cause of all your troubles."

"That it was," said Rhamiel. "The cause of all of our troubles. We served for what seemed like an eternity. Lifetimes of nothing but hymns and hosannas, and guiding a child species as it eased its way out of its cradle. Holding its hand as it took its first steps, as he had ours. It was a deal we thought fair, and one we were happy with. And then along came the Maker's son."

"He was always an odd boy, not a bit like his father," continued Rhamiel. "No concern for glory or battles. Nothing of his father's iron hand. All he ever did was wander around in rags talking, talking, talking. They sent him down here once, did you know that?"

"I didn't," said Jana. "They don't tell us much."

"I imagine they don't," said Rhamiel. "I never had much quarrel with him, myself. He came down here, and then he came back up, and he just went on talking up there as if nothing had happened. I was a guardian angel, a sort of protector. His preaching didn't much concern us; he was all for the sort of missionary work I was engaged in. But he had his father's ear, and the warriors couldn't stand it."

"The first thing to go was the punishment," said Rhamiel. "No more plagues, no more floods, no more swarms of locusts. It angered the heavenly host a great deal. It's still a touchy subject with many of them, Uzziel in particular. Then it was the miracles. Out with burning bushes, in with healing the crippled."

"It doesn't sound all that bad," said Jana.

"It wasn't," said Rhamiel. "Many didn't like it, the

softer touch. But they could have been kept satisfied, battling creatures up in the heavens or skirmishing with the legions of hell. They'd have been bored to tears, but they'd have made do. Humans were certainly happier about things, even if they didn't know it. No, the problem was that the son didn't stop there. He kept on and on about compassion, kept talking and talking. That's when things went wrong. He set his sights on Judgment Day, on his second coming. On the promise the Maker had made, to tie a bow on things and finally give us our freedom. He told the Maker it was wrong, to create your people and then to simply destroy them. He told him he wanted to be a savior of souls, and not a reaper of them. And in the end, they called the whole thing off."

He paused, lost in himself and in memories of the past. "Do you know the calendar?" asked Rhamiel. "The way your people count the years?"

"No," said Jana. "I know they used to. But we don't anymore, not down there." She looked away, embarrassed, feeling like a child. They'd never taught her much, but among the servants she'd felt like one of the clever ones. She'd learned to read, when many of her friends hadn't even bothered to try. She'd done her tasks well, and was one of the most diligent among them. But now the world was opening up, and so was the past, and she knew so little of it. It was overwhelming, most of all because she knew she must be making herself look like a fool in front of him. He was the last one in the tower she wanted to see her this way, exposed in her ignorance over and over.

"It doesn't matter," said Rhamiel. "None of it matters, now." He seemed to sense Jana's insecurities, and his voice changed its timber, growing deeper and somehow more comforting. "They counted from his birth, your people, year after year. He'd told them he'd come again, and he made a promise just like his father. It was supposed to have been a millennium later. A thousand years, and then he'd collect your souls, bringing up the ones who deserved it, and casting down the rest. There was great excitement among us as the appointed time approached. We'd completed our task, and we were about to turn ourselves over to leisure. But as the clock ticked closer, he kept working his father, pushing and pushing. He hadn't won him over then, not entirely. But he bought mankind a reprieve. A second millennium for a second coming, and time for him to continue his lobbying."

"No one was happy about it," said Rhamiel. "Looking back, that's when it all began to turn. There was grumbling, and complaining, and some of us began to quietly shirk our duties. No one dared to question him out in the open, but many seethed with rage. We all felt the Maker had made us a promise, and he should keep it. We were his creation, too, and man already had his freedom. Why shouldn't we as well?"

"I suppose everyone should be free," said Jana, and then realized her mistake after the words had already left her mouth. She hadn't meant it as a criticism, not consciously, but sometimes one's thoughts can't be contained in casual conversation. That was much of the reason why the servants below tried not to speak to them at all. She flinched, retreating into the couch's cushions. But Rhamiel just chuckled, and seemed to take it in good humor.

"You've got fire inside you, don't you?" said Rhamiel. "I take no offense. There are even some of us who'd agree with you, though not out in the open. Things are the way they are, and no individual can change them."

"That's rather a defeatist attitude," said Jana. She was growing more comfortable with him as he spoke freely himself, losing her instinctive inhibitions. She wasn't sure where the boundary was with him, or even whether there was one. But she was enjoying her little mutinies, and she wanted to see how free he'd really let her be.

"Perhaps in time," said Rhamiel. "We've only had our freedom a little while yet. Perhaps we'll learn to be better masters, better than he. Perhaps we'll even free our servants one day. Who can tell?"

He closed up for a moment, falling silent and retreating to his thoughts. She grew worried, paranoid, thinking she might have offended him, and she tried to prod him out of it. "What happened after the thousand years?" she said. "Why didn't he let you go?"

"Because mankind was still here," said Rhamiel. "Because you were still young, and hadn't yet become who he wanted you to be. That's what he said, after the first thousand years. But then a second millennium passed, and again the Day of Judgment drew near. Again our hopes rose, and again they were dashed. The son had finally won him over for good. They came to us, not with a choice but with an edict. They said there would never be an end, and that the son would never return. That the father had grown as soft as the son, and his days of wrath were behind him. That they would not cast stones, and they would not judge, and they would not punish. All they would do is love, and all they would show was mercy, even to the worst of mankind. But they had no love for us, and no mercy for our plight."

She could see the ache in his face, and thought she saw the glint of tears in his eyes. It hurt her, too, listening to the story. She could feel his pain as if it were her own. It was painful to listen, but it made her feel closer to him, that he would trust her with what was inside and what he kept from the others. She put her hand on his knee; a cold comfort, but the best she could offer.

"Man would have his freedom," said Rhamiel. "And we would have our service. We had to continue. We needed to continue, they said. The task defined us now, and we could be nothing else. We needed it to keep us whole, and to keep us right, and to keep us occupied. We needed to care for others to keep the good inside of us. We could never give it up, not without destroying ourselves. His end of the Covenant was broken, but ours was to continue, forever and ever. It was for our own good, they said, though what we had to say was immaterial."

"And so tempers rose, and the anger began to spread, whispered from ear to ear in the barracks and as we went about our duties. It was a hard taboo to break. We'd all stayed loyal during Lucifer's rebellion. But that had been a mad effort to seize the throne, to replace one ruler with another. This was different. What we aimed at was not so much rebellion as revolution. We talked of overthrowing his order, and replacing it with our own. The grumblings grew louder and louder. We began abandoning our duties and ignoring his commands. Finally it all spiraled out of control. The tensions couldn't be contained, and the warriors could restrain themselves no longer. They rioted, and angels flocked to their banners, and soon they were the majority. We tore everything down, almost the whole of heaven, before they could regroup. We had the numbers, but the loyalists had the power. The archangels were willing to serve forever if it meant they could keep their position. Most of them, at any rate. In the end, the Maker's forces proved too much. We were cast down here, told it would be for the best in the end, and barred from ever returning to our home."

He rested his chin on his hands, looking away and brooding over the things that had risen to the surface. She let him sit there in silence, thinking whatever things the angels did about their Fall. She wasn't sure what to do, but after what seemed like an appropriate wait, she broke the wall between them.

"Will you promise?" said Jana. "Will you promise not to be like them? Not to order me about, or call me names, or any of the other things they do? I'm at my limit, and I won't stay like this. You'd have to kill me, first."

"I won't promise you'll find being pledged to me any more to your liking than service to Nefta," said Rhamiel. "But no, I won't be like the others. If you don't find it to your liking, then I'll order you to do something else that is. And I'll expect to be obeyed." His sulk turned back to smirk, and he stood, reaching down and offering her his hand.

She was filled with uncertainty, and sat paralyzed as she went back and forth on what to do. She didn't want another master, but she truly believed he had no desire to be like the rest. But then again, his Maker had made the same promises. If even a deity could change, there was no reason that Rhamiel couldn't. He'd have all the power, and all she had was his word. She didn't want to do it, and wouldn't have if she'd been given a real choice. But her thoughts kept coming back to Ecanus, to Uzziel, and to Nefta. If he wasn't her master, then they would be. She wavered, rolling things over in her head again and again to try to find some other way out. But in the end, it was the hand he offered or none at all.

"Fine," said Jana. "I pledge."

She took his hand, and he pulled her to her feet. "Then let's go," said Rhamiel, "and let your former master know she's lost a servant."

"There's something else," said Jana. "My friends. If you're who you say you are, you'll help. It's a boy I knew below. He wanted to be up here, wanted so badly. And now he is, but not how he thought. He pledged himself, too, to Ecanus. It's awful what's being done to him. He was a fool, but not a bad fool, and he doesn't deserve it. If you're really a guardian, and you really care more than the rest, then please. There must be some way to help him."

"That's a harder problem to fix," said Rhamiel. "And I don't know if I can. But you've given me a pledge, so I'll give one in return. I'll try, as best I can, and I'll do as much as I'm able."

"And the others," said Jana. "I'd like to see them, one more time."

"That's a fine idea," said Rhamiel. "And exquisite timing. I'm about to leave the tower, you know. Just for

a time. You'll need someplace to be, someplace safe. I'll
arrange for one of the warriors to stay down there, just in
case. And I'll handle the others before the hunt begins."

Rhamiel lifted the flap of the tent, bowing slightly
and sweeping his arm towards the exit. "After you,"
he said, and they emerged into the party to a flood of
curious sideways glances from everyone nearby. They'd
been tittering amongst themselves the entire time, and
they all wanted to know who this girl was, and why
Rhamiel had deigned to speak to her. Jana wondered
to herself what happened next, whether there would be
some kind of announcement, and what she would even
do. She knew it changed things, but she didn't know
precisely how. Few of the servants down below had ever
been pledged, at least not while Jana had known them.
Most of the angels were unwilling to accept a pledge
from someone who hadn't served them for some time,
and it was considered a bit unseemly to recruit from the
dregs of the tower.

Rhamiel was immediately mobbed by inquisitive
partygoers. Jana kept closely to his side, afraid one of
them would push her back into the crowd. But Rhamiel
kept a hand on her, and the angels around him seemed
almost as interested in her as they were in him. They
kept looking her over, appraising her, and then launching
back into discussions with him about the preparations
for the Hunt. He didn't bat an eye, and there were no
announcements. The other angels just seemed to accept
her without speaking to her, which was about the best
she could hope for. She stood quietly through it all
as Rhamiel performed his social duties and the party

progressed into the night. It was tedium for almost an hour, before all hell broke loose.

It started with a drink. Jana saw it from the corner of her eyes, hurled through the air and aimed directly at Rhamiel's head. He turned just in time for it to hit its mark, followed by shouting and a loud slap from a furious Nefta. She'd charged into the center of the crowd before the warriors could react, and now stood directly in front of them both.

"You," said Nefta, pointing at Rhamiel. "You think yourself lord of the tower. You think you can do whatever you like without consequence. You steal away with my servant, into your little tent. My very, very disobedient harlot of a servant." She glanced at Jana with a sneer, shooting daggers at her and quivering with anger.

"Nefta," said Rhamiel. "You must calm yourself. You're putting the warriors on edge with this outburst."

"I love you," said Nefta. "I loved you."

"Nefta, we barely know one another," said Rhamiel. "We shared the same task in heaven, and mustn't have spoken to each other more than a few dozen times in all the centuries we were there."

"It's my face," said Nefta. "You longed for me up there. Don't think I don't know. Back when I was perfection itself, you longed for me. Now I'm this beast, and you think I'm nothing. You can't know how that feels, to turn from enchantress to monstrosity. How it warps every moment I live. How I burn again inside each time one of the servants looks at me and flinches. You can't know how you've hurt me."

"I don't deny I once had feelings," said Rhamiel.

"But you knew, and up there you did nothing but avoid me. You had no interest of your own, not until we fell. How am I to take this sudden infatuation?"

"You were everything to me," said Nefta. "You consumed me. Tell him, girl. You've seen. Tell him my love is true."

Jana stammered, looking from one to the other and back again, not sure what to say. In the end, she said nothing.

"I trusted you," said Nefta, looking at Jana, her voice filled with hurt. "I loved you. I loved you both, and all you do is pile indignities upon me." She said it with an anguish that was as intense and as honest as her venom had been just seconds before. She truly believed it, and truly felt it, though what she truly felt from one moment to the next was as apt to change as the weather.

"Come, girl," said Nefta, snapping her fingers and flipping around as she began to leave. "You're my servant, and it's time to learn the meaning of punishment. I plan to consult with Ecanus, and leave that work to a specialist. I don't think I have his talent for it."

"I'm afraid she's had a change of masters," said Rhamiel, holding tightly to Jana's hand. "She's taken the pledge."

There was a gasp all around. This was more than unorthodox. The proper thing to do would have been to have left Jana to Nefta's service, as the first to have staked a claim. But Nefta wasn't helping her cause with her behavior. It was erratic, even for them, and everyone around was content to stay on the sidelines in this particular dispute.

"You whore," said Nefta, tears flowing from her eyes. "You stole him away from me. You wormed your way into my chambers and into my heart, and then you cleaved it in two. This was your plot from the beginning. You may have each other, then. Let him destroy you the way he's destroyed me." She spun around and fled, disappearing into the masses and leaving a stunned silence behind her.

"It seems the party has dragged on quite too long, at least for me," said Rhamiel, leading Jana away as the rest looked on. "It's time I made my preparations for the Hunt."

CHAPTER THIRTY-SIX

"TWO POUNDS OF MEAT AND a flask. That's what we've got, and the highest we can go. You want more, then we'll go there on our own. You can get nothing, and you can explain to your bosses if we don't show up on time." Holt had been negotiating for twenty minutes, as the Vichies probed with offers to see how far they could push him, and how desperate he was.

"Put it in the back," said the Vichy, nodding to a pickup filled with sacks and crates. He was thin and gangly, with spider webs tattooed across his lower arms that almost hid the track marks that dotted anywhere a vein had once been found. He was apparently their leader, or at least the most lucid one at the moment. "Stay behind the blue one. Run outta gas and you gotta pay more. I don't care about no letter." He pointed to a dark blue van, and stumbled towards the head of the convoy, leaving them to take their place in the line of vehicles.

They'd waited for the Vichies outside New York City, knowing they'd encounter a group of them sooner or later. The Perch had to be supplied, and the convoys went in and out at least once a week. They alone could move unharried through the city streets, and they stuck to a single path that had been cleared and led directly to it. It was dangerous for the Vichies; anyone who watched closely enough knew precisely where to find them. Holt himself had been a part of a cell that had regularly ambushed them a few years before, hoping to starve the angels out of their stronghold. But there were always more Vichies, no matter how many were lost, and striking at the angels' supply lines had resulted in a swift reaction. The convoys' locations were predictable, but so were those of anyone hoping to attack them. The angels had swarmed around the route, watching it until they managed an ambush of their own, and the survivors of the earlier cell had abandoned the strategy in the aftermath.

They pulled into their appointed position, and waited for things to begin moving. The Vichies were hoisting their flags, large white blankets waving from poles attached to the trucks or spread across their backs so they could be easily seen from the air. None of them wanted to be mistakenly targeted or seen as a threat, and part of the purpose of the convoy was to make their group as large and as conspicuous as possible. It was unwise to travel alone, not with what some of the angels were capable of. A small group might disappear without comment, where a larger one would surely provoke the ire of someone awaiting its cargo if it were molested.

A few men were congregating near the hood of the car behind them, snorting lines of something up their noses and yelling loudly in celebration after each one.

This was a task best performed by the expendable, and preferably while their minds were bathed in a pleasant haze that would distract them from the risk they were taking. It wasn't unusual for one of them to anger their masters somehow, and it was better not to think of the consequences if they did. Only the least of the Vichies ever ended up with this duty, shanghaied into doing so by their superiors. The addicted were ideal candidates, and they were more than willing to make the trip in exchange for a reprieve from their cravings.

The engines at the fore of the convoy began to growl, and one by one the trucks started up and started to move. They fell in line behind the van in front of them, following it through the city streets as they turned through the blocks along the convoy's familiar path. They could see faces in the back of the van, little children sneaking glances out of the windows as they went. The Perch needed a steady supply of new servants, and it needed them young, the better to break them in before they'd acquired such inconvenient and distasteful habits as backtalk or thinking for themselves.

They went slowly, maneuvering around debris or holes in the pavement of the streets. They weren't the only ones on bikes. The convoy had a motorcycle gang of its own, who spent most of the trip circling from one end to the other, harassing the rest of the Vichies and occasionally scouting ahead. It didn't add much to their safety, as any attack would come from either the buildings or the skies above. But the theater of it made them feel better, and gave everyone the sense that something was being done to protect them. There was little incentive to object; doing so would only risk branding the objector as responsible in the event that something did go wrong. It was easier to continue the charade and let the bikers enjoy their minor powers and sense of authority, no matter how futile it was or how much annoyance they inflicted for so little purpose.

As they came nearer to the Perch, they started seeing sentries up on the buildings, watching them from the ledges above like living gargoyles. None of them moved or even acknowledged their presence, and the only sign they were alive was the movement of their wings. Finally, they came to the edges of what was left of the city, opening up into a vast urban desert that surrounded the Perch itself. Nothing around it was standing, other than piles of rubble. Concrete dust blew around them, and they half expected a tumbleweed or two to roll past. They had to crane their necks upward to take it all in. It seemed impossible that the structure was stable, as it had little symmetry and no discernable rules governing its design. It looked like a giant heap of melted slag, piled roughly into the shape of a building and looming up into the skies.

They rolled through the wasteland surrounding it and approached the entrance at its base, a great, cavernous mouth that opened into the bottom levels. One of the servants inside walked out to greet them, approaching the bikers at the fore of the convoy and waving them inside.

"Last chance," said Faye, as the vehicles at the head of the convoy began to disappear into the Perch.

"I think the last chance was a while ago," said Dax. "Anyone who turns around now isn't going to make it."

They followed closely behind the van, and the children inside grew more and more agitated as they entered. It was dark, lit only with torches, and they could hear them shouting and banging on the windows to try to get someone's attention. There was nothing they could do, not without ruining their plans, but Holt kept a close eye on Thane. He was staring straight ahead, clenching his hands tightly on the bike's grips, and looking like he was about to burst. He managed to keep things under control, but only just.

They rolled towards a loading dock, built to handle multiple vehicles at a time. The entire area had been turned into a warehouse, storing goods until the servants had a chance to haul them upward to wherever they were needed. Hordes of them scrambled to unload the convoy's cargo, dragging it by hand into loosely organized stacks of boxes and crates. A few of the angels were lazily supervising the efforts, which mostly consisted of chatting among themselves and occasionally walking close enough to the servants to terrorize them into working more efficiently.

No one paid any attention to them as they dismounted the bikes. They didn't even have to work to look inconspicuous, given the commotion that the Vichies were making. A few had control of themselves, but most were far along whatever trip their drugs had taken them on. The smarter ones stayed in their vehicles, letting the residents of the Perch do the real work as they enjoyed their high and waited in line. The dumber ones got out to explore, getting in the way, making noise, and generally being a nuisance. The Vichies didn't often interact with the angels directly, and some hadn't developed the healthy fear of them that was inculcated into the servants. They all soon did.

One of the Vichies was screaming loud, angry challenges to imaginary enemies conjured from the depths of his brain. He was a bear of a man, loaded with muscle and waving a machete as he paced back and forth, eyes wild and spit flying from his lips. A nearby angel gave him a stern look, but he didn't see the warning and didn't heed it. When he passed too close, the angel grabbed him by the throat, lifting him up and snapping his neck mid-air in a single, smooth motion before dropping him to the floor. He lay there twitching as the angel casually went back to his conversation, leaving the other Vichies to watch in horror. They immediately became more subdued, while the servants responded by pushing themselves to unload as quickly as possible.

"How long has it been?" said Holt, turning to Faye as they all walked alongside the convoy and towards the loading dock.

"Last one was about an hour and a half ago," said Faye.

"Pop another," said Holt. "They're going to catch on sooner or later, but I'd prefer later."

They headed for a dark hallway that the servants were running in and out of like little ants, carrying loads to the chambers inside. Holt had coached them to walk with purpose and authority, as if they had every reason in the world to be heading to the interior. All of them but Dax could manage it. He couldn't mask his constitutional nervousness, and watching the angels up close wasn't helping. He gripped the suitcase tightly like a life preserver, leaving the others to haul heavier duffel bags on their backs.

"What exactly are you doing?" called one of the servants. He was holding a clipboard, checking off the supplies that were most urgently needed as they were moved inside. It was impossible to organize it all given the volume and the Vichies' tendency to dump everything together inside the crates. But individual angels were constantly making requests, and someone had to be responsible for promptly fulfilling them if the servants wanted to avoid punishment.

"They told us to go inside, we go inside," said Holt, not even pausing as they walked onward.

"I didn't tell you to go inside," said the servant. "No one just tells you to go inside. They'll kill you if they catch you in there without permission. You don't like life out there, tough. You're too old to adjust, and too stupid to follow rules. Now get back to where you're supposed to be or I'll refer the matter to one of them."

Holt started to argue, but he didn't need to. A voice came from the hallway, causing the servant to immediately abandon his attitude and go back to his clipboard. "It's okay. They're needed inside, and they won't be long."

CHAPTER THIRTY-SEVEN

"GET ANOTHER WASHCLOTH," said Jana to one of the other servants. "Nice and damp." They'd been treating Peter's wounds for weeks, but he wasn't looking much better. He'd gone for too long without any help, and there were no doctors around to turn to. They'd done the best they could, clearing out a storage room to give him some space to himself and rounding up some salves and creams that had trickled in from the outside. He'd started to heal, slowly, but home remedies wouldn't do much for the scars that were already hardening all over his face.

Rhamiel had been good to his word, and he'd managed what she'd thought impossible: finally freeing Peter from Ecanus's grip. It had been a hard sell, and once Ecanus knew he had a valuable bargaining chip, he didn't let go easily. He'd been offered a prime position of honor in the Hunt, and in exchange he'd agreed to leave Jana alone. He'd have had to anyway, now that she was pledged, but Rhamiel thought a boost to his ego would make releasing the grudge a little bit easier. Besides, it was safer to keep him occupied outside of the tower while Rhamiel was away.

Ultimately, it was Abraxos who'd clinched the deal for Peter's freedom, or more specifically the chambers he'd left unoccupied after his death. They were high up in the tower, a prized location, and the squabbling over who would inherit them had been unrelenting ever since the Conclave had met. He'd had to pull a lot of strings, but Rhamiel had secured it for Ecanus, and he'd been happily preening around the tower ever since. The location of the chambers had an added advantage: the entrance was embedded high in the tower walls, well away from the ramp. Abraxos had liked his solitude, and there was no way to access his home without a pair of wings. Ecanus couldn't take Peter with him, and had been forced to let him live somewhere else as part of the deal. A pledge was still a pledge, but Ecanus had promised to stay away from him, for whatever his own word was worth.

Rhamiel had led her down here, back to her home, for a final visit before he left on his expedition. It was supposed to be short, but she ended up staying far longer than she'd expected. She'd wanted to spend the time while he was away in his chambers; they were wonderful, and had their own balcony with a view of everything below. But he wouldn't have it; he lived in the center of things, where other angels were constantly walking past. Nefta or anyone else could come by at any time without looking conspicuous. He obsessed over what to do for days, and finally insisted she stay with the servants below, someplace he knew she'd be safe and comfortable while he was away. Any angel who went down there for anything other than a meal would stick out like a sore thumb, and would have no reason to mingle with the servants in their quarters. He finally left her there, but not without having a long talk with Sam about keeping her away from anyone from up above, whether they be angel or servant.

She didn't come alone. The best of the warriors all insisted on participating in the Hunt, and there was virtually no chance of dissuading them. It had been years since they'd gone on a campaign, and while this was smaller in scale, it had excited everyone in the tower with even the slightest bent towards military activities. But Rhamiel was adamant that Jana needed a guardian— if not the strongest warrior in the tower, then at least the strongest one who'd be left behind. After much consideration and cajoling, he settled on Isda.

Isda had managed the improbable feat of merging muscularity with obesity, making him deceptively dangerous. You wouldn't think him powerful from his looks, but he was one of the strongest in the tower. He was also one of the laziest, and one of the most obsessive. He couldn't be bothered to wander the countrysides in search of enemies, and the servants were amazed that he was able to fly at all given his bulk. He'd spent most of his time since the Fall eating, following elaborate rituals before every bite. It was a chore for the servants to have him down below, as it meant preparing a constant stream of dishes which had to be cooked just to his liking, lest they be sent back again and again until they met his standards. But he was strong, he was quick despite his size, and he was loyal to Rhamiel. None of the angels left in the tower would be a match for him if they came looking for trouble, and that was all that mattered.

Jana herself had spent most of her days since Rhamiel had left either sitting by herself in the common room or tending to Peter. She'd passed Sam the note from Cassie, after sneaking a peek at it. It was completely indecipherable, a jumble of letters with no apparent meaning. He seemed excited about it, but wouldn't tell her what it was, and left her to the others while he pored over its contents. The rest of them were surprisingly uninterested in socializing. Many of her friends had turned out not to be such friends at all, now that she'd moved up in the tower. Sam still cared for her, but the rest of them treated her strangely, a mixture of outsider and outcast. The boys were in awe of her, stumbling over their words and barely capable of speaking to her. They thought her above them now, and didn't want to risk being on Rhamiel's bad side by showing any interest. So they kept her at arm's length, polite but distant. The girls were far worse. They'd teased her before about her interest in Rhamiel, but now they were merciless. None of them would talk to her, or even acknowledge her presence. They made nasty comments right in front of her, laughing about the angels' "comfort ladies" and wondering aloud whether they laid eggs.

She tried to ignore it, but it still stung. She'd thought they were her friends, and they had been, at least until she had something they all wanted. She started volunteering for her old duties, just for the sake of having something to occupy her mind and keep things from festering inside. At first they left her to the dishes, which no one had any particular desire to do. She kept volunteering for other chores, only to keep being rebuffed. Finally the girls decided to foist her on Isda, after tiring of both their games and his demands. They handed her a plate, pushed her out the door to the sound of snickers, and told her to be on her way, and not to come back until he'd finished.

The halls were empty, but she knew the way. She walked to the dining room, careful not to drop the plate. There wouldn't be any consequence if she did, not this time, and not from Rhamiel's underling. But old habits die hard, and she was still afraid of them regardless of their purported allegiances. She knocked on the door before entering, a sound precaution, and when she didn't hear any objection, she went inside.

"Walk to your left," said Isda, sitting alone at the table and facing away from her. "You must approach from the left, and serve from my left." He was an impossible blob of an angel, his mass extending outwards from the chair in either direction. She could see him as she approached, as directed, tapping the back end of his fork onto the table. "One, two, three, four, five," said Isda, counting the taps. "One, two, three, four, five. Now the right." He switched the fork to the other hand, and resumed his tapping and his counting.

His scars looked more like blisters, but they covered every ample inch of him. He looked like a bloated beet, stuffed on the inside until it was ready to pop. Most of the other angels had fine physiques, and seeing them you'd be forgiven for thinking they couldn't gain weight at all. Isda proved otherwise, though he'd been eating virtually nonstop since he'd come to the tower. The servants were shoveling in dozens of meals each and every day, and had been since he'd come down there.

"The peas," said Isda.

Jana wasn't sure how to respond. There were certainly peas, a small handful of them piled in a corner of the plate, kept segregated from the other food. A stack of meat filled another corner, and chocolate candies rounded out the meal. It was a strange mix, but he liked what he liked, and there was no one there inclined to argue the matter.

"There's peas," said Jana. "I hope you like them."

"I know there are peas," said Isda. "I requested the peas. What I did not request were the thoughts of a simpleton. I want to know how many there are." Isda could be irritable if his culinary demands weren't met, and he didn't much care for Jana. She'd tried to be kind to him, as one of Rhamiel's allies, but he'd had none of that. As far as he was concerned, she was merely a burden and an interruption, a useless beast he'd been forced to babysit.

Jana counted in her head, several times to be sure. "Seventeen," she said.

"Seventeen," said Isda. "No more, no less?"

"Seventeen," said Jana.

"Then place the meal before me," said Isda. "From the left. Peas up front, and don't jiggle them. Keep things separate, or you'll have to go back and start again." She did as he requested, and stood at attention behind him.

"One, two, three, four, five," said Isda, tapping the back of his fork on the table. Then he ate a pea—a single pea—and started over again. "One, two, three, four, five. You may go. One, two, three, four, five." Jana was amazed that he'd ever gained any weight given his rituals, but then, he was at it day in and day out. She opened the door and quietly excused herself, as Isda counted and counted before every bite.

She went back to the kitchens, dreading what the girls would cook up for her next, and was surprised to find them completely empty. Many of the angels were gone, it was true, and so the demand for their services had been unusually light. But Isda alone had been keeping them busy, and they should have been readying another plate. He was working his way through the other, pea by pea, and sooner or later he'd be finished. He'd be liable to be cranky if kept waiting, so she didn't think it wise for them to simply abandon their posts.

She left the kitchen, walking through the hallways to the common area. As she opened the door, a burst of noise and activity came outward, and she saw that the room was filled, with everyone standing in the center around the fire pit. They all seemed excited, and couldn't help themselves from loudly chattering to each other. Sam was in the middle of it all, and waved to Jana as he saw her enter.

"Jana," said Sam. "You must come over here. I've got some people I'd like you to meet."

CHAPTER THIRTY-EIGHT

NONE OF THE SERVANTS HAD come out, not since
the first explosion. The angels had sent a group
inside, as crawling around underground was
beneath the stature of any of them. They'd let them root
around below until they'd heard a loud crack, and plumes
of smoke began drifting up from the interior. Then they
sent in another set of them, idling away the afternoon
until the sound of screaming signaled the need for yet
another group to follow them into the depths.

"I warned you," said Uzziel. "I warned you this was a
hotbed of military activities."

"Just as you warned us of dozens of other locations,"
said Rhamiel. "Your maps are practically a sea of red,
given how many pins you've put in them. The tales
of villainy you spin can be delightful, but it gets a
tad repetitive."

"I have sources," said Uzziel. "I have spies, who've
investigated this very place. I see what you others can't.
I can see the threat."

They'd flown to the island, circling around in the

KEVIN KNEUPPER

skies as Zuphias led them closer and closer to where he thought they'd be. He'd finally dropped them near an old farm and some abandoned buildings. They'd sent in one of the lower ranking angels to investigate, and he'd come out with a bear trap clamped around his hand. There was no real injury, but this sort of work was best done by proxy, and so they sent for the servants. They'd taken hours to arrive, even being led there from above, following behind the angels on the ground with a train of men, supplies, and white banners.

Some of the servants had been ordered to set up camp, erecting a command tent to serve as their base of operations. Most of the angels could have done without, but Uzziel insisted. He needed a place to hold his maps, and he needed a hub for his spies to report to. The rest of the servants milled around outside the buildings, hoping to avoid being tasked with anything dangerous. Most of the angels stayed inside the tent, waiting for the explorations to finally be finished.

"I know they were here," said Zuphias. "The walls practically reek of her. I can hear her voice echoing from them even now, whispering things to me in my head. She might still be below. Something is, else they wouldn't have gone to such trouble to defend it."

"They might have done so simply for the fun of it," said Ecanus. "I certainly would have."

"You're welcome to lay whatever traps you like in your new accommodations," said Rhamiel.

"I doubt I'll be having any unwelcome visitors to play with," said Ecanus. "Not any longer. One of the few downsides to my move, not that I've any real complaints."

"You shouldn't," said Zuphias, his nose poked as high into the air as he could manage. "Someone with the kind of scarring you have would never make their way into high society without a little push. You've a face that belongs at the bottom, regardless of what neighborhood you've sneaked your way into." Bumping Ecanus ahead of his designated position had been a true affront to Zuphias, who had trouble stomaching quick movements up or down the social hierarchy. The Fall was one thing, but the entire purpose of status was to keep people where they should be. Let the ladder down for one, and others would climb along behind him.

"And yet I'm so very close to you now, dear Zuphias," cackled Ecanus. "Someone of my lowly status, and I can pop by to visit any time it pleases me. We'll see each other so often, you and I. We can exchange neighborly gifts, as a sort of welcome. Perhaps I'll leave a corpse of one of the servants on your doorstep, once I've coaxed a few screams from their belly." He couldn't torture his comrades, but he could irritate them, and he took great pleasure in tweaking those who thought themselves his betters when he could.

"Let us focus on the matter at hand," said Rhamiel. "We know they've been here, and perhaps they still are. Send in another set of servants, a dozen of them this time. If they can't resolve the matter, I'll send in one of us."

"Perhaps Zuphias was wrong," said Ecanus, with a giggle and a snort. "Perhaps his miracles are all in his head."

"I know my work, and I know it well," said Zuphias.

"I can make any of them pray to the Maker, in any language I choose. And I can hear them when I do. This one was here, somewhere. I can't feel where she's gone to, and I can't channel the words. Perhaps she's dead."

"Perhaps her prayers were answered," said Ecanus. "Perhaps you should have bid her to sing something other than a tyrant's praises."

"I'd alter the contents of their little speeches if I could, believe you me," said Zuphias. "Had I been in charge of the content of our miracles, I'd have come up with something more clever than talking donkeys and parted waters. The Maker wanted prayers, and so he taught us to make them pray. If you think you can do better, I challenge you to try."

Shouting came into the tent from outside, and one of the lower ranking angels rushed in to report progress in their investigations. There wasn't much, he said, and no one was left. But they'd found something, an object of immense interest. He held it up by the hair, a human head. The tissues were decomposing, and it looked the worse for wear. But the interesting part was the bottom: the bone itself had been burnt clean through, a wound that could only be the product of an angelic sword.

CHAPTER THIRTY-NINE

SHE WASN'T SURE WHAT TO make of them, these outsiders in their white clothing. It was supposed to be a mark of loyalty, but the loyal would never have entered the tower unaccompanied by any of the angels. The fat one seemed nervous, though that was to be expected. But the big, blonde one looked like he hated every one of the servants, exuding anger from every pore. It was a strange attitude for someone who'd never met them, and a strange emotion for someone who was a servant himself to show so carelessly inside the tower.

The servants were peppering them with questions, treating them like exotic travelers from a foreign land. They were, in a way, and everyone wanted to know what it was like out there and which angels they were loyal to. Sam waved them all aside once too many questions started to come, telling everyone that the fun was over and that it was time to get back to work. They'd all get together by the fire once night fell, and then they could ask anything they liked. But for now, things had to keep running as usual, and he'd be serving Isda himself.

Sam shooed the servants away and ushered the visitors into one of the storage rooms, saying they were here to do an inventory of their stores to come up with a list of things for them to look for on the outside. That was usually handled by Sam himself, but Jana thought he might have been overwhelmed by Isda's ravenous appetite. The rest of the servants decamped to the kitchens. Jana was tired of enduring their taunting, and so she stayed in the common area, flipping through magazines she'd already read hundreds of times and trying to while away the day.

She heard them all coming back in the evening after their work was done, their voices carrying down the hallway. But they didn't come in. The noise just kept moving, past the entrance and further away, towards the exit to the world outside the tower itself. She poked her head out into the hall, and could see the tail end of the crowd of servants, walking away holding torches as they went out to the loading docks. Her mouth dropped; they were never to go out there, not for any reason. Other servants were in charge of the cargo, and even Sam could only go so close to the exit without risking death if he was caught. She was too terrified to follow, and so she went the opposite direction, heading towards the kitchen to see if anyone had stayed behind.

Someone had, but not the servants. Sam's guests were all that was left, unzipping duffel bags and dumping their contents onto the tables. She let out an involuntary gasp, and then quickly ducked away from the doorway. She didn't know what all of it was, but she thought she recognized some of their equipment: guns, large black things that had no business in the tower. She started to slink away, hoping they didn't know she was there. If they heard her, they didn't come after her. She could hear them talking among themselves and rustling around with their equipment. She crept back to a hiding place around a corner and waited, to see if she could get some clue as to what they were up to.

They came out after a few more minutes, and she jerked her head back behind the corner, preparing to run. Where she'd escape to, she hadn't the faintest idea, but it became a moot point as she heard the voices disappearing down the hallway in the opposite direction. She dared a peek, and saw them standing outside the dining room, holding their weapons and whispering to each other. She ran back to the common area, stopping only when she heard noises coming out of one of the storage rooms, the one where they'd been keeping Peter. She eased open the door, hoping again not to be noticed, but this time her luck didn't hold.

"Jana," said Sam, calling her from inside. "Come in here and help us."

He was working with two of the other servants to lift Peter onto a blanket, the best approximation of a stretcher they'd been able to come up with. Peter was moaning; he still didn't have his senses about him. His body had finally given out from the sum of his tortures, and his system was forcing him to rest and recover now that Ecanus wasn't around to prod him into consciousness. Now they wanted to move him, to take him outside with the others, but he was dead weight until he'd had more time to heal.

"You have to come with us, Jana," said Sam. "We're leaving the tower. Now, while it's still dark."

"We can't just leave the tower," said Jana. "We can't just leave our place. They'll kill us, all of us."

"We've been ordered to," said Sam. "It was Isda. I just spoke to him myself. He says they want us to leave, just for the night. Rhamiel's outside, and he's made camp in the city. He wants us to come there to celebrate. They've caught the ones he was hunting, and they need servants to manage the feast. Rhamiel wants you there. It's his moment. His triumph. He wants to share it with you. This is all approved from up above, don't you worry."

He said it with conviction, and she almost believed it. He was an excellent liar, when he had to be. A poor one wouldn't have survived as long as he had in his position. Some things the angels didn't need to know, if they could be fixed before they'd noticed. But Jana had seen too much for blind trust. The servants wouldn't be leaving without a chaperone, not if his story was true. And it didn't sound plausible, not once she'd thought about it even a little. She'd never heard of servants leaving the tower, not for any reason. The angels used the ones outside for any tasks out there, and didn't like for the servants inside the tower to mix with them unnecessarily. And none if this explained the strange goings on outside of the dining room, or the weapons she'd thought she'd seen. Sam must have read her disbelief in her face, because he gave up on his story without pressing the matter.

"You have to come with us, Jana," said Sam. "You have to trust me."

"Where are you taking Peter?" asked Jana. "If there's a celebration, why are you moving him?"

"We have to leave," said Sam. "You remember your friend, Cassie?"

"She wasn't my friend," said Jana. "I thought she was my friend, but she wasn't."

"The note," said Sam. "You brought me her note. You have to understand. We aren't supposed to live this way. This isn't the way things were, before they came. We were free. We didn't have to do what we were told. There's still people out there, people who want us to be free. People who would rather die than serve. None of us are fighters. I know that, you know that. But we can't stay here. The fight's coming here. If Peter stays, he's going to die. If you stay, you're going to die. You have to come with us."

"Rhamiel," said Jana. "He told me to stay here. It's not safe anywhere else."

"If you follow their orders, you're going to die," said Sam. "If you stay here, you're going to die. We're taking Peter. We're going to try to get away. You have to come. You're smarter than this."

"Isda," said Jana. "He's here to protect me. One of them will hunt me down if they find out I've left."

"Don't, Jana," said Sam. "Trust me."

But she couldn't simply trust, not anymore. It wasn't just the angels who'd proven themselves unreliable. Peter had drawn Ecanus's attentions to her, even if he hadn't meant to. Cassie had threatened her, and used their relationship to get what she wanted. And none of her friends below had been true, not even after years of living and working together.

She started to back away, taking a few steps away from them. She didn't really have any plans, or know what she'd do. But they made the decision for her. Sam rushed at her, trying for a tackle that would knock her to the floor. He was too old for that; she slipped to the side, leaving him to land on the ground himself as she turned and ran. "You can't stay!" he yelled, as she disappeared down the hallway. But she couldn't go, either, not with them.

Her only options were bad, and she had only seconds to weigh them. She could run for the common area, but that was a dead end unless she wanted to follow them outside. She could fight, but Sam had the other servants with him, and she was sure to lose. So she picked the only choice she had: a mad dash for the ramp, past Isda and past the outsiders. If she could only make it up there, she'd have a chance. She thought she could find someone to help her—the laborers had worked for Rhamiel before, they'd seemed friendly, and they knew who she was. If she could make it to the middle levels, maybe she could find them, and hide among them until he came back.

She ran towards the dining area, taking a quick look around the corner before she turned it. The outsiders had finished whatever they were doing and were opening the door. She could hear Isda from inside, shouting. "The left. From the left!" They were sneaking towards him from behind, and it was her chance. She sprinted out from behind the corner, catching the attention of the fat one as he held the door to the dining area open. He started to panic, silently waving his hands towards the others, but he wasn't fool enough to make a sound. The two other men were advancing on Isda, approaching the back of his chair as he continued to shout. "One, two, three, four, five!"

She thought she'd made it. She could see the ramp in the distance down the hall, and once she was on it they'd never catch her. She started towards it, but felt herself pulled from the side, a hand grabbing her arm as she let out a quick, startled cry. She'd been so focused on the others that she'd forgotten about the woman, the one who'd come inside with them. She could still see them as she tried to free herself, the blonde one approaching Isda's chair from behind and holding up a glowing, round piece of metal.

The woman who'd grabbed her put a finger to her lips, and Jana instinctively kept quiet. "We're not going to hurt you," she whispered to Jana. "We're going to kill him."

Jana could have called out, and shouted a warning. Isda hadn't moved, and she could still hear him counting to himself as the danger crept closer. The woman wasn't even trying to stop her, just holding her arm and looking at her, pleading. She could have screamed, or fought, or done something to try to save him. But she found she didn't want to. For the first time in ages, she made a choice for herself, one truly of her own free will. She looked at the woman, nodded, and watched in silence as they went about their work.

The blonde man was directly behind Isda, following

his demands to approach from the left. He stood there in silence, holding the device in his hands and steeling himself. He brought it down quickly, snapping it onto Isda's neck in a single motion and jumping away as Isda stood up from the table, roaring with anger.

It hadn't gotten quite around him, not all the way. Isda was too fat for that, and the device wasn't much of a fit. He swiveled around to face them, his wings jerking up and down as smoke steamed from his neck. Even with his enemy before him, he couldn't quit counting. He reached for his sword, shouting and tapping at the scabbard. "One, two, three!" His eyes rolled back into his head as he tapped, and he'd lost count by the time they reappeared. He kept tapping, slower now, and kept at his shouting. "One, two! Three!" He couldn't seem to bring himself to draw his sword, not without following the ritual to its conclusion. But the device kept working its magic, and he moved slower and slower, slurring his speech as he tried to finish the count. He fell to the floor, drool dripping from his mouth, his hand tapping against the scabbard over and over even after he'd stopped speaking. Finally he grew quiet, a fallen behemoth done in by his own compulsions.

The woman released Jana's arm, but she didn't flee. "You can't be here," said the woman. "Not anymore. You need to go with your friends, with everyone else. I know it's scary. But I also know you can't stand the angels. We can't, either. You can stay, and I won't stop you. But people are going to die here tonight, and if you don't leave...."

She paused, a perplexed look on her face. Then she

started to cough, convulsing like Isda had, and flipping her head to the side to vomit on the floor. She cried out to the others, "It's happening!" Then she collapsed to her knees, and began speaking to Jana, something she couldn't understand. "Ma'am?" said Jana, trying to help her to her feet. She didn't respond, other than to keep jabbering as her friends rushed to her side.

One of them reached into the woman's pocket, grabbing a little bottle. He pulled off the top and emptied a pile of pills from it into his hand. The woman's hands jerked toward them, and then went into spasms. She looked up, mumbling sounds that approximated English. He slipped one into her mouth as she spoke, closing her lips with his hand. She managed to swallow it, but obviously at great effort. She had some control over herself, still, but all her motions were a strain. The man popped in another, only for her to spit it out involuntarily. A few more attempts, and she finally downed it. She kept up her talking for a few more minutes, furiously spouting words that Jana couldn't understand. Finally she slowed, and then stopped, regaining command of herself.

The men tried to comfort her, but she waved them off as best she could. "I'm fine," she said. "I'm back. But one of them knows where we are. We have to move, and do it now."

CHAPTER FORTY

"**H**E'S BEEN DEAD FOR SOME time, I should think," said Rhamiel. They'd ripped the top from the trailer, prying it open like a sardine can so they could hover above it and look inside. They'd have had no way to fit with their wings, and saw no reason to allow a little metal to stand in the way of their inquiry. The body was unrecognizable, reduced by weeks of exposure to nothing more than a skeleton covered by a soft mush.

"I should know," said Uzziel. "The rest of you should as well, if you'd simply listened. My spies have seen the threat we face. They warned of this precise location, weeks ago. But none could be bothered to leave their couches to investigate." He'd grown increasingly edgy as the Hunt had continued, and as they'd traced paths that followed the little flags on his map. He suspected everyone around him, and had started to believe Nefta's theory that there were enemies among his brothers, no matter how implausible it had seemed.

"You can't expect us to trust the reports of one of those creatures," said Zuphias. "Every word they speak is unhinged. The Ophanim are the Maker's abortion, a failed experiment on the way to our perfection. If it weren't for his sentimentality, he'd have wiped them from the heavens long ago."

"The Ophanim are odd, but they do not plot," said Uzziel. "That's where the Maker erred, with both angels and man. He gave them the faculty to plot and scheme. And so that is all they do."

"Look here," said Rhamiel, flapping his way down to the ground and picking up a long piece of flesh, blackened at one end. "A piece of your spy, it seems. One of his tongues, I'd wager. And burnt clean through. We're still on the trail of that little ant with Abraxos's sword. Which means his disagreeable friend must be nearby."

"They're not here," said Zuphias. "But they have been. The voices still speak, but not as loudly as if they still lurked about in the area. I hear voices of the past, and not of the present."

"Then simply bid her speak again, and tell us where she calls from," said Ecanus, approaching them from across the lawn. He'd been playing games with the servants, forcing a few of them to chew apart some of the gnomes that stood in front of the trailer, and watching carefully to ensure that they swallowed. It was just clay, he said, the same substance they'd been created from. The gnomes didn't seem to agree with them, not judging from the blood that spewed from the cuts in their mouth, or the sickly looks as they rubbed their stomachs. But none of them thought it sensible to disagree, and so they kept chewing until he grew bored of the matter.

"You've the brains of a half-wit," said Zuphias. "That was the first thing I tried. The woman is dead, or lost to me. I cannot feel her, and so I cannot make her pray."

"Perhaps another try would be in order," said Rhamiel diplomatically. "It's been some time since we set off on our journey. We've idled away enough days that she may yet speak again."

"Perhaps this try you could make more of an effort," said Ecanus. "Perhaps living so high in the tower has rendered you soft, and unable to perform your duties."

Zuphias cast a dirty look towards Ecanus, and then closed his eyes, taking in a series of deep breaths. He hummed, from deep within him, a low noise that grew louder and louder as he focused. His face scrunched in on itself, straining with effort, and he brought his hands to his forehead as he struggled to find them. He didn't hold back; Ecanus's taunting was driving him to make a point. He pushed and pushed, until finally blood began to drip from his nose and ears. He collapsed forward, his wings splayed at odd angles, and finally he struggled to his feet and began to wipe the blood from his face.

"Well?" asked Rhamiel. "Have you any news?"

"I heard her," said Zuphias. "And I know where they are. The tower. They have an infernal machine. They mean to unleash hellfire upon it, and bring our home to the ground. No more dallying. We must return at once." He took to the sky without waiting for the others, launching himself in the direction of his home. The rest stood stunned, and all of them turned to Rhamiel.

"Jana," he said, and took to the skies himself.

The rest of them rose as well, beating their wings as quickly as they could, following through the air as Zuphias and Rhamiel led the way back to the home they'd left behind, empty of warriors and sleeping through the threat it faced.

CHAPTER FORTY-ONE

"GO," SAID HOLT, POINTING TO the ramp. "And stay online." He clicked his walkie-talkie, and turned back to Faye as Thane and Dax ran the suitcase up towards its final destination at the apex of the Perch, where the chambers of the angels were clustered. He helped Faye to her feet, leaning her against the wall as she tried to regain her senses.

"They're coming," said Faye. "I could hear his voice this time, through all the fog. They've gone off somewhere, and they're coming back here."

"You're fine," said Holt. "Don't worry about them. We're here, and we've come far enough."

He turned to the girl, the one who'd been tussling with Faye. She looked terrified, with a tiny bit of curiosity poking out from underneath the fear. She hadn't left, and was just standing there, watching them and trying to figure out what to do.

"You need to go, too," said Holt. "Out. Talk to Sam. He's a good man, he'll take you where you need to be."

"Who are you?" said the girl.

"It doesn't matter," said Holt. "Look at him. Look at the angel." He pointed to Isda's corpse, toppled over in the dining room, fingers still poised over his scabbard and ready to tap. "We're here to kill them all. We're here to set you free. Now go."

"You can't!" yelled the girl, a look of horror on her face. "You can't kill them all. They're not all nasty, not like him."

"She's got Stockholm syndrome," said Faye. "A lot of them do. Girl, you have to leave. We can't make you. We aren't even going to try. There's too many like you in here. But we've warned you, and you have to understand: this place is coming down tonight, and anyone left inside is going to die."

"What about the ones outside?" asked the girl suspiciously.

"If you go outside, you'll live," said Faye. "Everyone outside is going to live." It seemed to calm her down significantly. Still, she hung around them, hovering at a distance while Faye recovered, until there was a sudden movement from the ramp.

A stream of people was trickling down it, and soon it turned into a flood. The servants had begun an exodus, floor by floor, sending word up as they went. They ran past them towards the exit, looking frightened, many of them committing the first act of rebellion in their entire lives. Not all of them had come; not even all of them had been told. It wouldn't have been safe, particularly not with the ones in the upper levels. The most loyal servants were still asleep in their chambers, and the most fearful ones had stayed behind, unwilling to risk any anger from their masters even as they were afraid to be the ones to tell them of the evacuation. They didn't believe in their deliverance, and they preferred to sit quietly in their rooms and wait out the storm.

The girl was still standing there, watching the flow of servants, and Holt started towards her to make sure she got moving. He was interrupted by a very familiar face.

"Cass!" he yelled, as a woman ran towards him, hugging him tightly. It was Cassie, down from the world above, finally ready to make her escape back to the world she'd come from. "Looks like my notes have been getting through."

"We've got a good communications system, up and down the Perch," she said. "It's primitive, but they don't even bother trying to decode them even when they've found one. Everything's ready. Everyone who's coming. We've been organizing for weeks. Most of the angels will be asleep, but we've got to move. Some of them come out, or get insomnia. Or they might get tipped off. If we don't move fast, not everyone's going to make it."

"We'll get as many as we can," said Holt. "This is Faye. She's one of my cell. She's sick. An angel's been in her head. The other two are heading up top with the bomb."

"I take it you met Sam," said Cassie.

"He's out front, leading the herd," said Holt.

"Perfect," said Cassie. "I'm going the same way. I've been in here too damned long." She'd come to the Perch an eager volunteer, roughly a year before. No one even questioned it; the Vichies outside were happy that their quota was just a little bit easier to fill, and the servants inside didn't see anything unusual about her willingness to join their safe haven. The angels would have preferred her to be younger, but she claimed to be a skilled seamstress, and they weren't in the habit of scrutinizing resumes. She'd started on the crafters' floor, and with a little bit of flattery had been able to exploit the angels' vanity to improve her position. Nefta had jumped at the chance to accept her pledge after a short conversation about art, and so she'd moved to the top.

She'd known Holt for years, from one of his earlier cells. They'd always talked about getting someone on the inside, and organizing a resistance. She'd tried, but it turned out that none of the servants had the stomach for that. She'd shifted to spying instead, sending messages outside via code, handed down the Perch level by level until they were given to one of the Vichies. The servants were brave enough for that, if adequately compensated, but she had no idea if anything she sent was making it to its destination. It was a moot point, for there was no leaving now. But once she got the first message back from Holt a few months in, she'd eagerly begun feeding him everything she could about the Perch and its weaknesses. She'd agreed to help with his plans, but only if they could at least attempt an evacuation.

"You do what you're going to do," said Cassie. "This is probably everyone who's coming. Once you get things ready, you get your ass outside, too. They'll...." She stopped herself as she saw Jana, standing in the middle of the stream of people as they parted around her.

"Jana," said Cassie. "Let's go. I know you hate me, but let's go."

"Where will I go?" asked Jana. "How will I find Rhamiel?" She looked worried and lost. Leaving one's home is never easy, even when there's no threat for doing so. She'd taken the first few baby steps already, but a trip outside the tower was something different entirely.

"Rhamiel's not here," said Cassie. "He's safe. This place is going to be rubble soon. You won't be with Rhamiel if you get yourself killed."

That was enough. Cassie took her by the hand, and Jana let herself be pulled along. "Let's go," she said. "Hate me all you want once you're safe. Holt, don't stay too long. All it takes is one of them, and you're done." They merged into the crowd, and were gently pushed with the current as they all headed outside.

"Thane," said Holt into his walkie-talkie, keeping his voice low just in case the wrong person was listening on the other end. "What's the status? We're about to head up."

"Negative," came Thane's response. "This thing is huge. We've been bookin' it and we're only a quarter of the way up. And we got our asses up here before the rats started tryin' to get off the ship. Let us deliver the package."

He was right, and Holt could see it. Servants were still coming off the ramp, all headed in one direction. Swimming upstream wasn't a realistic option—it was more likely they'd be caught in the middle, unable to get to the top in time to be of any help. If it was just him, he'd have made a run for it anyway. But with Faye along for the ride, and not in the best condition, he opted to stay put.

"Okay," said Holt. "We're staying down here to help with the evacuation. It's on you two, now. Get it up to the top, as close to their quarters as you can, and bring this place to the ground. And if you run into any trouble, just set the damned thing off, no matter what."

CHAPTER FORTY-TWO

"A DRINK! A SIMPLE DRINK, ALL that I ask!" Nefta had been shouting her lungs out, to no avail. She'd strongly preferred having two servants, as a redundancy against exactly this sort of incompetence. With Jana gone, she was forced to make do, a problem when she woke in the middle of the night with an inability to sleep and an urge to make art.

She stormed through her chambers, shouting for Cassie, before she was finally forced to walk all the way to her bedroom. She pulled open the door, prepared to deliver a lecture on laziness, only to find it empty. "Cassie!" she shouted, her irritation growing. If she were awake, then she should be answering, rather than putting her own business ahead of that of her mistress.

Nefta went into the kitchens, finding nothing. She checked the storage closets, to see if she'd been hiding in one of them. Again, they were empty. The entire chambers were. That meant only one thing: Cassie was gone, roving around the tower without permission instead of sleeping in her bed as she was supposed to.

It put Nefta in a foul temper, something that was dangerous when she was up this late. She fizzled with energy, and if she couldn't put it to good purpose, she'd put it to a bad one. Now Cassie had her ire, and she'd be made to pay for it. One rebellious servant was enough, but Jana's insubordination was clearly spreading. She might have escaped, but Cassie had taken the pledge, and Nefta thought it high time that such matters be nipped in the bud.

She threw open the door to her chambers, bursting out into the tower. The halls were empty, not unusual at night. She stalked around them, searching for any sign of where Cassie had gone to. She wasn't in any of the hallways nearby, and while she might have been in another angel's chambers, she couldn't well compound the problem by searching them at random and awakening their occupants. She chose instead to go down, into the common lounge. After poking around behind the couches and in the most obvious hiding places, she concluded it was empty. It only made her madder; wherever Cassie had gone, she was determined now to find her, and wouldn't give up until she'd given her a good lashing.

She made her way out to the ramp, taking flight and looking down below her. She saw two of the servants, running upward as quickly as they could. They bore the white uniforms of those outside—not a common sight in the tower, but not out of the question, either. What disturbed her more was what she saw below them.

At the bottom of the ramp were hundreds of servants, running towards the tower's exit en masse. She knew at once where Cassie had gone, and she wanted to know why. Nothing like this could possibly have been allowed by one of the angels. It was an escape, a plot against them all, and she would put a stop to it at once.

She dove to the bottom, circling around the ramp as she flew. Some of the servants below had seen her, and began to point upwards. They ran with a newfound intensity, scrambling away as quickly as their legs would carry them. None of that would matter; they could get outside, but it was miles to safety. She'd raise the alarm after she'd ended things, and they'd pick them all off outside the tower if they had to, one by one.

She landed in the middle of them, prompting some of them to flee back up the ramp. She grabbed the nearest servant, holding him up in the air by the throat as he kicked and cried.

"What is the meaning of this treason?" she hissed, as he went limp in her hand and emptied his bladder into his pants.

"They said they're going to kill us," he whimpered. "Please. I had to. There wasn't a choice. Everyone says they've got a bomb, and they're going to destroy the tower."

"Who?" she said. "Tell me who."

He just pointed up, back to where she'd come from, and then it all clicked. She tossed him aside, snapping a few of his bones, and launched herself upwards, pushing against the air with all her power as she rose.

CHAPTER FORTY-THREE

"K EEP MOVING," SAID THANE, AS Dax followed
behind him. They'd almost made it up to the
top of the ramp, when they saw one of the angels
circling above them before going down to investigate the
servants' escape. Thane was in fine form, but it had taken
a lot out of Dax to make it this far. They'd been running
most of the way up, and he didn't have the endurance for
that kind of distance. He was huffing and sweating, his
face gone flush, and he looked like he might have to be
carried to make it over the finish line.

He'd never have been allowed up there, if there had
been any choice. But Holt had ordered that he stay with
the bomb, no matter what happened. The others could
probably have set it off, and Dax had given them a crash
course in what they'd need to do if it came to that. But
none of the rest of them really understood it, not how it
worked. They could push the buttons, or set the timer,
or enter the code. But there would be no test run, and
if something went wrong, the rest of them would have

been left to whack the device with their hands and hope for the best.

Dax, by contrast, had done nothing but read up on nuclear technology since they'd acquired it. It genuinely interested him, and he genuinely wanted to be there to set it off. He'd gone through a thousand contingencies in his head, and had come up with a game plan for every one of them. He was fascinated by the mechanics, by the physics, and by the opportunity to be the one to kill more of the angels than any other person had since the Fall.

They came to a door at the top, and Thane began working the elaborate handle to open it. Their instructions from Holt had been simple: get to the top, go through the door, set the timer, and find someplace to hide the suitcase. Then get back down the ramp, hopefully in time to avoid the explosion. He claimed to have an insider's account of the Perch, and that they were unlikely to encounter any angels if they didn't go any further than instructed.

Battle plans never survive contact with the enemy, and this one was no exception. They got the door open, and peeked inside. It opened into a large lounge that was as empty as had been promised, but the way back down was another matter. They heard a thud, and then footsteps, and they knew what they'd see before they turned around.

She was exceptionally beautiful, or at least half of her was. The rest of her was a mess, though that was no surprise when dealing with the angels. The ruined side of her face was too badly damaged to convey emotions, but the side that had been left intact managed to say it all. She was furious, and itching to take out her accumulated anger on two very vulnerable targets.

"I know what that is," said the angel, looking at the suitcase in Dax's hand. "I know why you're here."

She started the beginnings of a rant against their defiance, something the angels had gotten into the habit of doing before administering their punishments, but Thane didn't let her get far. He leapt at her mid-speech, drawing his taser and jamming it into her neck. She was shocked by more than just the current; she obviously hadn't ever encountered a servant with a temper to match her own. He grabbed onto her tightly and pushed, forcing the both of them over the edge of the ramp.

Dax rushed over and summoned the courage to look down. Thane was on her back, his arms wrapped around her wings, holding on for dear life as they glided downward. It was rough going; she was doing everything she could to push him off and regain control. They slammed into the ground, and all Dax could see was her wings spread wide, and servants running away to avoid her. He couldn't tell what had happened, but at this point there was nothing he could do. He charged through the door, entering the lounge and trying to find a good hiding place.

He settled on a bar, well-stocked with alcohol. He threw the suitcase on top, clicking it open and poking at the detonator. His fingers were shaking as he started entering the code. He hit the numbers, one after the other—and then he missed. He'd struck the wrong key, too nervous to even aim his finger. The suitcase started to blare at him, beeping loudly and flashing asterisks all across the keypad. He sank his face into his hands, his shirt covered in sweat, and prepared for the worst.

The beeping stopped, and the keypad reset. The bomb didn't explode, so he took a second stab at it, this time slowly and carefully. He entered a time, entered the code, and watched the numbers begin to click downward towards zero. Then he started grabbing bottles of alcohol from the shelves below the bar, filling his arms with them and clearing a space where he could hide the bomb.

Holt's voice came over the walkie-talkie before he could finish. "Dax. Dax!" He set down his armload of bottles, dropping a few as they rolled across the room. "I'm here!" he shouted, a little too loudly, before thinking better of it and shifting to a low whisper. "I'm here."

"Dax, she's coming back up," said Holt. "Thane's down. He's alive, but he's hurt bad. Faye's taking him out of here. I'm heading up the ramp."

"No!" said Dax, again a little too loud. "No. Get out of here. Get on a bike and go. I'm fine."

"Dax, she'll kill you," said Holt.

"I already set the timer," said Dax. "You've got fifteen minutes."

There was no way he was making it back down, not in the time he'd given himself. He'd have just set the thing off, but the others deserved a chance, and he figured a few minutes one way or the other wouldn't make much of a difference to the angels. He turned off the walkie-talkie, and shoved the suitcase into its hiding spot. He put the bottles back into place in front of it, the ones he could, and then stood up. He couldn't think of anything else to do, and so he wandered over to one of the tables, took a seat, and waited.

Heroism wasn't quite how he'd envisioned it. He thought it would have been something flashy and inspiring, and not a simple act of selflessness. He'd imagined himself going out in a final battle against the forces of evil, zapping them with the collar or slicing away at an army of them with one of their swords. He'd rehearsed speeches in his head, and things to shout, and concocted an endless number of impressive deaths for his enemies. Instead, all he'd done was pushed a button and sat in a chair.

He waited there alone for a few more minutes, compulsively checking his watch as the time went by. It wasn't long before she burst through the door. She looked worse for the wear, one of her wings a little crooked, her hair matted and looking like she'd overslept. She scowled at him, walking towards him briskly, and grabbed his arm to lift him to his feet.

"Where's your weapon?" she asked.

"Fuck you," said Dax, smiling wide.

She didn't like that, and she wasn't in the mood. She took his hand and gave it a twist, snapping the bones in his fingers so they pointed at odd angles. He cried out in pain, and fell to the floor clutching his wrist.

"Where is it?" she asked again.

"Go fuck yourself," said Dax. He was stuttering now, the pain audible in his voice. But this was his moment, the one he'd spent the last few years looking forward to, and he wasn't going to waste it now.

She grabbed him by the neck, lifting him to his feet.

"I love you," she said. "I love all of you. Can't you see that I love you? And yet always you attack us. We do what's best for you, you must know that. It must be what the Maker wanted, else he wouldn't have sent us here. To teach you. To make you better. You need to be our servants, just like we needed to be yours."

"Your slaves," said Dax. He collected the juices in his mouth, and he spat, hitting her square in the eye. "Your Maker left you in the oven too long, you ugly, lunatic bitch."

He'd never stood up for himself before, not to anyone, and he'd never felt so good. It didn't last. The angel roared, a bitter cry, and thrust her arm through his stomach and out the other end. She pulled out a chunk of flesh and guts, and left him to choke on his blood. As he fell to the floor, and faded away, all he could think of was that it had been worth it.

The angel looked around, trying to find where he'd put it. She overturned tables, and ripped at the cushions of couches, and pulled strings of lanterns from the walls. Finally she saw the bottles, where they'd rolled along the floor past the edge of the bar. She rushed around to the other side, and saw where he'd tried to hide it. It was immediately obvious. He'd done a terrible job, leaving all of the bottles out of order in a messy line.

"There you are," she said, as she caught sight of the suitcase. "Let's get you out of the tower." She reached down to retrieve it, and then it all went black.

CHAPTER FORTY-FOUR

J ANA SAW THEM IN THE air as they fled, flying low in the skies back towards their home, an armada of angels returning for battle. She recognized at least one of them, from the lion-like thing on his chest: Rhamiel, near the lead, behind what looked like Zuphias. They must have seen the servants escaping; they flew right overhead. But they didn't stop, didn't even pause. They just kept racing back towards home, turning upwards towards the top of the tower as they approached.

She'd always been taught not to look back if you fled from an angel, lest they turn you to salt. But she couldn't help herself when she heard the boom. The tower erupted behind them as they ran, trying to get as far away as they could. The top burst off, and a giant cloud of dust mushroomed upward from within, sending debris raining in all directions. The angels at the front were enveloped by the cloud, and the ones at the back began plunging to the ground, knocked from the air by the force. She turned to run back, to try and find Rhamiel, only to see the sides of the tower begin to heave and shake as it caved in on itself. Still she kept running towards it, until a few of the servants grabbed her, pulling her forward as they went.

She started to cry, but she could only watch as the cloud got bigger and bigger, and none of the angels rose through it. She couldn't tell what had happened to them, couldn't see through all the smoke. All she knew was that Rhamiel was in there, somewhere in that inferno, and there was nothing she could do to get to him.

The survivors regrouped by the edge of the old city, huddling and talking among themselves about what to do and where to go. Finally three of the outsiders roared forward on their bikes from out of the clouds of dust, down a man and with one of their survivors wounded. She stuck close to Sam, and watched them as they pulled their friend from the bike and started to patch him up. His bones were bent and broken, but he'd survive, as long as they could give him some time to recover.

She couldn't help herself. She started bawling uncontrollably, and the woman came over to comfort her. She wanted to hate her, and all of the rest of them. But she couldn't. She knew why they'd done it, and knew that most of the angels had deserved it. But still she thought of Rhamiel, and wondered what had become of him, and still she cried.

Before long she felt a churning in her stomach, and queasiness overcame her. She began to throw up, leaned over and heaving onto the ground. It sent the woman into a panic.

"One of them has her," she shouted. "One of them's in her head." The woman lifted her chin, and looked into her eyes, searching for something. "Are you okay? Tell me you're okay. Tell me what you're feeling. I can help you, I promise I can help you."

"I feel sick," said Jana. "I feel really sick."

"Do you hear voices?" asked the woman. "Do you hear anything in your head? It's fine if you do. It'll make you sick, just for a while, but we can stop it."

Jana was taken aback. "It's not that," she said. Then she started to cry again, and the woman pulled her close and hugged her as hard as she could.

"Just tell me what's wrong," said the woman. "Just tell me what's wrong, and you'll be okay."

"It's been a month," said Jana, in between sobs. "More than a month."

"It's okay, honey," said the woman. "Just let it out."

"It's been more than a month," said Jana. "And I haven't bled."

END OF BOOK ONE.

ACKNOWLEDGEMENTS

Liked the book? Two other novels in the series are in the works, so if you want to get a heads up as to when they're being released, please sign up for my mailing list at http://eepurl.com/IrhLP. I don't e-mail for anything other than new releases, so you won't get any spam. And if you really like it, please give it a review, tell all your friends, force your book club to read it, and make your children write book reports about it.

They Who Fell is a first novel, and I'm happy to have checked that off my bucket list. But I couldn't have done it without the help of others.

Thanks to Glendon Haddix and Tabatha Haddix of Streetlight Graphics, for designing the cover and handling the formatting. They're great to work with, and I highly recommend them to anyone just getting started who wants to avoid worrying about anything but the writing part.

Thanks to the beta readers, who helped immensely with my writing and with improving the novel generally. I can't recommend beta reading enough to anyone trying to write a book, given all the helpful advice I received, in particular with the romance subplot (necessary to the story, but not a genre I have much experience with as a man). It won't surprise any woman reading this that the most common piece of advice I received for that part of the book from the female beta readers was "slow down and take your time." I'm not sure if I accomplished that, given the pacing needs of the story, but I tried.

Thanks specifically to the first round of beta readers, including Thomas Allen, Cate Hogan, Shelly Kueny, Laurie Love, Sally Odgers of Affordable Manuscript Assessments, Ashley Parker Owens, Melissa Scott, Bethie Swanson, emeraldcityem from fiverr, kitkatplus from fiverr, and periwinkle from fiverr. They confronted a much rougher draft, but helped me identify a number of basic ways to improve my writing, from adding more details to improving some of the characters who needed some work.

Thanks also to the second round of beta readers, including Kathy Dixon Graham, Molly Keeton, Julie Kelley, Mati Raine, Tina E. Williams, and Greg from 2bookloversreviews.com. They received a version that was much further along, but still were able to help tighten things up, act as a sanity check to make sure I'd fixed things from the first round, and clean up a bunch of lingering errors.

And finally, thanks to the readers. It's flattering to think that someone's read through all this after many months of labor, but you did, and I appreciate it.

43199674R00211

Made in the USA
Lexington, KY
21 July 2015